Doohickey

A Novel

PETE HAUTMAN

Simon & Schuster

NEW YORK   LONDON   TORONTO
SYDNEY   SINGAPORE

SIMON & SCHUSTER
Rockefeller Center
1230 Avenue of the Americas
New York, NY 10020

SIMON & SCHUSTER and colophon are registered trademarks
of Simon & Schuster, Inc.

For information about special discounts for bulk purchases,
please contact Simon & Schuster Special Sales:
1-800-456-6798 or business@simonandschuster.com

Manufactured in the United States of America

10 9 8 7 6 5 4 3 2 1

Library of Congress Cataloging-in-Publication Data
Hautman, Pete.
Doohickey : a novel / Pete Hautman.
p. cm.
1. Clothing trade—Fiction. 2. Arson investigation—Fiction. 3. Partnership—Fiction. I. Title.
PS3558.A766 D66 2002
813'.54—dc21   2002070671

ISBN 978-0-7434-0024-4

This doohickey is for Milla

Doohickey

One

Does chocolate go with champagne? Nick wasn't sure, but he knew that Gretchen loved them both. He put the bottle of Dom Perignon in the refrigerator, took out the chocolate torte, and placed it on the counter to bring it up to room temperature.

Six-fifteen. He walked through his apartment, trying to see it through Gretchen's eyes. He wanted everything to be perfect. If everything was perfect, then nothing could go wrong. He straightened and smoothed the bedspread and plumped the pillows and turned the overhead fan to low. He rearranged the flowers on the Mexican tile table by the front door. He put a vintage Smokey Robinson LP on the turntable.

He had made a reservation at Platanos, Tucson's priciest restaurant. Would Gretchen like it, or would she find it too pretentious? Maybe Caruso's, inexpensive and familiar, would have been a better choice.

No, it had to be Platanos. Tonight was too special for Caruso's. Tonight he would celebrate two years in business and six months with Gretchen. They would have a marvelous dinner, then back to his place. For chocolate and champagne.

He checked himself in the bedroom mirror: long-sleeved linen shirt the color of strong coffee, dark olive chinos, suede Bally loafers.

He slipped into his new sport coat, a natural-color vicuña/silk blend, casual but elegant. He turned away from the mirror, then quickly looked back, catching his reflection by surprise. Was his hair too long? Was he trying too hard? Was he too vain and shallow, or just vain and shallow enough?

The telephone rang, saving him from himself.

It was Gretchen. "Nicky, I just got back from Marana." She would be wearing grubby jeans and work boots and a sweat-stained T-shirt.

"That's okay," he said. "Our reservation isn't until seven-thirty."

"I just got your message. Nicky, I'm sorry! I forgot we had plans tonight."

Nick's heart shrank. "You're doing something else?"

"Yes. No. I'm doing something with *you*. Remember I told you my dad wanted to meet you?" Now she would be smiling, her teeth bright white against freckled tan.

"You mentioned that, yes."

"Well, I set it up for tonight. He's expecting us for dinner at seven-thirty. I guess I forgot to mention it to you. I'm really sorry. I know you wanted to celebrate your two-year anniversary."

"And our half-anniversary. You and me."

"Really? It's been six months? Now I'm even sorrier. Can we do it another night?"

"I suppose." Nick tried to sort out his immediate feelings. This isn't so bad, he told himself. Besides, he should meet the parent. Get it over with.

"Or I could call my dad and tell him we can't make it."

"No, no. I'd like to meet him. I really would."

"Are you sure?"

"I'm sure. Where does he live?"

"Out on the east side, just off Old Spanish Trail."

"I'll swing by around seven."

Nick hated it when plans changed, especially his own. He liked things tidy and predictable. How odd that he was with Gretchen, whose plans shifted with the desert breeze.

He called Platanos and canceled the reservation, then sat on his black leather sofa and stared at the flowers by the front door, feeling completely ridiculous in the vicuña jacket and two-hundred-dollar Bally loafers. Who did he think he was trying to impress? Gretchen hardly noticed his clothes anyway. What *did* she like about him? It was a mystery. Sometimes he thought she viewed him as a curious specimen: Homo sapiens, male, early-twenty-first-century clothing salesman. And how did he see her? Nick smiled and felt his internal temperature rise a degree or two.

He would wear his vicuña sport coat to meet the father. He would be charming and attentive. They would have a nice time. The chocolate torte would keep for a day.

Still, it was a disappointment.

The telephone rang again.

"Hello?"

"Hello. Is this Nicholas Fashon?" The voice was unfamiliar.

"Yes it is," said Nick.

"Caleb Hardy's grandson?"

Nick hesitated before replying. No good thing had ever come to him through the agency of his grandfather, but he could see no way around it, so he answered, "That's right."

"This is Hardesty Chin, Jr. I'm an attorney working out of Bisbee. I did some legal work for your grandfather?"

"Yes?"

"He never mentioned me?"

"Not that I recall."

"Oh. I have some . . . Are you sitting down?"

"Yes."

Nick heard the lawyer clear his throat. "I have some very sad news."

Two

Who is Caleb Hardy?"

"He was my grandfather," said Nick.

"Oh." Gretchen frowned. "On your mother's side?"

"Yeah, but I never met him till after she died. He shows up at her funeral. Ten years ago. I go to bury my mother and find out I have a grandfather. My mom didn't talk much about her family. Now he's dead, too."

They were heading east on Old Spanish Trail, winding out of Tucson toward the Rincon Mountains in Nick's '65 Corvette, cherry red, the sun low in the sky behind them.

"I'm sorry, Nicky."

"It's okay. We weren't exactly close."

Nick sensed a darkening at the edges, the shadow not of sorrow, but of guilt. He should be feeling grief and sadness at the old man's passing, but it was as though someone else's grandfather had died, someone he'd never met. Did that make him insensitive? Cold and heartless? He turned his head to look at Gretchen, something he did as often as possible. He loved the slight upturn at the end of her freckled nose, the way her mouth never quite closed, the faint creases left behind by laughter and too much sun, and her eyes, two perfect turquoise disks. No, not cold, not heartless.

Gretchen grinned, then looked away, running fingers through her short, sun-bleached hair. "So, you have to go to Bisbee tomorrow?"

"The lawyer said he wanted to meet with me. I'm Caleb's closest living relative."

"Maybe you inherited a fortune."

"Not from Caleb I didn't. He lived in a shack out in the desert. I saw the old man maybe a dozen times in the last ten years. He always hit me up for money. Always looking for people to invest in some crazy scheme. Last time I saw him, he tried to talk me into selling the store and going into business with him. He'd invented some sort of kitchen gadget and wanted me to help him sell it. He'd decided I was some sort of marketing wizard. Because of that article in the paper. I told him I was too busy with the store. He was pretty disappointed. I felt sorry for him. Gave him a few hundred bucks. No, I don't think I've inherited squat. Doesn't matter, though. I'm doing okay. Vince and I have been really busy at the store. We're thinking about expanding. Maybe even sell franchises."

"Maybe you'll be the next Gap."

"You never know."

Nick thought about his plans for Love & Fashion, the clothing store he and Vince Love had opened two years ago. Business was good. In another six months, after the Christmas rush, he planned to move out of his apartment upstairs from the shop and convert it into additional retail space. He'd be able to afford a house. He wondered what kind of place Gretchen would like to live in. Would she want to stay in town, or move up into the foothills? It was one of the many things he wanted to discuss with her. He felt as if his life was just beginning. Then he remembered Caleb and wondered how it felt to be dead.

"I suppose I'll have to pay for his funeral," he said.

"Can they make you do that?"

"I have no idea." He downshifted as they came up a rise; the growl of the Corvette's engine rose in pitch. "You know what was the last thing he said to me? He said, 'I ain't gonna live forever, Nick.' That was a month ago. He was right. Look."

Nick pointed at the Rincons. The ridges had turned the dark gold of buckwheat honey; the saguaros stood out like stubble. He pulled onto the shoulder and stopped, then turned to look back at the source of the light: the sun sinking behind the Tucson Mountains on the far side of the valley. The yellow orb slowly melted onto the jagged peaks, a cloudless sunset, turquoise kissing gold. Neither of them spoke. After a time, Nick put the car in gear and pulled out onto the road.

Gretchen said, "You know what I like? I like watching you drive. You try so hard to be perfect."

Nick did not know what to say to that.

Gretchen asked, "Are you the same person when I'm not with you?"

"No." Nick reconsidered. "Yes."

Gretchen laughed.

A mile later Nick asked, "Do I turn here?"

"No. The next one. Javelina Way. Nicky?"

"Yeah?" Nick hit the signal and guided the Corvette onto a wide street lined with identical low-slung side-by-side duplexes: slump block walls, flat roofs, decorative ironwork over the windows. Most of the homes had low-maintenance landscaping: crushed rock studded with assorted cacti. The neighborhood was a shallow cut above a trailer park.

Gretchen said, "When you meet my dad . . . he's kinda strange, okay?"

"I know, he's got underdeveloped social skills. You've been prepping me for months. I am fully prepared."

"We'll see. Just don't start talking about sex, okay?"

"Why would I do that?"

"You wouldn't. But Bootsie would."

· · ·

I've owned a few businesses," Nick said. "Had a little juice stand over by the U of A campus. Did that for two years. Had a detailing shop up on Grant. That was good until some Mexicans opened up down the block and undercut me, so I sold it to a Vietnamese family who undercut the Mexicans, and I got into jewelry: Mexican silver, Polish amber, Black Hills gold. Called myself Objects International." Nick laughed self-consciously, sipped from his glass of water. He talked too much when he was nervous. He hoped he didn't sound racist, talking about Mexicans and Vietnamese that way. The look Bootsie was giving him could have meant anything. The guy looked like a boiled potato.

Failing to get a read on the old man, Nick continued, "I had a booth at the gem show, and a spot out at the swap meet. Sold wholesale to some of the truck stops. It was a good business, but I was working out of my car. So I partnered up with a buddy of mine, and we opened Love & Fashion. Today is our second anniversary. Showed a profit both years." He hoped he didn't sound too boastful.

He and Bootsie Groth were embedded in matching burgundy leather recliners facing a television. An episode of *Star Trek* played silently across the screen. A TV tray between them held a bag of tortilla chips and a bowl of bean dip. Nick had the impression that their warp engines were about to come on-line.

Bootsie tipped his head back and poured most of a can of cream soda into his mouth. His hand wrapped the soda can, thick fingers overlapping the tip of his thumb. He belched, sending a tsunami up his prodigious abdomen. Bootsie was encased in burgundy warm-ups nearly the same color as his recliner. It was difficult to tell where one ended and the other began. Nick suspected it was mostly Bootsie.

"Gretie says you live there," Bootsie growled.

"I have an apartment above the store. It's just temporary.

Vince—that's my partner—Vince and I are plowing our profits back into the business. We plan to branch out, maybe open a store up in Scottsdale. Maybe sell franchises."

"You play any sports?"

"I'm pretty focused on business these days."

Bootsie's wide mouth shortened. His bristly gray hair seemed to stand up even straighter. "No sports?"

"I play a little racquetball."

"Huh. You got any hobbies? A guy has to have a hobby."

"Well . . . I collect Motown records. LPs. You know—Little Eva, the Four Tops, the Supremes . . ."

The old man stared at him, blinking small round eyes. "What's your last name again?"

"Fashon," said Nick.

"What kinda name is Fashon?"

Perfectly natural, Nick thought. The old man just wanted to find out what sort of guy was going out with his daughter. Nick wished he could offer something other than a list of his possessions and businesses. The problem was that Nick thought of himself in exactly those terms. He was a guy who wore Bally loafers and cotton chinos and listened to Motown records and drove a vintage Corvette and sold leather fashion accessories for a living. Probably not Bootsie's kind of guy, but it was who he was.

"It was my father's name. I never knew him."

"You look like a Swede. All that blond hair. I bet your old man was a Swede. You ever smile?"

Nick grinned, embarrassed. Was he coming across as too serious?

Bootsie stared at him, then grunted. "Now you look like a guy got away with something."

Nick's smile collapsed.

Bootsie grabbed a handful of chips. He gestured at the plastic carton of bean dip. "You're kinda skinny. Have some dip."

Nick scooped some bean dip with a single chip and ate it, feeling self-consciously dainty. He wondered what he might have been eating at Platanos. He wished Gretchen would come back into the room.

"It's got beans in it," Bootsie said, watching him.

Nick nodded, agreeing that yes, the bean dip did have beans in it.

"I bet the girls really go for a guy like you. Skinny and good-lookin'."

Nick washed the chip down with a gulp of water.

Bootsie leaned toward him and lowered his voice. "I hear you sell some kind of *sex* clothes." He laughed, a shrill *hee hee hee,* gripping the arms of his recliner. Coming from this obese old man, the high-pitched giggle was as incongruous as the name Bootsie.

Nick set his face in what he hoped resembled a smile. "We sell Mexican and South American leather goods. Purses, vests, jackets, sandals—stuff like that. A lot of exotic leathers—"

"Erotic leathers?"

"*Exotic.* Capybara, llama, lizard. Quality goods, not like that junk they sell down in Nogales. Not what you'd call 'sex' clothes."

"Gretie showed me that newspaper article. Looked like sex clothes to me." *Hee hee hee!* The old man's belly continued to slosh even after his laugh had faded. His hand dropped into the bag of chips.

"Not really," Nick said, keeping a close eye on himself. The article in the *Star* had been about how a few innovative shops like Love & Fashion were bringing retail customers back to downtown Tucson. Unfortunately, of all the items carried by Love & Fashion, the paper had chosen to run a photo of a matching goatskin bra and garter belt from Venezuela, a one-of-a-kind item that was more for display than for sale. The article had attracted some curious trade over the past few weeks.

"You know what you should sell? You should sell leather jockstraps." Bootsie dipped a fistful of chips into the bean dip, inserted them into his mouth, chewed.

Nick had been worried about making a good impression. If things with Gretchen worked out as he hoped, this creature might become his father-in-law. Nick stifled a shudder. If he could get out of there without upending the bean dip onto the old man's head, he would consider the visit a success.

"Our most popular items are purses and belts," he said. "We really don't do much in the way of intimate apparel."

Bootsie said, "What the hell. I got no problem with sex clothes. I use to be a cop. I seen it all."

Gretchen had just come into the room from the kitchen. "Don't mind Daddy, Nicky. He's an idiot."

Nick said, "You were a cop?"

"Twenty-five years. So how come you named it that? Love & Fashion?"

"Well, my partner's name is Love, and my last name is Fashon, so we added an *I* to my name and called the store Love & Fashion."

"Sounds like a couple of fairies," Bootsie remarked, blinking. "Gretie's last boyfriend was a football player."

"He was a rugby player, Daddy. And he was an idiot, too."

Bootsie shrugged. "What the hell do I know? I'm just the old man."

"You don't know much, that's for sure," Gretchen said.

Bootsie scowled at his daughter, then returned his attention to Nick. "So how old are you? Forty? How come you don't have a wife and kids, a guy your age?"

So what do you think?"

"About what?" Nick sped up to make the light at Alvernon.

Gretchen swung the back of her fist against Nick's shoulder. "About my dad."

Nick licked his lips. "I'm glad I finally met him."

"You're avoiding my question."

"I think your dad's a nice old guy."

Gretchen snorted.

"I liked his leather jockstrap idea," Nick said.

"Yeah, I'm sure it would be a big seller."

"How did he get that name?"

Gretchen crossed her arms over her seat belt. "His real name is Harmon. When I was a kid, we had a dog named Bootsie. Black with white feet. When the dog died, Dad decided he wanted to be called Bootsie."

"He must've liked that dog."

"He hated the name Harmon. But imagine bringing a friend home from school and having your dad come up, 'Hi, I'm Bootsie.' Imagine introducing him to your boyfriend. Imagine what my mother had to deal with. But you know what was worse for her?"

"It frightens me to imagine."

"Him being a cop all those years. He lived and breathed his job. Brought it home with him every night. It was all he'd talk about. My mother was like a spare hobby for him. First the job, then the dog, then me, then—maybe—her. It takes her twenty-five years to get him to retire; six months later she dies."

Startled by her vehemence, Nick said nothing.

"Thank God you're not like that," Gretchen said. Her frown suddenly became a smile. "But I'm glad to hear you like him, even if it's not true."

"I do have to say I was a little bothered that he thought I was forty," Nick said.

"He was only off by four years," Gretchen said, grinning.

"Four years is a long time," Nick muttered.

"Not to Bootsie. He's seventy-six."

"Yeah, and I bet he wouldn't like being called eighty. Also, what was with the chips and dip? I thought you said we were going there for dinner."

"That was dinner," Gretchen said. "There was a bowl of salsa there, too, don't forget."

"What was that? The salad?"

"Exactly. What's really sad is that he doesn't have to live like that. He's got plenty of money saved up, plus his pension, plus social security, and he hardly spends a dime of it. I worry about him. One day some con artist is going to sell him a desert time share or something."

"He didn't strike me as the gullible-victim type."

"He's getting older. When are you leaving for Bisbee?"

"I told the lawyer I'd be there at noon tomorrow. It's a two-hour drive. Vince is going to run the store. When he heard Caleb died, he was pretty upset . . . speaking of gullible-victim types."

"Who, Vince?"

"Yeah. A few months ago he invested in one of Caleb's inventions. The Inch-Adder. A belt extender. For middle-aged, horizontally challenged cheapskates who don't want to buy a new belt every six months. I warned him, but Caleb sold him on it. Poor Vince thought he was gonna strike it rich."

"Good thing your store's doing so well."

Nick nodded. It was true. Business was up. The future had never looked brighter. He was a successful businessman riding in his classic Corvette with a beautiful woman by his side. I am a happy man, he thought. Life is sweet.

It suddenly occurred to him that there was no real reason to put off the chocolate torte and Dom Perignon. Dinner with Bootsie Groth was not exactly Platanos, but the moment felt right. A few bites of chocolate, a glass of champagne, and who knew where the conversation might lead? Maybe Bootsie Groth would find himself with a son-in-law.

"Do you have room for dessert?" Nick asked.

"What did you have in mind?"

"A little place I know called Chez Fashon."

"I've heard of it. It's supposed to be *très* exclusive."

Nick turned west on Broadway, his heart racing.

"I think he likes you," Gretchen said.

"Who?"

"My dad."

Nick could not imagine how she had come to that conclusion, but he saw no point in arguing.

Gretchen sat forward. "What's going on?"

Nick slowed, hearing sirens. "I smell smoke," he said.

"There! Something on fire."

The sky glowed jagged orange with false sunrise.

"My god, it's up by the store." He sped up, turned at Sixth. "Oh." Nick let up on the accelerator, staring. He felt himself crumbling, collapsing from the inside. "Jesus." The car slowed, drifted across the center line.

"Nicky!" Gretchen grabbed the steering wheel, guided the car toward the curb. "Stop the car, Nicky."

Nick braked, but his eyes stayed with the fire trucks, the men in yellow slickers, the shouting and hoses, the flames. His front wheel scraped the curb; the car stopped. The firefighters were hosing down adjacent buildings while Love & Fashion, his apartment, his record collection, his clothing, the chocolate torte, everything he was and everything he owned, crumbled within a tower of flame.

Three

Nick sat up in bed and said, "I smell smoke."

The room was bright with sunlight. Gretchen's bedroom. Hopi baskets displayed on the walls, photographs of the Antelope Mesa site where Gretchen had done her thesis work in archaeology. A map of Arizona. A stone ax head she'd found as a kid. A coyote skull on her dresser.

He heard her voice. "Nicky? You up?"

"I smell smoke," Nick said again.

Gretchen appeared in the bedroom door—Nirvana T-shirt, jogging shorts, and a circlet of Hopi rain symbols tattooed around her left ankle. Her hair, bleached from hours spent in the desert, stood out as if infused with a static charge. She had the telephone in her hand.

"That's toast," she said. Nick sniffed, reevaluating the burned smell. Gretchen held out the phone. "It's Vince."

Nick took a breath, reached for the phone. "Vinnie?"

"Nick! Can you believe it? I can't believe it, man."

"Yeah."

"What a shock, man. I am devastated. I went downtown this morning. There's nothing left, Nick. Not so much as a coin out of the register. I feel like my heart got ripped right out of me. The whole building's just a soggy pile of ash. Thank God we got insurance, Nick. That's all I got to say. Thank God we got insurance."

"Yeah, we got insurance on the store. I wish I could say the same for my apartment."

"You don't have renter's insurance? Nick!"

"But you're right—at least we got insurance on the store. We can find a new place and be open in a couple months."

"Man, I am so sorry, Nick. All your stuff. Your clothes. Your books. Your record collection! You didn't have any of that covered?"

"We've got the policy on the business, I've got insurance on my car, and that's it. Artie tried to sell me a renter's policy, but I was feeling lucky, so I passed. I was stupid, okay?"

"Ouch. Okay. Do you need anything? Clothes? A place to stay?"

"I'm okay, Vince." Nick looked at Gretchen's alarm clock. "Listen, I have to leave pretty quick. I got to run down to Bisbee today—"

"Bisbee? Oh yeah . . . Caleb."

"I'll be back tonight, but in the meantime, could you call Artie? Get the wheels turning?"

"Already done. He said they'll get right on it. It's a good thing we just did our inventory. That'll make it easier."

"Artie's a good guy. He'll take care of us."

"I sure hope so."

"So, *mañana, amigo.* What do you say we start shopping for a new venue? Maybe something closer to the campus."

Vince took a couple seconds to reply. "Sure! Sure, we could do that."

Nick heard something in his partner's voice. "Vinnie? Something you're not telling me?"

"No! It's just . . . well, we gotta talk. Tomorrow let's talk. We gotta talk. Breakfast at Poca?"

Nick nodded, a sick feeling crawling up his gullet. He'd felt this way last night when he'd first seen the orange flickering against the night sky.

"Nick?"

"Yeah, I'm here. That's fine."

"Nine o'clock okay? I mean, since we don't have to worry about opening the store."

Nick said that would be fine. He hung up. Gretchen, leaning against the doorjamb, one Nike atop the other, was watching him, nibbling absently on her thumbnail.

"Going for a jog?" he asked.

She nodded. "You still heading up to Bisbee?"

"Up?" Nick had grown up in Detroit, where *up* always meant north. Up north, down south, back east, out west. Here in mountain country, "up" was a matter of elevation. Bisbee, an old mining town turned tourist destination, was south and east of Tucson but two thousand feet higher. "Oh yeah. Up. I'm going up to Bisbee. What else am I gonna do with myself?"

Gretchen shrugged, smiled. "I guess we're ahead of schedule."

"What do you mean?" Nick wasn't following her.

"I mean, we've moved in together. You and all your stuff." Inviting him to share the black joke.

Nick's smile died on his face. Him and all his stuff. His stuff. He didn't have any stuff anymore. A dark wave hit him broadside, a horrible emptiness. It was all gone. His clothes, his records, his 1960s sci-fi paperbacks, his shoes! Nine pairs of Bally loafers turned to ash. All he had left were the few items of clothing he'd left in Gretchen's closet, $2,200 in the bank, and his Corvette. And half of the insurance policy on Love & Fashion.

"It's not funny yet," he said.

Four

We called each other Hardy," said Hardy Chin. "We had some things in common."

"Oh?" Nick said.

"My great-great-grandfather came over from China in 1867 to help build the transcontinental railroad." He smiled, waiting for Nick to show signs of comprehension.

"Oh?" Nick said again.

Hardy Chin frowned. "You come from a railroad family also," he explained.

This was the first Nick had heard about it, and he said so.

Chin looked disappointed. "You should learn about your heritage," he said.

"I'm learning something today."

Hardy Chin blinked, then grinned, rubbery lips peeling back from large ivory teeth. Four generations in America had diluted the stereotype—Chin was about as inscrutable as a billboard. He had a huge smile, expressive eyes, and hyperactive eyebrows. Several dark moles dotted his wide cheeks. His black hair was combed across his forehead and over his ears, and he wore a cream-colored western-cut sport coat, a snap-button chambray shirt, and a bolo tie with a clasp of raw turquoise the size of a quail egg. He sat behind a heavy oak desk, the top of which held only a phone and one file folder. Framed diplomas from Palo Verde High School, the University of Arizona, and the William Mitchell College of Law hung on the wall behind Hardesty Chin, Jr.

Nick said, "You want to tell me what I'm doing here?"

Chin's face underwent a series of modifications, moving from small talk to business mode. He opened the file folder, looked down at it. "You are your grandfather's closest living relation."

"Yes, you said that. But I don't understand what that means. Practically speaking."

"It puts you first in line to inherit his estate. Of course, that's a moot point, since his will names you as the sole beneficiary."

"You told me that, too. What I'm wondering is, why did you want me to drive up here?"

"Don't you want to see what you've inherited?"

"A shack in the desert?"

Chin pursed his lips. "Actually, it's a caboose."

"A caboose?"

"That's the railroad connection."

Nick could not tell whether or not Chin was joking.

Chin said, "On three hundred acres."

"Really?" Nick hadn't known that Caleb actually owned the land. He had always assumed that his grandfather was squatting at the pleasure of some easygoing rancher. "Three hundred acres?"

"That is correct. He also left you his inventions."

"His doohickeys."

Chin nodded. "That's what he called them, yes."

"His automatic toilet flusher."

Chin nodded.

"His electric comb."

"Yes, the Comb-n-Clean. We were unable to obtain a patent on that one."

"His belt stretcher."

"I see you're familiar with his work."

"Hell, I'm one of his big investors."

Chin removed a small notebook from the file folder and opened it. "Five hundred twenty dollars," he read.

"What's that?"

"The sum total of your investment in the BassBoy II."

Nick sensed Chin's disapproval. "He kept track?"

"Caleb was quite thorough."

"I gave him some money for some kitchen gadget, too."

Chin frowned. "That could be. He wasn't actually *that* thorough. In any case, it doesn't matter. Everything that Caleb owned now belongs to you."

"His *stuff*," Nick muttered. Caleb had lost his life, but his stuff was okay. Nick had lost his stuff, but he was alive. Now he had new stuff. He shivered. It was as if he were about to crawl into another man's skin. He shook off the feeling. "Do I have to sign some papers?"

"Eventually, yes. Mostly I thought we should meet, since I've been named executor and you are the sole beneficiary."

"You just wanted to meet me?"

Chin sat back. "Yeah, but I didn't know you at the time," he said. The corners of his mouth compressed. "You know, I am perplexed that you have not asked me how your grandfather died."

Nick experienced an intense moment of guilt. He hunched his shoulders, cast it off. "He was about ninety years old," he said. "I figured it was his time."

"He was seventy-three, and it appears he had a heart attack."

Nick shrugged. "There you go."

"Although," Chin continued, "it was hard to say, since the coyotes had been at him. He was dead a week before his body was discovered. His girlfriend found him."

"Girlfriend?"

Chin smiled, displayed his palms. "She hadn't heard from him in two weeks, so she drove out to his place. Found what was left of him out in front of his caboose."

"He had a girlfriend?"

"That surprises you?"

"Yeah, a little." The Caleb Hardy he had known was a wild-haired, bearded hermit. Wild-haired, bearded hermits did not, as a rule, have girlfriends.

"You'll probably meet her at the funeral."

"Funeral?"

"Yes." Chin was openly frowning now. "Caleb made provisions to have his remains interred in a small cemetery here in Bisbee. The service is tomorrow afternoon at four. I'm sure I mentioned it to you."

"Maybe you did." Nick hated funerals.

"You will be there, won't you?" Chin's upper lip lifted away from his teeth.

Nick said, "Look, I hardly knew him, so don't give me that look."

Hardy Chin blinked and reset his features to neutral. "My apologies. It is none of my concern whether you choose to attend your grandfather's funeral."

"Don't worry, I'll be there," Nick said.

"Good." Chin pushed his chair back. "Would you like to take a look at your inheritance?"

Five

We drive all the way around the Mule Mountains, then come into this valley that looks like a meteor crater, only it's about five miles across, then turn onto this rutted road—my 'vette doesn't have the clearance, so we have to park and walk the last half mile, a hundred degrees out there, this clown of a lawyer in his sport coat and shitkickers. He just laughs when I say I hope the place has air-conditioning. We come up over this rise, and the first thing I see looks like a flying saucer."

Nick paused for effect. Gretchen sipped her margarita, waiting him out.

"I'm not kidding. It's like the top of a Chinese parasol, about thirty feet high at the tip and maybe eighty feet across, six feet off the ground at the rim, like it's floating. There's also a caboose, the real thing, painted red, wheels and all—God knows how he got it there. And a big pole barn, a couple of those little prefab sheds, a cattle tank full of goldfish, and an old Chevy pickup held together with strapping tape and clothes hangers. And a dark spot in the dirt where they found him."

"That's very dramatic, Nicky."

"Well, it was. We're out in the sun, and this damn lawyer never sweats a drop. He's smoking these little Dutch cigars, cigarillos, I guess, about half the size of a cigarette but they stink twice as bad. Showing me around like he's a real estate agent trying to sell the place. The place is off the grid, totally self-sufficient. There's a generator in one of the sheds, and a bunch of solar panels mounted on top of the caboose. Caleb was into that Y2K conspiracy crap, I'm sure it was a great disappointment to him when society didn't collapse at the turn of the millennium."

"A lot of us were disappointed."

"Then Chin walks me around back of the generator shed and shows me a packrat mound damn near as big as Caleb's caboose. Says it's a thousand years old." Nick held out his margarita glass. *"Uno mas, por favor."*

"You thinking of moving out there?" Gretchen refilled his glass from the cocktail shaker.

"Yeah, right. Me and the packrats. Thanks." He sipped his margarita. "We saw a snake, a big old rattler, curled up under the pickup. I about jumped out of my skin."

Gretchen emptied a bag of chips into a wooden bowl. "The snakes like the packrats."

"A thousand years. You'd think the rats would all be gobbled up by now."

"I'm sure plenty of them were." Gretchen began chopping serrano peppers, cilantro and garlic together, chopping and rechopping to a fine mince. Nick watched her, the second margarita drawing a gentle mist across his eyes. She scraped the pepper mixture into a bowl, added a couple of chopped tomatoes and a pinch of salt, squeezed in half a lime, and turned the mixture gently with a wooden spoon. "What about the flying saucer?"

"Oh yeah. We get closer, and I can see that it's a roof made out of corrugated steel supported by a bunch of steel posts. No walls, just a curtain of chicken wire. The lawyer says it's Caleb's workshop. We find a door and duck under the eaves and go inside. It's like walking into a giant oven. If it was a hundred degrees outside, it must've been one-twenty under that roof. He has about ten picnic tables in there, all piled high with some of the strangest stuff you ever saw. A hundred projects half done, tools, you name it. Black widows everywhere. I saw one must've been the size of a mouse."

"The spiders like the packrats, too."

"Spiders eat rats?"

Gretchen set the bowl of salsa on the table. "Where there are rats there are insects, and where there are insects you find spiders."

"Spiders aren't insects?"

"Spiders are arachnids."

"You are a wealth of information."

Gretchen loaded a chip with salsa. "You spend a few years digging holes in the desert, you learn a lot about things that bite." She popped the chip in her mouth and crunched. Nick followed her example.

"The only thing that was halfway organized was— Oh man!" He slurped his margarita. "That salsa's mean!"

"I left the veins and seeds in. They've got some heat."

"No kidding. Whew. Anyway, as soon as we get in there, I want out, but Chin goes to the middle of the building or tent or whatever it is and turns a hand crank attached to a pipe. A second later I hear it starting to rain, and this misty drizzle is coming down all around the edge of the roof, and a few seconds after that, this cool breeze hits us. Turns out Caleb mounted a couple of lawn sprinklers up top. The whole building works like a giant evaporative cooler. The water falls into a trough and gets recycled."

"What a great idea."

"The old man had a lot of ideas. The workshop had a couple dozen of those big steel storage cabinets, every one of them full of weird inventions and boxes full of junk, all of them labeled. That was one thing he was organized about. All his doohickeys. He was really serious about them. According to the lawyer, he actually made money on a couple of his fishing lures. He was living off the royalty checks, a few thousand bucks a year. Plus he made money on his coffins."

"Coffins?" Gretchen gave a theatrical frown.

Nick shoved another chip in his mouth, this one only lightly dipped in the salsa. He made a time-out gesture and ran out to his car. A minute later he returned with a coffin-shaped cardboard carton about thirty inches long. Nick set it on the table and lifted the lid. The inside of the box was printed with cartoon bones and running mice.

"Pet coffins," Nick said. "This particular model is a Number Four, for cats or small dogs up to sixteen pounds. He sold them mail-order. That pole barn I mentioned? Full of these things. Six sizes, from gerbil-size all the way up to one big enough to bury a Dalmatian."

"What if you have a golden retriever?" Gretchen asked. She liked golden retrievers.

"I don't know," Nick confessed. "It might fit in the Number Six. I just got into this business."

"You're going to sell coffins?"

He shrugged. "I have to do something with them. Caleb ran ads in the back of *Cat Fancy* and some other pet magazines. I don't know how many of the things he was selling. Couldn't have been too many. He didn't have any money, or if he did, he spent it. Here, look at this." He reached into the coffin and pulled out an object that looked like a flashlight with a steel comb jutting from one end and an electric cord trailing from the other.

Gretchen drew back. "I don't know what that is, but I'd rather you didn't point it at me."

"It's an electric comb."

"That's what I was afraid of."

"You use this, you don't need shampoo. Caleb called it the Comb-n-Clean."

"Uh-huh."

"Caleb once had Vince seriously interested in investing in this thing. It actually works, but it has a design flaw. If your hair is a little too wet or greasy, it can spark."

"It can set your head on fire?"

"Something like that."

"That's a pretty serious design flaw."

Nick put the Comb-n-Clean back in the coffin. "Check this out." He brought out another object, a curiously shaped white plastic contrivance slightly larger than a human hand. He held it out to her.

"What is it?" Gretchen asked, taking it gingerly.

"Remember I told you Caleb had invented a kitchen gadget he wanted me to market? This is it. He showed it to me the last time I saw him. He was pretty excited. Chin said they applied for a patent a few months ago."

"What does it do?"

"I'm not sure," Nick said. "Chin's going to get me a copy of the patent application."

Gretchen inspected the device. Formed from a single piece of hard plastic, the object was both complex and simple. There were three oddly shaped holes, two sharp edges, and a ridged, cup-shaped protrusion. Gretchen tried several handholds, turning it this way and that. "Is it part of something else? Like a mixer part?"

"Nope."

"It looks like a . . . I don't know what it looks like."

"Hardy Chin said it looked like an IUD for elephants."

Gretchen made a pained face; her hand drifted to her abdomen. "How about an alien dissection device?"

"A French windshield scraper?"

"A fan blade that the government pays nine hundred dollars each for."

"The part that's left over after you assemble your kid's bicycle."

"A spatula from Betelgeuse."

"A boomerang from the Bizarro World."

Gretchen laughed. "Does it have a name?"

"It's called the HandyMate."

Six

Vince Love had commandeered their usual table near the back of the tiny, brightly painted restaurant. He was shredding a paper napkin into fettuccine, then reducing the strips to confetti with his manicured nails. He had a pretty good pile going.

"Waiting for a parade?" Nick asked.

Vince started, dropping the napkin. He recovered quickly and smiled, showing small, regular teeth. "You never know. Could be one any minute now." He pushed the confetti aside, picked up his coffee mug, looked into it, frowned, set it back on the table.

Nick pulled out a chair and sat down across from his partner.

Like Nick, Vince was thin, handsome, and well dressed. Unlike Nick, he had short, dark hair, small black eyes, and a precisely trimmed mustache. When seen together, they were often mistaken for a gay couple. That didn't bother Nick, but Vince couldn't stand it. He made a point of flirting with the waitresses, occasionally giving Charlene or Nan a pat on the hip as they passed in and out of the kitchen, making sure they knew which side of the male sexual divide he favored. Since he was a regular customer and a generous tipper, this behavior was tolerated, somewhat cheerfully, by the staff at Café Poca Cosa.

Charlene came by with a pot of coffee. She topped off Vince's mug and left without further incident. Vince was not in a flirtatious mood this morning.

Nick asked, "What's going on, Vince?"

"What do you mean?"

Charlene reappeared with a mug of coffee for Nick. He ordered the *huevos rancheros*. Vince asked for a tamale. "Just that and some salsa," he said.

Nick said, "You sounded kind of funny on the phone yesterday. And you don't look so good."

"I don't? Can't imagine why. I mean, just 'cause our store burned to the ground. Fucking burned to the fucking ground." Vince's face contorted into an anguished grimace for a fraction of a second, then snapped back to normal.

"You okay?" Nick had never seen Vince's face do that.

"I'm fine. No I'm not. I'm worried about the insurance, Nick. I talked to Artie again this morning. He said they have to sift the ashes. What the fuck does that mean? Sift the ashes? Fuck!"

"I don't know." Nick had never heard Vince use the word *fuck* so liberally. It embarrassed him, especially in this café, so small that private conversation was impossible. "You want me to talk to Artie?"

"Hell yes, I want you to talk to him."

"He must know we're going to need some cash pretty quick," Nick said.

"No shit."

"We have to rent a new space, and reorder, and . . . damn, I forgot all about Pertsy and Caroline." Pertsy and Caroline were their employees, or rather their employee, as the position was more like a shared full-time job than two part-time jobs. Nick never knew which one would show up for work on any given day. He took out his cell phone. "I'll call them right now."

Pertsy and Caroline lived together, dressed similarly, and lived on the same diet of tofu, brown rice, and seaweed. Vince was certain they were lesbians, but Nick believed their bond to be asexual. One day, he thought, they might both marry the same man.

Pertsy, the more dynamic of the duo, answered the phone. Nick told her what had happened. He let her explore a range of emotions, got her calmed down, then told her that they would be reopening soon at another location—possibly within a few weeks. He noticed Vince shaking his head sorrowfully.

"I'll be in touch, Perts. Gotta go." He pocketed the phone. "What's the matter?"

Vince lowered his eyes to the confetti hill. "I've been thinking, Nick. Maybe we shouldn't make any promises about reopening the store." He drew his finger across the pile, splitting it into two lesser hills. "We were partners, what, five and a half years? We made a few bucks, didn't we? Had some good times?"

Nick, noting the past tense, said nothing.

"You ever think of maybe doing something different? Maybe go off on your own?" Vince raised his eyes to meet Nick's gaze. "Maybe we ought to let it go. Take the money and run."

Nick said, "This is not good timing, Vince."

"Why not? Maybe the fire was a sign."

Nick took a deep breath, then another. "Okay, you want to split up. I respect that. I don't want to be in a partnership with a guy who doesn't want to be there. But first let's get the business back up and running, then let me buy you out. Or you buy me out, I don't care. But this isn't the time to quit. We've got a name, a product line, a customer base. We've got that guy up in Scottsdale who wants a franchise. We've got that buyer for Nordstrom who was talking about licensing our name—"

"That was just talk."

"That's where it starts, Vince. You know that. We've got something going. We walk away now, all we got is the insurance settlement, and that's it. We get nothing from our name, our goodwill, our momentum. You hear what I'm saying?"

"I don't know." Vince resumed his napkin-shredding. "I'm burned out, Nick." He gave a sick laugh. "I need a vacation. I need the cash, too. I'm kinda overextended. I invested ten grand in the Inch-Adder, and now Caleb's dead, too. I can't believe you let me give him the money."

"I tried to stop you. Look, Vince, stick with me six months. Six months, then I'll buy you out. Or we can sell the business together. We do it right, sell the goodwill and the name and the label, we can each take a nice chunk of cash, enough to start something else, or just sit back and do nothing. But if we just walk away now, we'll net maybe sixty, seventy thousand from the insurance settlement after we pay everybody off. Probably less."

"I gotta think about it."

"Fine, you do that."

Charlene arrived with Nick's *huevos rancheros* and a lonesome tamale for Vince. Nick stared at his plate, overflowing with rice, sliced fruit, and a salad of lettuce and red cabbage. The eggs and tortillas were under there someplace. It was a beautiful presentation. He didn't think he could eat a bite.

Vince said, "I'm really worried about this insurance thing."

"I'll talk to Artie."

Nick, you gotta look at it from their point of view. I mean, I can talk all I want to, tell them I know you since I was a kid, they don't listen to me. They got to do their thing. Sift through the ashes, you know?"

"Yeah, but yesterday you told Vince there wouldn't be any problem." Nick was sitting on Gretchen's porch watching the constant stream of U of A students pass by, his butt deep in a sagging butterfly chair and bare feet propped on the wrought-iron railing. He imagined Artie Nagel in his office leaning over his desk squeezing the telephone handset, sweat beading his ridged forehead. Artie was anxious by nature.

"Well, hell, Nick, what do I know? I never had a client's business burn down before. I do mostly auto and health work. They got procedures they got to go through."

"How long, Artie?" Nick said. "I've got expenses. I've got employees."

"I don't know. Could be they find out it was some electrical thing, give us the all clear tomorrow." Artie made some *putt-putt* sounds with his lips. "Or it could be six, eight weeks."

Nick groaned. "Two months?"

"Maybe not. Maybe not, Nick. Look, I know you got a problem. I'll do what I can, but I'm telling you, don't count on nothing soon."

Nick focused on his feet. He had good feet. "Thanks, Artie."

"You're welcome, man. Listen, you want to play some racquetball Friday?"

"My racquet is ashes." Nick's feet were slender and well formed—no corns, warts, or unsightly lumps. He could be a male foot model. If there was such a thing.

"Add it to your claim. Say you kept it in the store. Listen, I'll loan you one a mine. Whaddya say?"

"Sure, Artie. I'll give you a call." Nick hung up, trying to think of who might need a male foot model. Maybe a sandal company. Or Dr. Scholl's. Or one of those drug companies that marketed nail-fungus treatments. He scowled. The market seemed to be limited. No doubt there was a male-foot-model guild that had the opportunities sewn up. After all, how many male foot models did the world need? Two? Three?

He sat and watched a young man with a backpack zip by on a motorized scooter. Gretchen's tiny three-room double bungalow was just off Campbell, two blocks from the university. Always plenty going on.

The phone rang. Nick answered.

"Is this the *leather* guy?"

Nick hesitated, trying to place the voice.

"Hello? Leather guy?"

"Bootsie?" Just what he needed.

"I heard your place got *torched.*"

"It didn't get torched. We had a fire. Um, Gretchen's not home right now. You want me to have her call you?"

"I used to know a guy did that for a living."

"Did what?"

"Torched businesses. I was a cop. I seen it all. Arson, homicide, vice, I worked 'em all. Especially vice." *Hee hee hee.* "I still got my service revolver, so you better treat my little girl good, kid." *Hee hee hee.* "Just kidding."

Nick said, "Uh . . ." He didn't know which part, if any, Bootsie was kidding about.

"Where's my girl?"

"Gretchen? She's up in Marana doing a survey."

"Digging up dead Injuns?"

Nick frowned, knowing how offended Gretchen would be by her father's choice of words. He said, "Something like that. There's a new development going in, so she's up there with a couple of grad students walking the site."

"Well, you tell her to call her old man."

"I'll do that."

"You treat her good."

"I'll do that, too."

"Or I'll shoot your ass." *Hee hee hee.*

Seven

Yeah, one of each color, except for the orange. And two black. Do you have two in the black?"

"Let me see . . ." Gordo Encinas, owner of Adobe Rags, flipped expertly through the rack of linen shirts. "One olive, one straw, one sea urchin, two black . . . You sure you don't want one in the burnt peanut?"

"Who the hell comes up with these names? You mean the orange? No thanks. What have I got so far?"

Gordo carried the shirts back to the counter where Sheila, his assistant manager, was folding and wrapping Nick's other purchases.

"We got the five shirts, three pairs of chinos. You sure you don't need shorts? I've got some great retro-look silk Bermudas. Just in. They'd look great on you, Nick."

"When's the last time you saw my knees?"

Gordo shrugged. "You need any boxers? I got some great boxers."

"Just add up the damage, Gordo. See if my Visa card melts."

"Okay. We've got the belt, a very nice tooled calfskin. Not as fancy as a Love & Fashion belt, Nick, but not bad for thirty-nine bucks. Your shirts, one-twenty each, the pants—what are these chinos at, Sheila?"

"Eighty-five on sale."

"Three of those. And the jacket. It's a hell of a nice jacket, Nick. I could only get a dozen of them, could've sold three times that. You're lucky I had one in your size."

"When's that gonna be ready?"

"I'll get Gloria to do the sleeves tomorrow, okay? No charge on that."

"Okay. Where are we at here? Bottom-line me."

Gordo went around to the other side of the counter and rattled the keys on an adding machine. "Comes to seventeen forty-nine . . . twenty-five percent discount to the trade—you're still trade, right, Nick?—plus tax . . . call it thirteen hundred even. How's that sound?"

"Like a *ganga*." Nick slapped his Visa card on the counter, watched Gordo swipe it and key in the amount. "Listen, Gordo, Vince and I have put our orders on hold until we can find a new place."

Gordo waggled his head, watching the machine for an approval code. "I just can't imagine, Nick. What a shitty thing to happen to you guys."

"But we've one shipment in transit, some llama vests and jackets out of Peru. Right now the stuff is sitting in customs—anything out of Peru gets held up, you know—but they'll probably release it any day now. I'm going to need a place to store them. I was wondering if you might have a hundred square feet or so we could rent. Just till we get a new place."

"Rent? No way, Nick I couldn't take a dime, not with what you guys have been through."

"Really? That's generous of you."

"Only thing is, I'm jammed up. I haven't got the space, Nick."

"Oh."

"You want me to buy them off you? Cover your cost?"

"I don't know. We might have our new place open in a month or two. I'm gonna need inventory. Besides, I thought you didn't have the space."

"I've got space for *my* inventory."

Nick sighed. "Forget about it." He signed the charge slip, wondering how he was going to pay the bill when it came.

"Anything else I can do to help you out?"

"Yeah. Don't steal all my customers while I'm down."

Gordo laughed.

You've got orders," said Hardy Chin.

"What do you mean, orders?"

Chin's response was obscured by static; Nick set his jaw and kept driving.

". . . and two Number Threes."

"I missed that," Nick said. "Are we talking about those pet coffins?"

"Yes. You have orders to fill. I am—" More static.

Nick pulled into a Circle K parking lot. "You there?"

"What's going on?"

"I'm on my cell. Look, you're the executor. Can't you fill the orders?"

"I ship your coffins myself, I got to charge you a hundred bucks an hour. You lose money. Look, you come out here, I'll help you figure it out. You got to drive out tomorrow for the service, anyway. Come early. I'll drive you out to Caleb's, help you get up to speed."

Nick said nothing.

Chin went on, "You're the heir, Nick. You get the benefits, but you also have certain obligations. Your grandfather had an ongoing business. You've got customers."

"Okay, okay. What time should I come by?"

"How about ten?"

"That early? You sure this can't wait till next week?"

"I don't think so. People have a dead pussycat in their freezer, they get antsy."

Gretchen touched her fingers to her lips, restraining a smile.

"You don't like my new clothes?" Nick asked, posing in the mouse-gray brushed-cotton chinos and black linen shirt. Bally slip-ons. No socks. No watch, no jewelry, no hat.

"You look great, Nicky."

"What's so funny?"

"They look just like all your other clothes. Pleated chinos and a long-sleeved shirt. You're in the clothing business, but you only wear one thing."

Nick shrugged. "I found my look."

"You should try wearing shorts sometime. Step out." She did a little dance move, her battered hiking boots clomping on the red tile floor of her kitchen.

"I bought a new sport coat, too. Pure Scottish wool gab, woven in Italy, feels like silk. And hey, I bought you something."

"You— Oh!" Gretchen took the velvet box, obviously jewelry, opened it, took a breath. "Nicky . . ." She held the pendant, an intricate, asymmetrical mosaic of turquoise and coral, in her hand. It was about the size and shape of a eucalyptus leaf. She held it up to the light. "It's beautiful!" She opened the clasp, fastened the chain around her neck.

"It made me think of your eyes," Nick said.

"It feels alive. It feels *old*."

"It's a Zuni piece from the twenties," Nick said.

"It's beautiful, Nicky. I love it. How did I get so lucky as to find you?"

"It was your Fashion sense."

Gretchen unfastened the pendant and returned it to the box.

"You aren't going to wear it?"

"I'm going to take a shower. Look at me! I just got home. I'm covered with desert." Her jeans and Arizona Wildcats T-shirt were mottled with dried perspiration and dust. Nick, showing off his new clothes, had hardly noticed.

"Sorry. You find anything interesting?"

"A few scattered potsherds is all. I'm sure there's a habitation site nearby—probably several—but we haven't located any yet. Of course, you could put your finger anywhere on a map of Pima County and say the same thing. Only three of us to survey nine hundred acres, and they want us to do it in a week. It's absurd." She sat down and untied her boots, kicked them off. "They've got five of those enormous earthmovers, tires twelve feet high, crouching there waiting for us to finish. Hyenas the size of *T. rex.*" She moved toward the bathroom, stopped, gave him a kiss. "Thanks for the necklace, Nicky. I'd hug you, only I know you don't want desert all over your new shirt."

"I don't mind."

"Yes you do."

Nick followed her into the bathroom.

"What are you doing?" she asked.

"I want to watch."

"Oooh. Kinky boy." She pulled her T-shirt up over her head. Nick felt the air leave his lungs. No one had ever looked better in a farmer's tan. Six months now they'd been seeing each other, and Gretchen Groth still took his breath away. Her body was perfect—even the scar on her shoulder, the one slightly crooked finger, the raspberry birthmark like a pawprint on her belly, and the tattoos, of which she had several, all Native American symbols. She had interpreted them for him once. Most of them called for rain, luck, and fertility. She loosened her jeans, slid them down her white thighs, stepped out, watching him, her lips parted in a half smile. He remembered to breathe in; the smell of her hit him like morphine; his legs went weak as blood rushed to his groin. She hopped into the shower and closed the frosted glass door.

Nick listened to the water come on, heard her gasp as it hit her cold. He imagined her hand on the knob, adjusting, warm water hitting her neck, sheeting around her brown nipples, over her flat belly, through the forest of pubic hair and down her pale thighs, swirling into the round brass drain. Rain, luck, and fertility. He tugged and pulled and pushed and shrugged and left his new clothing on a pile on the floor, then he joined her.

Nick heard the sound of a blind man tapping. A woodpecker hammering. Someone knocking at the door. He opened his eyes, sat up naked on the bed, looked at the clock: seven P.M. He had been asleep only a few minutes; the tapping and scraping were coming from the kitchen. Nick found his chinos puddled on the bathroom floor. He pulled them on and brushed back his hair, still limp from the shower. He put on a clean shirt, the olive, as his mind idly attempted to identify the noises.

When Nick came into the kitchen he found Gretchen, wearing an oversize T-shirt and nothing else, scraping a pile of chopped tomatoes into a bowl.

"Making more salsa?"

She nodded happily.

Nick opened the refrigerator and grabbed a bottle of spring water. He watched Gretchen break apart a bulb of garlic with the heel of her hand. She brought her other hand up and, with a rapid series of movements, chopped off the ends of two cloves, smashed them across the cutting board, and, using a rocking motion, reduced the garlic to a fine mince. Nick experienced a moment of disorientation, then recognized the white object in her hand.

"The HandyMate!" he exclaimed.

Gretchen grinned. "I thought I'd try it out."

"You can cut with that plastic edge, huh?"

"Yeah. I think it's the way the serrations are designed. It cuts better than some of my good knives." She sliced off the stem end of a jalapeño, cut it lengthwise, turned the HandyMate ninety degrees, and used a spoonlike protrusion to scrape out the seeds. "No matter what little thing you want to do, this thing does it. So far I've figured out that it chops, scrapes, peels, cores, measures, grates, and pounds. It has a bottle opener, and I'm pretty sure you could use it to separate eggs."

"No kidding."

"It really is handy."

I have to leave for Bisbee first thing in the morning," Nick said.

"Oh?" Gretchen looked up from her magazine. "I thought the funeral was in the afternoon."

"It is. But I have to ship some pet-coffin orders. Hardy Chin—the lawyer—offered to drive me out there in his Bronco and help."

"You sure you don't want company?"

"Nah. You've got your survey to finish. I'll be fine."

They were sitting on Gretchen's front porch, enjoying a cool early evening breeze. Nick was playing with the HandyMate, imagining new uses. Gretchen held the latest issue of *American Antiquity.* They had printed one of her letters criticizing an article about the diets of pre-Columbian Hopi and Navajo peoples. Gretchen was a prolific letter writer; she never tired of seeing her opinions expressed in print.

She let the magazine fall to her lap. "At least it'll get your mind off the insurance thing."

"I better call Vince tonight, let him know what Artie said. He's gonna freak."

"Why is he so anxious about it?"

"I don't know." Nick laughed dryly. "Maybe he torched the place."

Gretchen echoed his laugh, picked up her magazine, then set it back down. "You're not serious, are you?"

Eight

Nick spent most of the drive to Bisbee thinking about Vince Love.

Vince had not answered his phone when Nick called him the night before. Nick, somewhat relieved, had left a message relating Artie's news—that it might be a month or two before they got the insurance money. One good thing about this funeral: it gave him an excuse to get out of town while Vince had his temper tantrum.

Nick had known Vince Love for twelve years, ever since they'd been vendors on the U of A campus, Nick selling fruit juices and smoothies out of a pushcart, Vince with his espresso stand just up the street. Their businesses were complementary—Nick made his money on the hot days, Vince raked it in when the weather turned cool. After a day of selling drinks, they often met at the Shanty for a beer. Vince had been a lot of fun back then. They'd talked a lot about getting rich, about cars, about music, about women.

Nick got off the freeway at Benson and drove south on Highway 80. The roadsides, green from the summer monsoons, were speckled with red and orange poppies.

The pushcart business went bad a year later when the university gave an exclusive contract to a vendor out of Phoenix. Nick and Vince were banished to the campus fringes. Nick sold his juice cart in disgust and started detailing cars in the alley behind his rented duplex. Vince took a job selling condos to snowbirds. Every now and then he would drop by with a six-pack to drink and talk.

Eventually Nick got serious about his detailing business, which he had named White Glove Auto Magic. He rented a garage up on Grant, hired a couple of guys part-time, put out some advertising. Vince moved to San Diego to work for a company that imported Peruvian handicrafts, and got married to a girl ten years his junior, barely legal, named Carlotta. He showed up with his bride one hot summer day at White Glove. Carlotta was a ball of fire, talking and chewing gum, bright red lips, tossing her mop of curly black hair and slashing the air with multicolored fingernails. "You can call me Lotta," she said. "Lotta Love." She wanted to be an actress. Vince thought she was a goddess.

As a belated wedding gift, Nick detailed Vince's MGB. He found a dozen lumps of used chewing gum stuck beneath the passenger seat. Three years later Vince turned up again, single.

Nick's detailing business outlasted Vince's marriage, but only by a few weeks. He soon found himself in the jewelry business, selling Mexican silver at the Tanque Verde swap meet. He invested his profits in additional inventory: Black Hills gold, Polish amber, South American freshwater pearls—whatever he could pick up cheap. A few months later he rented space at the annual Tucson Gem Show. Nick was showing a gaudy but unique necklace of coral, lapis, and freshwater pearls to a professional intuitive from Sedona when Vince Love reentered his life with a new woman by his side.

Nick didn't remember her name. What he *did* remember about that meeting was the realization that he and Vince had once again wound up in complementary businesses. Vince, having learned a thing or two during his stint with the San Diego handicrafts importer, was bringing in belts, wallets, and leather hats from Ecuador and Peru. They were both in the imported personal-accessories trade.

"We oughta swap stories sometime," Vince said. "I'm living up near Sabino Canyon now."

A few days later they met at the Shanty and sampled some of the new brews on the menu. Vince kept asking the bartender if he had Mohoxo, an obscure Peruvian brand. The bartender kept telling him no. Nick told Vince about a woman he'd been seeing, Kathy something, and Vince told Nick that he'd just broken up with the woman he'd brought to the gem show. Nick congratulated himself on not remembering her name. Vince noticed a humidor behind the bar and bought two cigars, nine bucks each, and smoked them, talking about how easy it would be to get rich in their respective businesses if only they'd work a little harder and catch a break or two. At some point during the evening, the notion of forming a partnership came up, and Love & Fashion had been conceived.

They hadn't really known each other then, Nick thought as he approached Tombstone, a dusty little town notable for an abundance of tall cemetery trees and an even greater abundance of bars and gift shops. During the past century, Tombstone had evolved from a mining town into a tourist trap, with numerous businesses claiming connections to the town's colorful past. Nick drove slowly past Boot Hill, and the town's main claim to fame: the OK Corral. He thought he might visit the site sometime and form his own opinions as to whether the Clantons or the Earps had held the high moral ground that day.

He wondered as he left Tombstone whether such a tourist destination might support a new Love & Fashion. He liked the idea of opening a store in an unfamiliar location. It took him back two years to the day he and Vince had opened the original.

Two weeks after that night of brainstorming at the Shanty, Nick and Vince rented a storefront on Fourth Avenue and laid out their wares, an eclectic mix of amber beads, Peruvian belts, Mexican silver, and assorted wallets, earrings, leather bracelets, and other articles of personal adornment. Nick rolled metallic gold paint over the old shoe-repair sign, and the next day lettered LOVE & FASHION in silver. The sign was all but unreadable, which got it noticed. Over the next few months Nick and Vince discovered each other's strengths and weaknesses.

Vince knew the import business inside and out. Nick had always used brokers to bring jewelry into the country, but Vince found and worked with original sources. By the time they celebrated their six-month "anniversary," they had goods coming in from seven South American countries. Vince also had a handle on their company finances—back in the pushcart days, he had taken a few classes in accounting.

Vince's personal finances, however, gave him constant problems. He was always broke, triple-mortgaged, maxed out on his credit cards, and complaining incessantly about his bad luck. Vince had a gambler's heart. Usually he lost his money at the local track, but two years back he had made his first investment in one of Caleb Hardy's products: the NoseGard, a reusable flesh-colored patch that adhered to one's nose to prevent sunburn. After spending a few thousand dollars of Vince's money, Caleb discovered that the patches were the wrong color, shape, and size for 98 percent of the population, and that the adhesive left behind a greenish stain. Fortunately, Vince kept his personal finances separate from those of Love & Fashion. He was fastidious in that regard. In business matters, he was a practical pessimist.

Nick's talents lay in sales and marketing. He had an instinct for what would move; he knew how to display the merchandise; and he knew who would buy it. Although they often mystified each other, both men recognized that they made a good team. The store was an immediate success. After a few months on Fourth Avenue, they leased a small two-story building downtown in what they hoped would become Tucson's new arts district. Nick converted the upstairs of the building into his apartment, and for a time all was well.

Nick learned early on that Vince Love had a tendency to overreact to minor problems—one slow afternoon at the store or one unhappy customer could throw him into an emotional tailspin. He relied on Nick to lead him back to the sunny side of the street. Two or three times a week Nick had to make a serious effort to lift his partner's spirits. At first Nick hadn't minded the role. It made him feel useful and important. But after a few months he came to resent it, feeling as though Vince was feeding off his positive energy.

In some ways, Vince Love's gloom-and-doom side had served their partnership well. Without it, Nick realized, he would have continued to overpay his suppliers, carried too much inventory, and priced the merchandise too low. Vince's tendency to see the downside of every transaction had saved the business from some horrendous mistakes.

Their partnership had been working for two years. Nick did not want to let it go. He did not seriously believe that Vince had anything to do with the fire. The insurance investigators would eventually discover that the fire had started in some antique wiring, or a pile of rags in the basement, or a freak lightning strike. The delay was just the insurance company's way of holding on to their money for as long as possible.

He would have to work on Vince, get him pumped up again. The fire might turn out to be a good thing after all. They could reopen the store at a new location. The Fourth Avenue area between downtown and the university was ripe for gentrification. They could update their look and bring in that line of emu purses from Argentina.

By the time he reached Bisbee, Nick had convinced himself that Love & Fashion would be up and running in no time. He would make it happen. It was either that or go into the pet-coffin business—a career that lacked appeal. He decided to liquidate the coffin business as soon as possible. Maybe Hardy Chin could find him a buyer.

He turned off the highway at Tombstone Canyon and drove slowly down the steep, twisted thoroughfare that ran the length of

Old Bisbee. Chin's office occupied a narrow brick building wedged between a vintage clothing store and a palm reader, a few doors down from the AAA Bonding Service. In Bisbee, where funky tourism, copper mining, and correctional institutions all contributed equally to the local economy, such a mix of businesses was typical.

Nick walked in riding a wave of self-confidence. The receptionist, an older, diminutive Asian woman with prominent teeth and a pockmarked complexion, directed him with a jab of her thumb toward Hardy Chin's open door.

Nick entered Chin's office prepared to issue a raft of instructions, but stopped dead when he noticed that the person sitting behind the desk had longer hair, bigger eyes, and a lot more estrogen than Hardy Chin. Better-looking, too.

She said, *"Buenos días,"* giving the words an authentic buzz, crinkling her black eyes, her mouth widening to a crooked smile. Nick thought he'd seen her someplace before.

"Good morning," he said, looking left and right. "I'm looking for Hardy Chin?"

"He'll be right back." She stood up and thrust out a hand. Short red nails. "I'm Yola." She looked about thirty, maybe thirty-five. Maybe older. With the makeup it was hard to tell. Her eyebrows were painted high and arched. An enormous quantity of dark auburn hair spilled over smooth shoulders; her bosom strained the black chiffon of her sundress. A woman flattered by her extra pounds.

"Nick Fashon," Nick said. He liked her handshake—crisp, dry, and firm. "Do you work with Hardy?" He watched her hand slide away. The olive skin of her wrists was spattered with tiny pale dots, like reverse freckles. He had seen marks like that before, burn marks on the arms of a fry cook. This Yola did not look like a fry cook.

"I am just a client, like you." She sat down. "Chin went next door to make some copies for me. He'll be right back." She pushed her hair back over her shoulder. "And I'll be out of your hair." She grinned, her mouth tilting up toward her left eye. "I know you got an appointment."

"I'm a few minutes early," Nick said. He wasn't sure whether he should leave, or take a seat and wait. He decided to remain standing and make conversation. "You live here in Bisbee?"

"Sierra Vista," she said, naming a town twenty-five miles west of Bisbee. The way she was smiling made Nick feel as though she knew something he didn't.

"Ah. I've never been there. I mean, except just driving through."

"Is nothing special. Lots of military."

"Ah."

They regarded each other for a few heartbeats. Nick decided that she was older than she looked. Late thirties. He wished she would stand again so he could get a better look.

As if reading his mind, Yola got up and walked past him. Nick slowly pivoted on one heel, following her progress, watching the way her hips rippled the inky fabric. She stopped in the doorway, looking out into the reception area. Her weight was marvelously distributed. The shape of her calves made Nick want to take up sculpture. He imagined forming her from slick clay.

"I know your grandfather." She looked back at him over her shoulder. "I am very sorry."

"You knew Caleb?"

"He was a friend of mine. He would fix things for me. Hey Chin, what you do, take it to some monk to copy?"

Hardy Chin appeared, handed her a thin sheaf of papers, looked past her, and saw Nick. "You two meet?" he asked. He was wearing a straw cowboy hat, jeans, and an embroidered denim shirt.

"We're good buddies by now, okay?" Yola winked at Nick, then said to Chin, "I see you later."

"Okay then." Chin watched her leave, then turned to Nick and said, "Nice ass."

Nick gave a noncommittal shrug. He agreed with Chin's assessment, but he was not prepared to discuss it.

Chin said, "So, Nick Fashon, you ready to ship some coffins?"

Nine

Would you do me a favor?" Nick asked.

"Sure," said Chin as he simultaneously lit one of his cigarillos and pulled into the left lane to pass. They were in his Bronco four-by-four, coming up fast on a white sedan.

"Slow down, please."

Chin, still in the left lane, eased up on the gas and looked at Nick through sunglasses with lenses the size and color of ripe olives. "You don't want me to pass?" The two vehicles were abreast, traveling at eighty miles per hour.

"Just slow down."

"I'm billing the estate for my time, you know."

The man in the sedan was looking up at them, his expression hovering between anger and fear.

"Just ease off, okay?"

Chin shrugged, took his foot off the accelerator, slipped back behind the white sedan. "How fast you want me to drive? Speed limit okay?"

"That would be fine."

Chin puffed on his cigarillo, filling the Bronco with smoke. Nick cracked his window. Chin patted the thick manila folder on the console between them. "You got a lot of orders last week."

Nick picked up the folder and extracted a handful of smaller envelopes, about twenty of them, all addressed to C.H. Enterprises at a Bisbee post office box. Each of the smaller envelopes contained a check or money order and a request for one or more coffins. Most of the orders came from individuals or small-town pet shops. There was one for four dozen coffins in assorted sizes from Pet Rest Cemeteries, Inc., and another for two dozen Number Ones—the gerbil size—from a pet store in Colorado.

"This is a lot of coffins," Nick said.

"Pets die, man." Chin had loosened up since their last meeting.

"How many of these things did he sell?"

Chin shrugged. "What you've got in your hands is about three weeks' worth. Maybe a couple thousand bucks a month? I don't know. Caleb wasn't much of a bookkeeper."

Nick shuffled through the orders, adding them up. "Looks like a little over sixteen hundred dollars. What do you think they cost? Cardboard's cheap, right?"

"He was making money," said Chin.

"I wonder what he did with it."

"Probably put it all back into his doohickeys."

Nick noticed that they were traveling at eighty miles per hour again, but the road had straightened out, so he said nothing.

Chin said, "So what you think of Yola? Pretty hot tamale, isn't she?"

"You always talk about your clients like that?"

"Just Yola. You recognize her?" He turned his black-olive sunglasses on Nick.

"Should I?"

Chin grinned. "You don't watch TV?" He slowed abruptly and turned on to the narrow dirt track that led to Caleb Hardy's homestead.

"I thought she looked familiar," Nick said, his fingers white on the armrest. "What does she do?"

"¡Vamanos!"

"Vamanos?"

"The cooking show. Every Thursday afternoon. ¡Vamanos!: South of the Border with Yola Fuentes."

Nick nodded, remembering. He had never watched the show, but he'd seen the promo spots.

Chin said, "She's got a restaurant over in Sierra Vista. El Otro Lado. I handled her divorce for her. Her husband, man, he's a psycho. One time he came into my office waving a gun."

"He shoot you?"

"Nah. I got her a good settlement, too. Anyway, she got to keep the restaurant. By the way, I got a copy of that patent application for you. We submitted about nine weeks ago. It'll be a few months before we hear back."

"The HandyMate?"

"Yeah. Most of Caleb's inventions never got submitted, you know. It's an expensive process. But he was hot on this HandyMate. It's supposed to do everything. I still say it looks like birth control for elephants."

Caleb Hardy's spread came into view. Nick, looking at the UFO-shaped workshop, said, "I see it hasn't departed for Betelgeuse."

Chin nodded. "Since Caleb built it, you can never be sure."

Nick slid the ten-foot door all the way open, holding his breath against the hot-cardboard reek that came rolling out of the pole barn.

"I don't suppose this thing has a sprinkler on the roof."

Hardy Chin said, "I don't think so." They stepped inside. The side walls were lined with metal shelves piled high with die-cut, prefolded coffins. A long table at the end of the barn held a tape machine, labels, packing lists, and other shipping miscellany.

"Okay then," Chin said, handing Nick the folder full of orders.

"Looks like everything's here. You get started. I got to make some phone calls."

"What? Hold on, I don't know what the hell I'm doing here!"

"You'll figure it out. You got the orders." Chin spread his arms. "You got all the goods. Just pack, label, and ship. That's all you have to do."

"How? I can't even wrap a birthday present."

"You'll figure it out."

"How do I ship the stuff? UPS? Will they drive all the way out here?"

Chin laughed. "Probably not."

"If you're not going to help, then why are you here?"

"I'm executor. Got to keep an eye on you." Chin smiled. Lots of teeth. "I gotta make some calls." He walked back to his Bronco.

Nick stared helplessly at the orders, at the shelves of folded coffins. He looked out the open door. Chin was already sitting in his air-conditioned sport utility vehicle with the phone to his ear. "Jerk," Nick muttered. He picked up the first order. One Number Three coffin—bunny-rabbit size. Nick walked down the row of shelves, found a stack of Threes. Now what? Did he put the cardboard box inside a cardboard box? Wrap it in kraft paper? Or just slap a label on the coffin and ship it?

He heard the beep of a horn. "Hey, Nick!"

Nick walked to the door. Chin had rolled his window down. "I can't get a signal." He jerked a thumb back up the driveway. "I'm going to have to drive back to the ridge. I'll be back!" He drove off, spinning his wheels. A cloud of dust drifted slowly toward Nick, becoming invisible as it surrounded him. He could feel it sucking the moisture from his body.

An hour later Nick had packed all nineteen orders. Chin had not returned. He looked at the stacked cartons. There was no way they would fit into Chin's Bronco. He remembered Caleb's old pickup truck parked beside the caboose. He could load it up and drive himself back to Bisbee—if he could find the keys. If the truck worked. He left the pole barn and walked out to the pickup. The left rear tire was flat. Nick found the spare tire tied under the truck bed with bungee cords and packing tape. He began to remove it, then decided he should first see if the engine ran. He found a large ring of keys in the caboose, tried several, finally identified the ignition key, and cranked the engine. It started instantly. Nick was pleased. He let the engine run while he jacked up the rear end and disentangled the spare tire. He was tightening the lug nuts when two packrats ran between his legs. Nick yelped and jumped back. He noticed the smoke coming from under the hood. He turned off the engine and popped the hood. The engine compartment was packed solid with smoldering cactus parts, tufts of grass, twigs, and feathers. The rats had made the truck their home.

He used his hands and the tire iron to clear most of the smoldering vegetation from the engine. The plug wires had melted. He slammed the hood.

So much for that idea. Now what? He could hear angry voices in his head, future conversations with Hardy Chin. He imagined himself trying to walk the twenty miles to Bisbee, staggering across the high desert. Realizing that he was already becoming dangerously dehydrated, Nick returned to the caboose to look for water. He was pleased to discover several ice-cold Coronas in Caleb's small refrigerator, which was apparently powered by the solar panels on the roof. He drained one bottle on the spot. The interior of the caboose was neat and efficient-looking, like a well-kept houseboat. The shelves were crowded with books: *The Inventor's Bible, The Inventor's Guide to Patents, How to Market Your Big Idea,* and other books on the same theme, plus several Ernest Hemingway novels and a dog-eared copy of *On the Road.* Next to the shelves, a collection of photographs was pinned to a cork bulletin board.

Two of the photos were of Nick's mother: one as a teenager, looking very 1950s, and the other as he remembered her, much older, still looking very 1950s. Nick was surprised to find several pictures of himself. Five were old school photos, from elementary school up through his senior year in high school. His mother must have sent them to Caleb over the years. The sixth was clipped from the *Arizona Daily Star* article about Love & Fashion: Nick standing in front of the Venezuelan goatskin bra and garter belt. The only other photo was a Polaroid of Caleb and another man of similar vintage astride Caleb's Harley-Davidson. The photo had been taken in front of the caboose, at the exact spot where Caleb had died. Nick shivered, feeling the presence of Caleb's ghost. He turned away from the images, grabbed a second Corona, and carried it out to the UFO, as he had come to think of Caleb's steel parasol. He turned on the sprinkler system; artificial rain hissed on the hot steel roof. A few seconds later a mist began to fall from the eaves, cooling the desert wind. The air temperature beneath the steel parasol began to drop.

Nick wandered through the workshop on an unguided tour of a dead madman's mind. From what little he had learned, it seemed Caleb had settled here in the late fifties, shortly after abandoning his wife and daughter. For over four decades he had devoted himself to inventing gadgets in hopes of getting rich. Nick recalled his second meeting with Caleb, three years after his mother's funeral, back when Nick had owned the detailing shop.

Nick had been working on a Porsche 911, trying to get a stubborn spatter of road tar off the fender skirt, when a bearded, shirtless, barrel-chested old man in greasy, beltless blue jeans, lace-up boots, and an antennaed helmet rode up on a Harley-Davidson a few years older than Nick. The man stopped in front of the open garage door and pressed a button on the handlebar. As if by magic, the bike rose up onto its stand and turned itself off.

Nick had not recognized his grandfather. He'd only met the old man once before, at his mother's funeral. At that time Caleb Hardy had been beardless and fully clothed.

The old man removed his helmet, which appeared to have a radio built into it, and hung it on the handlebar mirror. He ran thick fingers through his gray and white beard, combing out the bugs, then detached himself from the motorcycle and stood beside it for a moment, slightly bent forward, as his body prepared itself for a new form of locomotion.

Nick said, "We don't do bikes, pop."

The man grinned, displaying a set of teeth that had been heavily repaired with silver and gold. He lumbered over to Nick and threw his arms around him in a powerful hug.

Astonished, Nick ducked out of the embrace, his face dragging across a forest of curly gray chest hair.

The old man was cackling with inordinate glee.

"What's so funny?" Nick wiped his face with the back of his hand.

"You are, you young pup. Don't you recognize your granddaddy?"

"Grandpa Caleb?"

"Damn straight, boy." Caleb delivered a short punch to Nick's shoulder, knocking him back a couple feet. He then looked from the rag in Nick's hand to the road tar on the Porsche. "I got something that'll take that right off."

Caleb Hardy hung around all afternoon prattling on about his ideas and inventions. When the old man finally got around to putting the touch on him, Nick was sufficiently charmed to hand over a few hundred bucks for a share in the BassBoy, a fishing lure made from recycled beer cans.

Caleb returned to Nick's detailing shop a few days later with a sample of the BassBoy and a one-quart mason jar full of blue liquid.

A cheap black-and-white label pasted to the side of the jar identified the contents as GUNKOFF®.

"Take that road tar right off," Caleb promised. He wore the same jeans and hat but had traded in his boots for a pair of shredded sneakers. Nick thanked him, looking doubtfully at the fishing lure, which had been fashioned from a can of Tecate. Caleb said, "That'll be ten bucks for the GunkOff." Nick paid up and put the jar on a shelf with his other cleaning chemicals.

A few days later he had occasion to try the GunkOff on an '88 Mercedes that had been badly spattered along the rocker panels. The tar came off as promised. Nick finished the job, delighted with his new find, but when the customer picked the car up that evening, he noticed that the paint was blistering wherever it had been touched by the GunkOff. The repaint cost Nick six hundred dollars.

He hadn't seen Caleb for another year after that.

Nick found several jars of GunkOff in one of Caleb's steel cabinets. Another cabinet held a collection of handmade fishing lures. Nick wandered among the tables and cabinets, sipping his beer, looking out toward the driveway, wondering whether Chin would ever be back. He looked at his watch. The funeral was supposed to start at five; Chin would have to return soon if they were going to make it. He sat down at a table where Caleb had been working with a Dremel tool, carving curious shapes from white, waxy-looking blocks of plastic. Nick examined the half-finished forms, trying to puzzle out Caleb's intentions. He might have been working on another version of the HandyMate.

Of all Caleb's inventions, the HandyMate was the one that really interested Nick. The pet coffins—despite their promise of immediate cash flow—did not excite him. Nor did the NoseGard, the fishing lures, the Inch-Adder, the Comb-n-Clean, or any of Caleb Hardy's other weird brainstorms. But the HandyMate . . . The more he thought about it, the easier it became to imagine a HandyMate in every kitchen drawer in America.

He didn't know much about injection molding, but he was pretty sure that the HandyMate could be made for a buck or two. Nick allowed himself to fantasize numbers. Say the HandyMate cost two bucks to make, and he could sell it wholesale for $3.50. Two hundred million kitchens in the United States implied a potential profit of $300 million . . . and that was just the U.S. Or he could import them from China, get them for fifty cents each. Better yet, he could *sell* them to China. What was that, another eight hundred million kitchens?

Nick drank the last of his beer. He was still thirsty and was getting a headache. He walked back to the caboose, where he remembered seeing a plastic jug of water in the refrigerator. He tipped up the jug and drank. He drank until his belly felt tight. He was thirstier than he'd realized. He sat down on a wooden chair in the tiny galley, the water jug hooked on his forefinger. He wanted more but was suddenly beset by the fear that Chin might never come back for him. He would die out here, just like his grandfather, devoured by vultures and coyotes. Nick smiled, shaking his head at his own folly. He was being ridiculous. Of course Chin would return. Nick's eyes fell again upon the bulletin board, at the photos of his former selves, of his mother, of Caleb astride his Harley-Davidson.

Where was the Harley?

Nick stood up and peered closely at the photo. In it, Caleb looked much as he had the last time Nick had seen him. Ancient and bearded. His companion, whoever he was, looked even older and hoarier. Nick unpinned the photo and put it in his shirt pocket, then went out to search the compound for the missing motorcycle.

Half an hour later, Hardy Chin's Bronco came bouncing up the driveway. Nick set his jaw and left the shade of the UFO.

"Where the hell have you been?"

"Hey, I'm sorry, man. I had a flat tire."

Nick looked at Chin's hands and fingernails, which were immaculate. "Yeah, right."

Chin shrugged. "You want to load up? We've only got an hour till the funeral starts."

"There are more boxes than we can fit in here. I'll have to rent a truck, or try to get UPS to drive out here."

"Good luck, man. Caleb always had to drive the stuff into town himself." Chin turned the Bronco around and headed back up the driveway. "That what you're going to wear?" he asked, looking askance at Nick's dusty, sweat-stained clothing.

"Don't worry about it."

"I just was wondering."

"I've got a change of clothing in my car, so you can stop wondering."

"Okay, man, *sorry!*"

"I can't believe I'm going to have to drive all the way back out here."

"Life's a bitch, man. Hey, you need to hire a truck, I got a cousin, he's got a Suburban, lots of cargo space, four-wheel drive, get you in and out like corn through a goose."

"I'll think about it."

"He'll be at the funeral."

"He knew Caleb, too?"

"Nah. He's gonna be driving the hearse."

They rode the rest of the way to Chin's office in silence. Nick got his bag out of his 'vette; Chin let him use the restroom to wash up and change into a black linen shirt, black chinos, black slip-ons. Nick liked the all-black look but usually felt it was a bit too East Coast for Tucson, Arizona. Of course, for a funeral it was perfect. He wet his hair and combed it back, then looked himself over in the mirror. His lips were rimmed pink with dryness. His eyes were bloodshot from dust and heat, making his irises look bright blue. He covered them with a pair of dark sunglasses. The bereaved grandson.

Chin was waiting by the front door. He, too, had changed, adding a navy blue sport coat to his ensemble and replacing his white straw hat with a black one. He held the door for Nick and locked up. He pointed at Nick's Corvette. "You follow me, okay?" he said, heading for his Bronco.

"Just a second, Chin."

Chin stopped.

"Where is Caleb's bike?"

"Bike?"

"He used to have a motorcycle. A Harley."

Chin shrugged. "All I ever saw him drive was that old pickup truck."

Nick took the photo of Caleb on his bike from his pocket and showed it to Chin. "He had a bike."

Chin squinted at the photo. He pointed at the other man on the motorcycle. "That's Herb Jenks."

"Who's Herb Jenks?"

"Herb? A real old-timer. Prospector. Only I don't think he prospects much. He has a shack up in the Mules, I heard. Shows up in town every couple months to get drunk. Likes to get in fights. I got him out of jail a couple times, at your grandfather's request." Chin handed the photo back to Nick. "Caleb wasn't too picky about his friends. Herb might show up at the funeral, but I doubt it. He probably doesn't even know Caleb died."

"I'm mostly interested in where Caleb's motorcycle went to," Nick said. "Maybe this Herb Jenks stole it. Are you sure it wasn't there when he was found?"

"How do I know? Ask the one who found him."

"The girlfriend?"

"*Sí*, man."

The sparsely attended service was held at a cemetery three miles outside of town. The young priest, Father Michael Delany, had never met Caleb. He went on for nearly forty minutes intoning passages from the Bible while the living crowded beneath a cottonwood, seeking shade. Nick figured the priest was there simply to log some flight time, or because no one else would do it.

Bored, Nick passed the time by observing his fellow mourners. He knew Hardy Chin, of course, and the receptionist from his office. The other Asiatic face in the crowd, a blocky young man in an ill-fitting dark suit, would be Chin's nephew the hearse driver.

The only other face he recognized was that of Yola Fuentes, who stood as close to the coffin as she could without leaving the shade of the cottonwood. He wondered what she was doing there. Briefly, he allowed himself to think that she had come to see him, drawn by his magnetic personality and good looks. Too bad he would have to disappoint her, he thought, then let go of the fantasy.

The other six mourners were all older women. Nick tried to figure out which of them had been Caleb's girlfriend. He was pretty sure it was either the tall one with the tight jeans and the blond wig, or the one who looked as if she could take down a longhorn steer using only one hand and her powerful-looking dentures. Nick played with that image, repressing the smile that threatened to ruin his funeral face.

The priest was ten minutes into an impromptu sermon concerning the nature of the soul when Nick became aware that Hardy Chin had eased up beside him.

"You doing okay?" Chin asked in a low voice.

Nick shrugged. He was still angry about being left to pack all those cartons himself.

Chin whispered, "I don't know how come this Father Mike got to be here. He's a real asshole. Caleb's probably got his ghost fingers in his ghost ears."

The priest droned on. Nick finally turned to Chin and asked, "Which one was Caleb's girlfriend?"

"Man, I thought you met her."

"Met who?"

"Yola. Man, you don't pay attention much, do you?"

Nick opened his mouth, but words failed to materialize. He looked over at Yola Fuentes. She was staring back at him, eyes shining, mouth slightly curved into a smile that was half Mona Lisa and half Courtney Love.

Gretchen was awake in bed, reading the latest issue of the *Journal of Field Archaeology*. She lowered the magazine to her lap, watched Nick kick off his shoes.

"Long day?" she asked.

"Interminable."

"You okay?"

"I'm filthy." He stepped out of his chinos. "I spent three hours in an uncooled metal barn packing cardboard coffins. That damn Chin didn't lift a finger to help. He was supposed to walk me through it, help me get up to speed, then he spends the whole morning sitting in his car talking on his phone. He'll probably bill me for it. Then we have to go to the funeral, which is pretty bleak, and then I have to hire a truck—one of Chin's never-ending supply of cousins—to follow me back out to the ranch to pick up the packages on account of UPS won't drive all the way out there, and we get stuck, and—ah, hell. I should just haul the inventory up to a fulfillment center. Let them do the work."

"Good idea."

"I've got a business to rebuild. I don't need this running out to Bisbee twice a week."

"I don't blame you. It's a long drive."

"You're damn right it is." He sat down on the edge of the bed and peeled off his socks. "I need a shower."

Gretchen leaned forward and massaged his shoulders. She kissed his back. "I've smelled worse."

Nick felt the muscles in his back and shoulders relaxing beneath her probing fingers. "I saw the patent application for that thing, that HandyMate. You wouldn't believe all the stuff it does."

"I used it to make supper." She put her arms around his chest and pulled him against her. "It cores apples."

"Yeah, and about forty other things."

"Artie Nagel called. He said he'd call back first thing in the morning."

"Oh. Anybody else?"

"Just Vince." Gretchen laughed. "About six times." She traced a circle around his left nipple with a fingernail.

"Oh." Nick took a breath. "Hey, you ever watch that cooking show ¡Vamanos!?"

"I saw it once. That Mexican woman."

"Yeah. I met her. Yola Fuentes. She's one of Hardy Chin's clients. Chin told me she was Caleb's girlfriend, but then I talked to her after the funeral, and she says she and Caleb were just friends. Caleb used to do some odd jobs for her, fixing stuff at her restaurant. I guess he was sort of her HandyMate."

"Really?" Gretchen's hands slid down his chest, over his belly. "Do you think she's pretty?"

"No," Nick said quickly.

"She looks pretty on TV."

"Yeah, well, off camera she looks about eighty years old. No teeth, scabby lips, three nostrils."

"That's what I thought." Gretchen put her palms against his back and gave a shove. "Go take a shower, HandyMate. I got a job for you."

Ten

The morning arrived gray and tumultuous; lightning flickered over the Catalinas, and the dull roar of distant thunder filled the air. Gretchen sat in the living room watching the usually complacent TV weather forecasters jabbering excitedly over the possibility of flash floods, damaging winds, and hail the size of softballs. Nick was in the kitchen making *huevos rancheros.*

"They're saying three to four inches possible," Gretchen said. "They're getting dumped on west of the Tucsons." Gretchen picked up the phone. "I'm calling John and Valerie to tell them to take the day off. Marana will be one big mud puddle." She punched in the number.

Nick cracked a pair of eggs into a sauté pan, spooned warm salsa around the edges, covered the pan. While the eggs cooked, he used the HandyMate to chop some onion and cilantro. He heated four tortillas over the gas flame, slid them onto two plates, topped them with the cooked eggs and salsa, garnished them with the onion and cilantro, and set them out on the counter that divided the living room from the small kitchen.

Gretchen finished her brief conversation with Valerie, asked her to pass the message on to John, then joined Nick at the counter.

"Looks good." She cut a wedge of egg and tortilla, and ate it. "Mmmm. You are a HandyMate indeed."

"I do my best."

"We're good together, aren't we, Nicky?"

"Better than good."

"I'm sorry you're having such a hard time."

"I'll get through it. The fire might turn out to be for the best. Maybe I'll let the retail business go and devote myself to marketing the HandyMate."

"Really? You loved your clothing shop."

"Yeah, I did. But since Vince isn't interested in reopening, I'll only have half of the insurance settlement to work with. Besides, I've been thinking about this thing." He picked up the HandyMate. "Maybe it will make me a rich man. Would you still love me if I were a rich man?"

"I'd certainly try." She pointed her fork at Nick's plate. "Your eggs are getting cold."

Nick applied himself to his breakfast. They ate without speaking, listening to the sounds of fork hitting plate and an occasional soft grunt of pleasure. Nick was mopping up the last of the egg and salsa with a folded tortilla when the phone rang.

It was Artie. "Nick? I don't got nothing good to tell you, kid."

Nick's *huevos* turned to ice.

"I talked to Clint Pfleuger, our investigator. He was down there at your store with the police. It looks like your place might have been torched."

"Torched?" To Nick's ears, his voice sounded extremely calm considering what was going on with his heart.

"I'm not supposed to be telling you this, Nick, so anybody asks, you don't know anything. It looks like there was something in the basement, some kind of incendiary device. Did you keep any, like, alarm clocks or gas cans or anything like that down there?"

"Gas cans? No! There was some old furniture down there, and

some excess inventory. I guess we had some boxes full of display props, stuff like that. No firebombs."

"Well, Pfleuger says it looks like arson."

Nick's mind had gone numb. "Am I going to have a problem getting my money?"

"Nick, you're not hearing me. Here's how the company looks at it: it was you, or it was your partner, or it was your landlord. That's how they see it. You ought to get yourself a lawyer."

"But I didn't . . . why would any of us . . . why would we burn down our own store? We were making money! I lost all my *stuff!* My Motown records! My clothes! Why would we burn ourselves out?"

"I'm not saying you did."

"What about a disgruntled customer? Or a firebug?"

"They look at those things, too. Only they don't look very hard."

Nick slumped in his chair, his chin coming to rest on his fist.

"It's business, Nick. If they weren't assholes about it, everybody who wanted to redecorate would torch their own businesses. A lot of them do anyways."

Nick nodded, grinding chin stubble into his knuckles. Artie went on talking for a time, but Nick wasn't taking it in. When Artie stopped talking, he hung up the phone. Gretchen was staring at him. Nick stood up and walked out onto the porch. Water had begun to fall from the sky. The mist softened the edges of the houses across the street. The clouds grew thick and dark, and the rain fell harder, turning the air gray. He sensed Gretchen's presence behind him, but he continued to look out into the rain. It came down in sheets, pounding the tile roofs, filling the street, roaring in his ears.

Eleven

Vince Love was drinking rum and Coke when Nick arrived at his apartment.

"Nick. What's going on, man? Christ, you're all wet. Is it raining? You hear from Artie?"

Nick looked around Vince's living room: rumpled sofa, coffee table studded with empty glasses and beer cans, one leather chair covered with newspapers and discarded clothing, another holding up Vince's oversize gray cat.

"I ever tell you that you live like a pig?"

Vince shrugged. "Sounds like something you might have said." He held up his glass. "You want a drink?"

"It's a little early for me."

"It's after noon in New York."

"No thanks."

"Whatever. Siddown." Vince scooped the pile of papers and clothing from the chair and dumped it on top of the cat. The cat didn't move.

"Is she alive?" Nick asked, sitting down.

"She perks up around dinnertime." Vince sank into the sofa. "I don't always drink like this, you know."

"I didn't figure you did."

"I'm just sort of freaked about, you know, everything." Staring into his glass.

"I talked to Artie."

Vince looked up; hope flared briefly, then died. "Oh shit," he said. "What did he say?"

"They think it was arson."

Vince stared back at him, his black eyes wide. "Arson? What're you talking about?"

"You don't know?"

"Know what?" Leaning forward. "Jesus, Nick, how come you're giving me that look?"

"The building was torched, Vince."

Vince sat back as if punched in the chest. "Torched?"

"They're not going to pay us until they do their investigation. And if they decide one of us did it, they won't pay, period."

"One of . . . *us?*"

Nick said, "How bad do you need money, Vince?"

Vince shook his head, fear, anger, and confusion playing across his face. His lips tightened and his eyes narrowed, anger winning out. "Christ, you don't think *I* did it, do you?"

Nick held Vince's eyes, then shook his head. He did not really believe that Vince Love was responsible for the fire. Vince was a lousy housekeeper, a gambler, and a doomsayer, but Nick simply could not see him as an arsonist.

"Jesus, Nick, how can you think I'd do something like that?"

"I'm not saying you did it."

"Yeah, but you think I might have."

"No." Nick tried to make it forceful and sincere. "I do not think you did it. Okay? The question is, who did? Artie said they found some sort of incendiary device in the basement. Somebody burned us out on purpose. Who?"

"Well, if it *was* me, then I'm a fucking idiot, because you're making it sound like the insurance company isn't gonna pay up."

"Who else would profit? Henderson?" Nick said. Henderson was their landlord, a decrepit, seldom seen octogenarian who lived in a country-club condominium in Desert Springs, California. He answered his own question. "I can't see it. He doesn't need the money. Besides, it's not something he would do."

"Maybe it was some kids just getting in their kicks. Or maybe one of our customers got pissed at us."

"Can you think of anybody like that?"

"We get a lot of weirdos. Or maybe it was the competition. That asshole Encinas."

Nick shook his head. "Gordo Encinas feeds off our customers, and he knows it. He'll just lose business with us gone."

Vince drank the rest of his rum and Coke in one swallow. "They really aren't gonna pay us?"

"Not as long as they suspect us of setting the fire."

Vince stared into his glass. "I am so fucked," he said.

Gretchen had left a note on the refrigerator: *Back at 7. Dinner at Caruso's?*

That sounded good to Nick. Caruso's had become a Friday-night ritual for the two of them. Checkered tablecloths, red sauce, and cheap Chianti. He opened the refrigerator and poured himself a glass of juice, tasted it, frowned, read the label on the bottle: Mango-Cranberry Passion. How Gretchen. He looked around the small kitchen, at the pans hanging above the stove, the crockery-lined shelves, the collection of cutting boards, all too small for serious cooking. He had been thrust into an alternate reality. This was not his world. His world had become smoke and memories. He sat down at the counter with his glass of Mango-Cranberry Passion. Here, he was a visitor. A bowl of fruit caught his eye. Mangoes, kiwis, oranges. He would have chosen apples, plums, and bananas. Next to the fruit bowl, holding down a stack of mail, was the Handy-

Mate. Nick picked it up and ran his fingers over its smooth, sculpted surfaces. One surface, really, since its basic structure was that of a Möbius strip. Nick selected an orange from the bowl and used the HandyMate to peel it. The tool felt completely natural in his hand. Using it seemed to relax him, perhaps because it was the only object in sight that belonged to him.

Nick ate the orange slowly, trying to imagine the rest of his life. With every turn of thought, he found fog and darkness. The one shred of consistency was that every time he looked down, he was holding on to the HandyMate.

He was on his last segment of orange when his phone rang.

"Yeah, hey, it's me, man." Hardy Chin. "I'm in town tonight, staying at the Holiday Inn down on Palo Verde. I thought since I'm in town, I'd give you a call."

"I'm honored."

"You're special, man. Yola thinks so, anyway. Listen, you want to get rich?"

"Yola thinks— What? Rich?"

"How about you buy me dinner?"

"I, ah, I've got plans, actually."

"Okay. I'll buy *you* dinner."

"What are we talking about?"

"You want to talk, let's do it over a beer. How about you meet me at Kanaka's, five o'clock."

"Kanaka's?"

"You don't know Kanaka's? I thought you were this hip dude."

"I guess I'm not as hip as you thought."

Chin gave him directions.

Nick said, "By the way, I've got a little problem with my insurance company. They think I burned down my store."

"That's not good. Listen, whatever you do, don't talk to them. Come down to Kanaka's, we'll discuss it."

Ten seconds after Nick disconnected, his phone rang again.

"Mr. Fashon? Clint Pfleuger, Pima Life and Casualty. How are you today?"

"I'm fine. What can I do for you, Clint?"

"Right down to business, eh? I like that. The fact is, Mr. Fashon, we're looking at your claim for the, um, property damage."

"Is there a problem?"

"Well, the fact is, Mr. Fashon, I need to ask you a few questions. When would be a convenient time for you to stop by my office?"

Nick thought about putting him off as Chin had advised—but why should he? He was innocent. The sooner he cooperated, the sooner the company would settle the claim. "How about this afternoon?"

Clint Pfleuger was one of those guys, Nick could tell just by looking at him, who hated anyone with a full head of hair.

"You're late," Pfleuger said, turning his desk clock for Nick to see: 4:07. Seven minutes late.

"Sorry." Nick entered the tiny office and sat down across from Pfleuger. The chair was chrome-plated steel with a hard black vinyl seat. He crossed his legs, then uncrossed them. Pfleuger watched from behind his desk, saying nothing.

Nick said, "So . . ."

Pfleuger nodded, unsmiling but encouraging. The skin on top of his head had crackled like dried mud—a bad sunburn or some sort of fungus infection. It was hard not to stare. Nick forced his eyes to explore the walls of Pfleuger's office. There was little to look at. Lots of nubbly gray carpet, a calendar, assorted memos, and three cheaply printed diplomas stating that Clinton Vernon Pfleuger had completed company-sponsored seminars in Arizona Insurance Law, Claims Investigation for the Twenty-first Century, and Maximizing Personal Power.

Nick asked, "You got your personal power maximized?" Pfleuger frowned, and Nick realized that, in this venue, wisecracks wouldn't play. "Just kidding," he said.

Pfleuger shook his head sadly. "I've been in this business a long time, Fashon. There's not much that gets by me. I've been to a lot of fire scenes. I've seen fires that were started by rats chewing on electrical wiring. I've seen fires started by spontaneous combustion. I've seen fires caused by cigarettes dropped on cheap carpeting. I've seen fires caused by birthday cakes. I've seen fires caused by Molotov cocktails, pipe bombs, and a packet of firecrackers left in a sunny window. I once investigated a fire set by a woman who filled her teapot with paint thinner, turned the stove burner on high, then went shopping, leaving her boyfriend asleep on the sofa. The reason I wanted to see you, Fashon, was to talk about what started your fire. Do you have any idea?" Pfleuger produced a ghastly smile.

Not wanting to get Artie in trouble for alerting him to Pfleuger's suspicions, Nick shook his head.

Pfleuger sat back in his chair and gazed at Nick. He looked very disappointed. "There's not much that gets by me, Fashon."

"You already said that."

"It bears repeating."

"What are you getting at?"

Pfleuger opened the red folder on his desk. "We know the fire started in the basement. We have ways of determining these things. The police have identified the ignition device. Never seen one quite like it, but I know arson. I can smell it. That fire was no accident. It's only a matter of time before we find out who did it." Pfleuger raised his eyebrows, waiting for Nick's response.

"You're saying that you think the fire was deliberately set."

Pfleuger nodded.

"You're looking at me like you think I did it."

"Did you?"

Nick said, in as calm a voice as he could manage, "Why would I do that?"

"Some people do such things to collect insurance settlements."

"Our store was making money."

Pfleuger shrugged.

Nick said, "Look, I spent twenty years collecting Motown records. I had more than five hundred of them, many of them irreplaceable. All gone. I lost the last letter I ever got from my mother. I lost nine pairs of Bally shoes. You know what those things cost? And none of the stuff in my apartment was insured. Why would I burn up everything I own? It makes no sense. If I'd planned to set that fire, I would've at least taken out some renter's insurance."

Pfleuger, unimpressed, made a note in his file. "Do you know of anyone who might have done it?"

"No."

"Hmm. I have been trying unsuccessfully to reach your partner."

"Vince didn't burn the store down."

"Why do you say that?"

"I've known him for years. He just wouldn't."

Pfleuger shrugged. "He hasn't been answering his phone."

"That doesn't mean he did anything wrong."

"Who then?"

Nick shook his head. He couldn't imagine Vince burning the store down. But then, he couldn't imagine *anyone* doing such a thing.

Nevertheless, someone apparently had.

Twelve

Hardy Chin was building himself a depth charge when Nick found him bellied up to the bar at Kanaka's. The karaoke stage was not in use. Nick watched Chin pour half a bottle of Kirin into a mug, leaving two inches at the top. Chin then filled a small sake cup and dropped it—cup and all—into the beer. He saluted Nick with the mug and tipped it back, gulping and increasing the mug's incline until the submerged sake cup slid down to clack against his incisors. He belched and set the glass back on the bar, his eyes bright, his lips stretched tight across his face. He gestured to the bartender for another depth charge, and one for his friend.

"That your second or third?" Nick asked.

Chin flexed his brow, doing the numbers. "You mean this one or the one I just ordered?"

"Never mind."

The bartender brought them each a Kirin and a small pitcher of sake.

Chin said, "This place is supposed to have the best sushi this side of Phoenix. At least that's what Yola says."

"You're saying, then, that it's better than what you can get in Mexico."

"I guess so. Hey, you want to get a table?" He signaled the hostess, a long-legged beauty of Asian ancestry. Seconds later, she led them to a table, Chin following too close to her. They sat down at a small table near the empty stage. Several of the other tables were filled, mostly by Asian men. The hostess handed them menus and glided off.

"Man, we don't see that kind of stuff in Bisbee."

"What's that?"

"Check her out, man. You see those legs?"

Nick turned his head, caught a glimpse of the hostess heading through swinging doors into the kitchen.

"Nothing like that in Bisbee," said Hardy Chin, clutching his chest. "You see her? She's a fucking goddess."

"She's a pretty girl," Nick agreed.

"I would eat her shit."

Nick did not reply. He liked to think of himself as a tolerant, worldly fellow, but Chin's hound-dogging brought out the Puritan in him. He buried his nose in the menu, holding it up to give himself relief from Chin's flushed, goatish face.

"I hear tuna sushi is the best," Chin said, easing from the carnal to the carnivorous. "So, Nick Fashon, what you want to see me about?"

Nick lowered the menu. "You called me, remember?"

"I know that, man. But you came, didn't you?" He poured the last of the sake into his beer.

"Yeah, because you said you wanted to see me."

"No shit?" Chin's grin had a dangerous looseness to it.

A waitress appeared to take their orders. Chin ordered the deluxe sushi tray and another depth charge. Nick asked for an order of *edamame*. The steamed soybeans would help absorb some of the alcohol, and he still hoped to leave in time for dinner with Gretchen. After the waitress walked away, Chin said, "She's not so bad, either."

"On the phone you said something about getting rich."

Chin blinked himself back into focus. "Oh, yeah, hey, you know I was talking to Yola, man. She really likes you."

"Great. Is she going to shower me with gifts?"

Chin's mouth curled into a leer. "I bet she'd shower—"

"I don't want to hear it," Nick said, cutting him off.

Chin frowned, hurt. "Hear what?"

"Never mind. What about Yola?"

"Well, she's interested in that thing."

"What thing?"

The waitress returned with Chin's beer and sake, and the *edamame*. Chin looked at the bowl of soybeans, picked one up, and bit into the pod. "Kind of tough," he observed.

Nick showed him how to pop the beans out of the pod. Chin picked up the technique instantly. Nick watched Chin empty a half-dozen pods into his mouth then wash them down with more beer and sake.

"What thing?"

"Thing?"

"What thing is Yola interested in?"

"Oh. That kitchen-gadget thing."

"The HandyMate?"

"Yeah. She got this idea she wants to feature it on her TV show."

"Really?" Nick took a gulp of his depth charge.

"You could get rich, man."

Nick sat back, letting his mind spin free. If Yola Fuentes featured the HandyMate on her TV show, she might sell tens of thousands of the things. Maybe millions. The HandyMate could outsell Chia Pets.

"What does she want?"

"I don't know. You should talk to her. You maybe could make a lot of money."

"That would be nice," Nick said. "My insurance company is making noise like they won't pay for the fire."

"Fucking insurance companies. Who you with?"

"Pima Life and Casualty."

Chin nodded. "I've dealt with those assholes. They don't have to pay you, they won't. Like trying to squeeze *cerveza* out of adobe."

The sushi tray arrived, an enormous blue platter covered with variously shaped seafood and rice confections. Chin examined the collection suspiciously, picked up a tuna roll with his fingers, and took a bite, not bothering with the condiments. He chewed and swallowed. "I got insurance stories you wouldn't believe," he said, frowning at the half-eaten tuna roll. "Help yourself, man."

Nick poured a tablespoon of soy sauce onto one of the small plates stacked at the end of the table. He used his chopsticks to stir a dollop of wasabi into the soy sauce. Chin watched, interested, as Nick lifted a tuna roll with his chopsticks, dipped it into the wasabi-soy mixture, and popped it whole into his mouth.

"That how you do it?"

"You never had sushi before?"

"We don't get this kind of stuff in Bisbee." Chin tried another roll, this time following Nick's example. "Not bad," he gasped, gulping beer to wash down the spicy wasabi. "So what's the insurance company saying?"

"I just met with the investigator."

"What's his name?"

"Clint Pfleuger."

"I know Pfleuger," Chin said. "He's a stone."

"He thinks we burned down our own store."

"Really?" Chin displayed a flicker of alertness. "Did you?"

"No!"

"But you got torched?"

"That's what they tell me."

Chin was staring at Nick, his eyes dilated, something inside straining to break through the alcoholic haze.

"You know what you should do, man?" Chin thumped himself on the chest with his chopsticks. "You should hire me."

"Oh yeah," said Nick. "That sounds like a *real* good idea."

"I'm serious, man."

Nick decided it was a good time to visit the restroom. Excusing himself, he made his way to the back of the restaurant, hoping that by the time he returned, Chin would be off on another train of thought. Did he still have time to get back to Gretchen's for dinner at Caruso's? It was almost six-thirty—how had it gotten so late? Maybe if he left right now . . . but he wanted to hear more about Yola Fuentes. He called Gretchen and got her answering machine.

"Hey, it's me. I'm meeting with that lawyer. We're, ah, actually, I'm showing him how to eat sushi. Sorry. I should be back in an hour or two. How about we do Caruso's tomorrow? Sorry. See you . . ."

Answering machines brought out the worst in him.

He was returning to the table, telling himself that Gretchen would be okay with his message, when the first nasty guitar lick of "Bad to the Bone" came over the sound system. Nick arrived at the table. Chin's chair was empty.

His first thought was that Chin had stuck him with the bill. His second thought was that something awful had happened to George Thorogood's voice. He looked up at the stage and there was Hardy Chin, writhing his hips and snarling into the microphone.

B-b-b-b-b-b-b-b bad . . .

Chin sobered up, relatively speaking, after cranking out his unique interpretation of the song. His voice sounded like a bloodhound-Chihuahua cross, and his stage presence was that of an Asian Mr. Bean, but he had a lot of heart. After such a performance, Nick felt compelled to buy another round of depth charges. They finished the sushi tray and ordered another, along with a third—or was it the fourth?—round. Chin launched into his collection of stories about insurance companies, all of them with Hardy Chin as the hero. Then he told a story about Caleb's early efforts to market the NoseGard. Caleb had demonstrated the prototype to a potential investor who had been most impressed until he tried to remove the device from his nose. The adhesive Caleb had used had proven to be overly aggressive, and the investor had left the meeting with the NoseGard still firmly attached.

"Far as I know, he's still wearing it," Chin said.

After listening to a graying Mexican businessman regurgitate a version of "MacArthur Park," Chin returned to the stage to perform "My Way." For a while, Nick forgot all about his troubles, giving in to laughter and drunken banter. Hardy Chin could be a lot of fun. Or maybe the critical factor was the number of drinks Nick had consumed. At one point he nearly took the stage himself, thinking that he might rip off a passable rendition of the classic Supremes number "Baby Love." Fortunately, he experienced a moment of clarity and decided to cut himself off. It was after midnight when Nick, still relatively sober—or so he told himself—drove Chin back to his hotel.

Nick eased himself into Gretchen's bed, hoping not to wake her. He'd done nothing wrong, he told himself. A business dinner with his lawyer. He pulled the covers up to his chin and closed his eyes. He was sinking into an alcohol-infused dream when Gretchen's voice yanked him back.

"You have fun tonight?"

"I thought you were asleep."

"I was. The sweet scent of beer breath must've woken me up."

"Sorry. I had to meet with that lawyer, Chin. He was in town and wanted to have dinner. I called."

"I got your message."

Nick didn't like the tone in her voice. Had he done something wrong? He did not think he had, but now that he was living with her, albeit temporarily—at the moment it felt *very* temporary—the rules may have changed.

Gretchen said, "You know what you smell like? You smell like my dad when he used to come in and kiss me good night."

"He was a drinker?"

Gretchen said nothing. Nick laid very still, breathing shallowly. He felt as if he were sleeping next to a bottle of unstable nitroglycerin. After a few minutes of silence he heard the sound of air being expelled from flared nostrils.

"By the way, some policeman called. I wrote his number down."

"Oh," Nick said. "What did he want?"

Gretchen rolled away from him, onto her side. Nick began to rehearse several conversations that might occur in the morning.

None of them went very well.

Thirteen

His head hurt. With every throb of his heart, a ripple of pain rolled from one temple to the other, back and forth across the top of his head. How many depth charges had he consumed? At least four. Maybe five. If he couldn't remember, it must have been six. It felt like seven. He never should have driven home. Several years back, he had promised himself he would never again drive drunk. Another promise broken. Gretchen was gone, no note, no hot coffee waiting for him. Nothing but the day, empty and forbidding.

So he'd had some bad luck. He had lost his business and all his possessions. He had needed a place to stay, and Gretchen had invited him into her home. So he was staying there for a while, no big deal, he'd move out as soon as he got things settled. It wasn't as if they were living together by choice. Before, if he'd wanted to go out to dinner with, say, Vince—a business dinner—he'd just go. No explanations or apologies required. Nick did not understand how things had changed. He'd been staying with Gretchen for less than a week. They weren't married. They weren't even engaged, and already he was fantasizing divorce.

Nick put water on the stove to boil. He picked up the phone and dialed Artie's number. The machine answered. Nick left a message. He looked at the pad by the phone where Gretchen had scrawled the name and number of the policeman. William Hoff. Nick didn't think he could handle a conversation with a cop, not this morning. He thought about calling Vince—but why? Vince would only make him feel worse. Nick turned away from the phone and went to stand before the teapot. He opened the spout to prevent it from whistling.

In time, even a watched pot boils. Nick made himself a cup of green tea, which he had heard was good for hangovers. He used it to wash down three aspirin tablets. Almost immediately, he felt like throwing up, but forced himself to sit quietly, waiting for the caffeine and aspirin to enter his bloodstream.

He wondered, again, who had set his store on fire. He did not really believe it had been Vince, or Henderson the landlord, or an overzealous competitor. And no one else he could think of had a reason to do such a thing. It had to be some thrill-seeking kids. There was no other explanation. But how could he make a guy like Clint Pfleuger believe that? He couldn't. Not without proof. On the other hand, wasn't the burden of proof on Pima Life? If they couldn't prove that Nick or Vince had started the fire, they would be obliged to pay up. Or would they?

Maybe he should hire Chin to negotiate with Pima.

He recalled the image of Chin singing "My Way."

Maybe not.

He could drive out to Bisbee and fill some more coffin orders. Put in some time with Caleb's junk, maybe start to organize it, figure out what he could throw away, what was worth saving.

His eyes fell upon a white plastic shape sitting on the counter.

The HandyMate.

El Otro Lado was busy. Nick had the feeling that it was always busy. One o'clock on a weekday afternoon in Sierra Vista, middle of nowhere, and he had to wait for a table. He spent the time watching trays of food go by and trying not to think about his headache.

Most of the other diners looked like migrant retirees from Tucson and Green Valley—representatives of the pre-baby-boom generation who had chosen southern Arizona as their final resting place. The golf was good, as was the dry heat, and you could afford to live there. Most of these folks, Nick had found, were refugees from the Midwest, feeling collectively smug about their migration. Nick, the youngest customer in the place, was the only one eating alone.

All the other diners seemed to have ordered either the Topopo Salad, a showy local specialty, or the Fiesta Plate, a shrine to melted cheese. They were drinking colorful blended drinks from stemware with bowls the size of melons. It could have been any Chi-Chi's in, say, Detroit—but it was not. El Otro Lado was owned by the famous TV chef Yola Fuentes, who made Mexican cooking look fun and easy, and it was a wonderful Saturday-afternoon adventure to drive there on the curvy two-lane highway, and an even greater adventure to drive home again after a few Margarita Grandes.

After about twenty minutes, the hostess led him to an undersize table at the back of the restaurant near the kitchen door. Ten minutes later, a surly looking waitress brought him a wooden bowl full of chips and a smaller bowl of tired-looking salsa. She offered him a leatherette-clad menu.

Nick refused the menu and ordered a bowl of *menudo*, the mouth-searing tripe and *posole* soup that was reputed to perform Saturday-morning miracles.

"We don't have no *menudo*," said the waitress.

"You don't have no *menudo*?"

The waitress shook her head. "We got Spicy Chicken or gazpacho."

Nick sighed. *Menudo* might not have cured his headache, but it would certainly have taken his mind off it.

"Just bring me a chicken burro enchilada-style, frijoles, and a Pacifico."

"You want red or green sauce?"

"Red. Is Yola here today?"

"Uh-huh."

"Tell her Nick Fashon is here, would you please?"

Nick Fashon! What are you doing back here in Chiapas?" Yola Fuentes grinned, wiping her hands on a towel tucked into her apron tie. The kitchen door was still swinging, missing her by inches.

"Chiapas? Thought I was in Sierra Vista."

"We call these tables Chiapas. You know, the Mexican Siberia." Her hair was tied back. She wore a pair of running shoes and no lipstick. Nick would not have recognized her on the street.

"Oh. I get it."

"Restaurant humor. Let me get you a better table, okay?"

"This is fine—"

"Fine for you, maybe, but you want to talk to me, don't you?"

"Well—"

"Dolores!" Yola's voice cut through the restaurant clamor and caught the attention of the hostess, whom she instructed to set up another table. Returning her attention to Nick, she asked, "Have you ordered?"

"Yeah, I—"

"What did you order?"

"Well, I ordered *menudo*, but—"

"I talked to Chin this morning. He said you were bad boys last night."

"I wasn't that bad."

"We don't get much call for *menudo* here. Listen, you go over to table three—see where Dottie's setting up? I'll be with you in a couple minutes." She winked and blasted back through the swinging door. Feeling buffeted, Nick sat still for a few seconds to let his brain settle. Yola and Chin rattled him the same way. It was a bit like stepping onto a moving sidewalk. Old Caleb, Nick remembered, had

had a similar time-warping effect, bringing the future on at dizzying speed. They all made him feel sluggish and dull.

Table three was one of six tables along the windowed front wall of the restaurant. Seconds after he sat down, the hostess showed up with a cold Pacifico, a fresh bowl of chips, and an assortment of salsas. Nick ate a few chips and washed them down with the beer. It felt good to get something in his stomach. He was sampling the third salsa, a cilantro and green chile puree, when Yola reappeared. In the space of a few minutes she had transformed herself from dowdy chef into sexy Madonna. Her dress, which before had been concealed beneath her apron, was a black scoop-neck that made the most of her ample bosom. She had traded in her sneakers for a pair of stiletto heels, and had performed a feat of makeup magic that enlarged her dark eyes, widened her full lips, and created a seductive glow on her cheeks and neck. He hair was still tied back, but not so tightly. One strand had been artfully neglected to hang loose against her cheek.

She posed for a second to make sure he noticed her transformation, then slipped into the opposite seat.

"So, Nick Fashon, you came to see me!"

"I was in the neighborhood."

Yola reached across the table, put her right hand on his arm, and laughed, her teeth so bright against carmine lips that they left him with a crescent-shaped afterimage. Nick felt as if he had said something remarkably witty.

He said, "I'm headed up to Bisbee. I thought I'd stop by."

"That's nice," said Yola, giving his arm a squeeze, then letting go. "You going out to Caleb's place?"

"I'm planning to."

"You know, a month ago I give him one of my tortilla presses that was broken. He was going to make it better, you know? Only I'm short a tortilla press now. If you see it, maybe you could grab it for me." Her tongue appeared for an instant, wetting her upper lip.

Next she'll start playing with her hair, Nick thought. "You were out there, weren't you? Aren't you the one who found him?"

Yola's eyes dropped to the table, and she seemed to shrink. "Yes. It was very bad. I was frightened."

"Did you visit him often?"

"No. Maybe two, three times. Caleb did not encourage visitors."

"Chin told me you were his girlfriend."

Yola's eyes widened, and she laughed.

"I guess he was just kidding," Nick said.

"Caleb and I were very close, but he was not my boyfriend."

"You didn't happen to notice a motorcycle while you were there, did you?"

Yola squeezed her lips into a knot and shook her head. Nick showed her the picture of Caleb and Herb Jenks on the Harley.

"I took that picture," she said, touching the photo lightly "It is Caleb and his crazy friend Herb. A few months ago. Caleb was teaching him how to ride. Herb, he is crazy for motorcycles."

"I wonder what happened to the bike?"

"I do not know." She dropped her hands to her lap.

Nick put the photo back in his pocket. "Hardy Chin said you wanted to talk to me about one of Caleb's inventions."

Yola straightened up and smiled, suddenly animated. "I was thinking I might use it on my show." She touched her hair. "Would you like that?"

"We're talking about the HandyMate, right?"

"That was one name. But Caleb told me once he was going to name it after my restaurant. El Otro Lado."

Nick blinked. "Really?"

Yola nodded. "You know. 'The other side'?"

"I know what *el otro lado* means."

"See, because you use the *other side of it*." She held an invisible HandyMate in her hand. "You turn it one way and do one thing, then you turn it the other way and do something else."

"I get it."

"So I was thinking, my TV show, right now I have sponsors—Garcia Foods, Herdez, South of the Border—underwriters, actually. But I've never used the show to sell anything directly. Except getting people to come to my restaurant, of course." She leaned forward, giving him a panoramic view of her cleavage. "What if I used the Otro Lado while I'm cooking, then at the end of the show I tell my viewers how they can order one?"

Nick nodded carefully. "I could see that. To order their Handy-Mate, they call an eight-hundred number, just like one of those infomercials."

"Exactly. I move my show from PBS to the Food Network. *Millions* of viewers. The Otro Lado could be *huge*. I'll bet—" The waitress interrupted by sliding a bowl of soup in front of Nick: pale strips of tripe floating on a sea swimming with *posole*. Dime-size slicks of chili-infused oil dotted the steaming surface. He eased his spoon into the broth, came up with a disk of carrot and a swollen *posole* kernel. *Menudo*.

"I keep some in the freezer," Yola said. "For emergencies."

Nick tasted the soup. A river of fire scorched his esophagus. He coughed and took a swig of Pacifico.

"What do you think?"

Nick cleared his throat. "Man! It's *menudo* all right."

"I mean about featuring the Otro Lado on my show. Do you know that I once made a five-course meal for Caleb using nothing but two sauté pans and the Otro?"

Nick sampled another spoonful. "Outstanding," he said, swallowing. It really was good—for *menudo*. He could feel beads of sweat forming on his forehead. His belly was warm, his headache receding.

"He designed the original prototype to fit my hand."

Nick nodded, eating more soup.

"I actually helped him design it."

Nick looked up, alarm bells clanging in his head. "The Handy-Mate?"

"The Otro Lado," she said. "We were going to be partners. Me and Caleb. That was what I went out to talk to him about that day. But he was not talking."

Nick set his spoon on the table and sat back, sensing danger.

"What do you have in mind?" he asked.

"An arrangement," Yola said. "Fifty-fifty. I sell it; you make it."

Nick pursed his lips, hoping for a kitchen fire, an earthquake, a Border Patrol raid, *anything*.

"So what do you think? Fifty-fifty?"

"Tell you what," Nick said. "Let me do some research, find out what it'll cost to make the thing."

"We have a history, Caleb and I. We work together on many things."

"Oh?"

"We made a thing for the ovens. A thing to change the way the thermostat controls the gas jets." Seeing Nick's blank look, she explained, "It is very important when baking that the oven temperature is flat. You know, not so up and down. Most ovens, the thermostat turns the gas on and off, so the temperature goes up and down, up and down, up and down. This is not good, and I am complaining to Caleb, so he made a little thing. Now the thermostat doesn't turn the gas on and off, it adjusts it gradually. Is very clever. I sold it to the oven manufacturer. Partners. We made a lot of money."

"I didn't know Caleb ever made any money. What did he do with it?"

"Money was not important to Caleb."

"He always seemed to need it."

"Trust, that was important to your grandfather. He trusted me." Yola leaned toward him, her breasts coming up over the edge of the table. "So . . . we have a deal?"

Nick kept his eyes glued to her forehead. It was way too soon to be striking deals. "Let me get back to you."

"Okay. When?"

Light reflected from minute drops of perspiration on her brow. Avoiding her eyes, Nick dropped his eyes to her mouth. Her upper lip was moist, too.

"I'll call you," he said.

"Tell you what. How about I call *you?* Tomorrow."

"Okay." Nick just wanted to get out of there. "You call me tomorrow."

"Uh-oh, now I got a better idea." Yola grinned; her breasts slid another inch closer to Nick's *menudo.* "I got to go to Tucson to tape some shows next week. How about I take you to dinner?"

Fourteen

So, you talk to Yola?"

"I talked to her."

"How'd it go?" Chin, slumped behind his desk, had given up his usual western accoutrements in favor of a black nylon jogging suit and a purple leather baseball cap. His eyes were hidden behind a pair of dark, oversize sunglasses; his cheeks looked slack and pale. The blinds were drawn, the room was lit by a single desk lamp, and the air-conditioning was set cold enough to keep milk from souring. A plastic twenty-ounce bottle of Coca-Cola stood in the precise center of the desk blotter.

"Not so good. She thinks she invented the HandyMate herself, so she thinks she owns half of it. She wants to name it after her restaurant."

"Really?" Chin seemed genuinely surprised. "She didn't say anything like that to me."

"She's saying it now." Nick stood up and walked to the window. He thrust his hands deep into his pockets and hunched his shoulders. Through a crack in the aluminum miniblinds, he watched a small dust devil pick its way up Main Street. "It's too bad, because I think she could sell a ton of them on her show. But there's no way I'm giving her half. And I'm *not* calling the HandyMate the 'Otro Lado.'"

"What did you tell her?"

"I put her off." Nick turned to look at the hungover lawyer. "I don't have a problem, do I? With the rights?"

"No, man, that's just Yola. The patent application is in Caleb's name. She's pretty aggressive, you know? But she likes you. She didn't like you, you'd know, man. You can do some kind of deal with her, only don't let her run over you." Chin reached out and adjusted the Coke bottle, turning it a few degrees, moving it a quarter inch to the left.

Nick felt himself making a decision. He said, "I don't know if you remember, but last night you mentioned that you've butted heads with Pima Life?"

Chin stared back at him, inscrutable, for once, in his shades.

"Remember?" Nick prompted.

"Sure," said Chin. "What did I say?"

"You said you could pry some money out of them for me."

"Oh. I could do that."

"What would you charge me?"

"Depends. Maybe I'd charge you nothing. I could charge it to the estate. That way you don't get taxed twice."

"Is it okay to do that?"

Chin shrugged. "Probably." He lifted the Coke bottle, put it to his lips and took a tiny sip, set it carefully back in the center of the blotter. "Like today, you stop by, we talk for twenty minutes, I bill the estate."

"I just stopped by to see how you were feeling," Nick said.

"And to ask me about Yola."

"*You* asked *me* about Yola."

"I did? Well, I wasn't really going to charge you anyway. Tell you what, how about I write a letter to Pima for you. Lots of times, they see you got yourself a lawyer, they'll cave. Just like that."

"Okay."

"You going out to the ranch today?"

"Yeah, I thought I'd look around some more. I'm thinking about moving the pet coffins to Tucson. Rent a space in town. All the rest of the stuff I'm going to put in storage."

Chin, nodding, said, "I got a cousin owns a mini-storage up in Benson."

"I was thinking of something closer to home."

"I hate to be the one to break it to you, man, but you don't got a home."

"That has not escaped my notice."

Nick contemplated the hot, dusty half-mile walk ahead of him. The Corvette's engine labored at idle; icy air blew from the dash vents as the afternoon sun sliced through the window, baking his neck and left shoulder. Nick felt completely unprepared for the rest of his life. He wanted to go home. But the closest thing he had to a home was Gretchen's little bungalow, and who knew *what* was waiting for him there. He'd probably find himself locked out. Not that he'd done anything wrong. Damn it, he *hadn't* done anything wrong.

Maybe he could stay in Caleb's caboose. What the hell, it was *his* now. He tried to imagine sleeping in Caleb's bed, but his mind recoiled from the thought. He needed a place of his own. A place he could come and go from as he pleased. A place with indoor plumbing, air-conditioning, no rattlesnakes, and a coffee shop no more than five minutes away. Was that too much to ask? Nick thought not. After all, he had the HandyMate. He was going to get rich.

Money. It always came down to money. Maybe he could borrow a few thousand against the land. What was the price of dirt out here? Two hundred bucks an acre? Maybe less. Maybe Chin knew somebody. Maybe he could sell off the pet-coffin business. Maybe the insurance company would pay off. That was what he really needed, what he *deserved*. And if they did? Would he reopen Love & Fashion? Without Vince Love? Or put the money behind the Handy-

Mate? He tore his thoughts away from the insurance money. Money he might never see. He had to focus on what he *had*. His car, his connections, his business savvy, his inheritance.

The vibration of the engine traveled up his spine. The Handy-Mate was his best shot. He should focus. Forget about resurrecting Love & Fashion. Sell the pet-coffin business. Put everything he had behind the HandyMate and let it rip. The thought was liberating: set all of his other problems aside and devote his life 100 percent to the HandyMate.

He raised his eyelids. Sunlight on rock and dirt. Jagged hillsides dotted with juniper and mesquite. Relentless blue sky. The rumble of the big engine and the hiss of the air conditioner.

He shut down the engine, got out, and began to walk toward Caleb's strange domain.

Fifteen

Gretchen had decided to pretend that nothing had happened, that she'd never been mad at him, which left Nick both relieved and confused. They were sitting in her undersize living room at each end of her undersize sofa. Nick held her foot in his lap, massaging it. The delicacy of Gretchen's feet always surprised him, since she spent so much time in the desert in her beat-up Red Wing boots.

"You spend the day at Caleb's?" she asked. She was drawing with a technical pen in the spiral-bound, grid-lined notebook she used to record field data.

"I've been all over," Nick said. "I met with that restaurant owner in Sierra Vista, I met with the lawyer, and I drove out to the ranch— spent a couple hours going through Caleb's files."

Biting her lower lip, Gretchen leaned into her drawing, filling in a shape. "What were you looking for?"

"Anything I could find about the HandyMate. I think I'm going to go ahead with it. You know. Try to sell the thing."

"You mean sell the idea?"

"I mean actually manufacture it and market it."

"Really?" She looked up, surprised. "Are you giving up on Love & Fashion?"

"Just on Love."

"Never give up on love," Gretchen said.

Nick smiled and began to knead the soft spot behind the ball of her foot. "I'm meeting with a guy at Rincon Plastics tomorrow," he said. "I found a business card tacked up above Caleb's desk, so I called and made an appointment. I want to get some idea of what it'll cost to make the thing." Nick looked at her drawing. "Swastikas?" Three of them, arranged in a triangle.

"Not swastikas. Whirling logs. The Navajo have used them for thousands of years. It's a good-luck symbol."

"Looks like swastikas to me."

"That's because you're ignorant, Nicky."

"A lot of ignorant people out there."

"That's not my problem." Gretchen held the sketch up to her shoulder. "I'm going to put it right here. What do you think?"

Nick thought that Gretchen had enough tattoos, but he had learned not to offer even a whiff of negativity about her skin art. The odds were, she would not go forward with this one. She was just messing with him. He was forgiven, but that didn't mean she wouldn't take a few shots. Keep him on his toes. Besides, Gretchen could shave her head, put a bone through her nose, dye herself green, and he would still find her attractive.

"I think you're beautiful," Nick said.

The first time Nick met Gretchen, he had mistaken her for a street person. He'd been minding the store on a slow Thursday afternoon when a very dirty person of indeterminate gender came into the store, walked directly to the display of Peruvian handbags, and began to paw through them. Nick approached cautiously.

The very dirty person wore a filthy baseball cap over sun-bleached hair pulled back into a stubby ponytail, a U of A sweatshirt with mud crusted on the elbows, faded jeans that held more dust than cotton, and a pair of well-worn leather boots. Nick's eyes went to the hands touching his merchandise and was surprised to see that they were feminine and, except for a bit of grime caked beneath the nails, clean.

"Can I help you?"

The mud woman turned her face to him and smiled, and Nick felt a cold nugget of fear plant itself behind his ribs.

"Are you aware," she said as she lifted a handbag by its strap, "that these symbols are not Incan?" Her voice was slightly hoarse, her eyes clear blue. The smile lines at the corners of her mouth were embedded with dust. She smelled of earth and sweat, the aroma of hard, healthy work. The fear in his chest grew tendrils and clutched at his lungs.

He said, "Uh, actually, they're Peruvian." He couldn't look away.

The woman laughed at him. She returned the handbag to the display and walked out of the store.

As soon as she was out of sight, Nick's fear lessened but did not leave him entirely. Her sun-blasted face with those white teeth, that upturned nose, those crystalline eyes remained in his memory. He sincerely hoped that he would never see her again. He did not want to fall in love with a soiled creature who would track mud into his store and disparage his merchandise and laugh at him. She won't be back, he told himself. His heartbeat slowed. A close call, nothing more. He'd let his own imagination frighten him. Besides, he was enjoying being between girlfriends. The store was keeping him busy. He did not need or want a woman in his life, especially one who did not know how to keep herself clean.

Later, when Vince showed up at the store, Nick pointed to the handbag display and said, "Did you know that the symbols on those bags aren't really Incan?"

Vince looked surprised. "So?"

"So they're from Peru, right? Isn't that where the Incas come from?"

Vince shook his head. "How the hell should I know?"

Two days later, Nick was rearranging a display of slow-moving leather and wool tunics when she showed up again, this time wearing blue jeans and a sleeveless white linen top. Her hair, just long enough to show some curl, brushed her cheeks. Nick recognized her as soon as she smiled. She wore neither dirt nor makeup. In fact, she looked exceptionally clean. He felt his throat swell, and he could hear his heart pounding.

"How's it going?" he said, keeping his voice and expression carefully neutral.

"Not bad," she said. Her voice was huskier than he remembered. He could feel it.

"Looking for anything in particular?"

She shrugged and looked away; her eyes landed on the four belt racks along the north wall. "You have a lot of belts," she said, moving toward them.

That was when Nick knew that she had returned not to shop but to see him.

He waited on the edge of the abyss, watching her hands go through the belts, long brown and black leather strips slithering against one another, the soft metallic chatter of buckles. The store was otherwise quiet. He wished he had left the sound system turned on.

After spending a minute or so with the belts, the woman turned to him and said, "I came to apologize."

"Oh?"

"I was here a couple days ago—"

"I remember you."

"Oh!" She looked away. "Well, that's what I wanted to apologize for. I mean, you're just trying to make a living, right?"

Nick said nothing. The woman thrust out a hand. Nick shook it. Her grip was firm, that of a woman who has had to learn to be one of the guys.

"My name's Gretchen Groth. I teach archaeology here at the university. I, ah, one of my students told me you had an interesting collection of contemporary Incan crafts here. That's why I stopped by. I'm afraid I was rather rude."

"Not really."

"Yes I was. I was tired and cranky, and I guess I was disappointed. I look at a lot of modern Native American crafts. It saddens me how many of them have lost touch with their traditions. Those purses I was looking at"—she indicated the handbag display—"most of those symbols are gibberish. They look vaguely Incan, but they aren't."

"They might be Chinese," Nick said.

"They . . . Why do you say that?"

"I was visiting a factory one time, down in Sinaloa. All they did in this place was unload containers of Chinese leather attaché cases and portfolios, peel off the 'Made in China' stickers, replace them with '*Hecho en Mexico*' stickers, then ship them out to shops in the border towns and resort cities. We imported these handbags from Peru, but it's quite possible that they were made in Shanghai. By the way, my name is Nick Fashon."

Gretchen Groth grinned. "I suppose you have a partner named Love."

"As a matter of fact, I do."

They both laughed. They talked about belts and bags and vicuña and the endangered sea turtles, and Nick asked her to have dinner with him. Wanting to impress her with his worldliness and sophistication, he took her to a pretentious and overpriced restaurant.

He could not remember what they ate or what it had cost, but the evening had been a great success.

Six months later, his hopes and fears had come to pass. They were living together. Not the way he had envisioned it, but living together nonetheless. Nick lay in Gretchen's bed, content for the moment, his thoughts free of fires and insurance and inventions. He closed his eyes and imagined Gretchen's body, knowing that he could move his hand a few inches and touch her. He thought of them floating together in space. He listened and heard the sound of her breathing. Was she asleep? He moved his hand, slid it up over her hip. She stirred and made a soft sound and wriggled against him. He tasted her shoulder.

Gretchen said, "I was mad at you, Nicky."

"You were mad at me?" He had almost forgotten.

"You stood me up."

Nick didn't remember it that way, but he didn't want to argue. "I'm sorry," he said.

"Stood me up and then came home shitfaced."

"I wasn't that drunk."

"You weren't that sober."

"That's true. Anyway, I'm sorry."

"It scares me when you change. You never stood me up before. I never saw you drunk like that. I don't want you to change, Nicky."

"Okay, I won't change."

"I like you the way you are."

"I like you, too. And I love you."

"Okay then."

"Good night."

"G'night."

Sixteen

You know, we've looked at this part before." Lew Krone rotated the HandyMate, frowning at its contours.

"You have?"

"A year or two ago." Krone set the HandyMate on the worn black composite top of his gray metal desk. His fingers were long and spatulate, his hand mottled with liver spots. He gave Nick a level gaze, his bristly gray eyebrows elevated by a suspicious one eighth of an inch.

"Caleb Hardy?" Nick asked.

"That's right."

"He was my grandfather."

Krone's brow furrowed. "Was?"

"He died a few weeks ago," Nick said.

Krone compressed his lips and shook his head sadly. He reached out and stroked the cutting edge of the HandyMate with his forefinger. "That old man. That old man was a character."

Nick nodded in agreement, somewhat surprised by Krone, who had to be in his late seventies himself, describing Caleb as an old man.

Lew Krone sat back in his wooden office chair and gazed at a point in space a few inches above Nick's head. "Did you know that he invented Velcro?"

Nick laughed.

"I'm serious," said Krone, still staring into space.

"I thought Velcro was invented by some French guy."

"It was." Krone's eyes caught on Nick's face. "But your grandfather invented it, too. He brought a prototype to me back in the sixties. A patch of the stuff no bigger than a business card, little plastic hooks sewn onto a backing by hand. Must've taken him weeks. Asked me if I could make the stuff. Called it SpaceStick. He thought he could sell it to NASA. You know, so the astronauts could walk around in zero gravity. Problem was, I'd just returned from a trade show back east, where the newest sensation in the fastener industry was this stuff called Velcro. Identical concept. Told Caleb about it, and you know what he did?"

"He probably just laughed," said Nick.

Krone smiled, showing a beautiful set of yellow dentures. "You really are his grandson," he said. "That's exactly what Caleb did. Laughed and tossed his prototype right in my trash can. That old man was a real character, even back then, when he wasn't all that old." He picked up the HandyMate again. "So you want to know whether I can make this part?"

"And what it'll cost."

Krone nodded and stood up. He was tall. "I believe we ran a sheet on it. It was pricey, as I recall. Wait here."

He walked out of his office and returned a few minutes later with a manila folder. "I ran a lot of numbers for Caleb over the years, but none of the ideas he brought me ever went into production." He sat down and opened the folder. "These numbers are old, you understand. Just to give you an idea. Let's see. The material. We talked about a number of options there. Your prototype is hand-carved out of Delrin—easy to machine, but not all that durable for an application like this. You need something harder. I ran the numbers for nylon and ABS."

"ABS?"

Krone picked up the handset of his phone and whacked it against the metal edge of his desk. Nick jerked back, startled.

"ABS," Krone said, displaying the undamaged handset. "Tough stuff." He hung up the phone. "Okay, I got your per-unit cost—no printing, shipped bulk, no packaging—at about ninety-four cents."

Nick nodded. "That's good."

"That's assuming we shoot it one-up and run lots of ten thousand—two-up would knock a few cents off. Your big cost, of course, is going to be your tooling."

Nick said nothing, not wanting to reveal the extent of his ignorance, but Krone waited him out. After several seconds, Nick asked him to explain.

Krone said, "You know how injection molding works?"

"Not really."

"Basically, we inject molten plastic under high pressure into a steel mold. The mold is your big investment. A mold with one cavity makes one part per injection. The more cavities you got, the cheaper your part is. Something like a plastic golf tee, we have a mold that'll kick out thirty tees per shot. Tees are cheap. Larger items, like automotive trim or telephone casings, we run one-up. Your part, we'd like to run that two-up, but molds cost. Larger and complex costs more. A mold for your— What are you calling it?"

"The HandyMate."

"Yes. It's complicated. You got all these curves, and we'd need to build in a cam for this hollow here . . . it's a fussy little piece. Your mold, one-up, will cost you about fifty-two thousand."

"Fifty . . . you serious?"

"Of course, you sell a million of the things, that only adds about a nickel per. You still come in under a buck."

.   .   .

Nick said, "I figure I need about a hundred twenty thousand to get the mold made, run some samples, open an office, and so forth."

"I'm not the wealthy woman you take me for," Gretchen said. She propped her bare feet on the dashboard and stared out at the road between her knees. They were traveling south on 90, the lights of Sierra Vista coming into view.

"I'm not asking you for money. Actually, I was thinking about Bootsie. Didn't you say he had some money? Maybe he'd like to invest."

Gretchen frowned. "I don't think I like the idea of you borrowing money from my dad. In fact, I'd rather you didn't. Bootsie is . . . well, he just isn't very realistic sometimes."

"It could be a good deal for him."

"I don't want you asking my dad for money, Nicky. Besides—believe me—you do not want Bootsie as an investor. He'd never leave you alone."

"I suppose you're right."

"Can't you just go to a bank? Isn't that how it's usually done?"

"Banks won't even talk to a guy like me unless I can show them some collateral."

"What about the land you inherited?"

"According to Chin, no bank will lend against the estate until it's out of probate, which will be another three or four months. The thing is, I don't have a lot of time. I need to get something going now, before I starve to death."

"I won't let you starve."

"I'm starving right now."

"You're the one who wanted to drive all the way to Sierra Vista for dinner."

"I thought it would be fun. I'm trying to make up for not going to Caruso's with you."

"I'm just kidding you, Nicky."

"Oh." He wasn't always sure. "Anyways, I've got this opportunity, and I don't want to blow it. If Yola puts the HandyMate on her show, who knows? I could be the next Ron Popeil."

"Who?"

"That guy that sells rotisserie ovens on TV."

Gretchen shook her head. She didn't watch much TV.

"One way or another," Nick went on, "I'm going to make this thing fly. I just need a little money. Here we are."

He turned in to a crowded parking lot in front of a long, low adobe building. The illuminated sign at the entrance read EL OTRO LADO—FINE MEXICAN CUISINE SINCE 1993.

"I expected it to be bigger," Gretchen said.

"It's bigger than it looks." Nick got out and opened the trunk. He lifted out a heavy brass and wood contraption.

"What on earth is that?" Gretchen asked.

"Yola's tortilla press. Caleb was supposed to fix it for her."

Inside the restaurant they were directed to wait at the bar. Nick set the tortilla press on a bar stool and ordered two margaritas. When he saw the bartender reach for the sweet-and-sour mix, he stopped her and delivered a specific set of directions: two shots of Centenario Silver, a single shot of triple sec, a half-shot of freshly squeezed lime juice. Shake with plenty of ice, then strain into salt-rimmed martini glasses. He watched the bartender follow his instructions, gave her a liberal tip, then turned back toward Gretchen with a margarita in each hand.

Yola Fuentes was standing between them, so close he nearly dumped the margaritas into her décolletage. Yola was not dressed for cooking—tonight she was in hostess mode.

"I didn't know you were such an old-fashion guy, Nick Fashon. That's how my papa use to make them back in Hermosillo."

"Why alter perfection?" Nick said. He looked past her to Gretchen. "This is Gretchen. Gretchen, this is Yola."

As the two women shook hands, Nick imagined he heard a *scree*

scree screee sound, something like the music from the shower scene in *Psycho*. The moment passed, and he was able to hand Gretchen her margarita.

Yola, spotting the tortilla press on the bar stool, said, "You found it! Thank you very much."

"You're welcome."

She took a closer look. "It's still broken. Oh well." She turned to Gretchen. "Your boyfriend comes from unreliable stock." She laughed. Gretchen returned a flat smile. Nick gulped his margarita and wondered what the hell was going on.

Yola said, "I have a nice table for you two. Very romantic."

They followed her out of the bar and across the dining room to one of three small, arched alcoves set into the far wall. The alcove contained one small table and two chairs and was lit by two Mexican ceramic sconces.

"See? Very nice, very cozy," said Yola. Nick and Gretchen stepped up into the alcove and sat down. Yola beamed at them. "I'll send Teresa over with some menus," she said, and left them.

"I feel like I'm onstage," Gretchen said. "I thought you told me she had three nostrils."

"I must have miscounted."

Gretchen laughed. "Don't worry about it, Nicky."

Salsa, chips, and menus appeared. For the next few minutes they ate chips and discussed the menu offerings.

Nick, still concerned about Gretchen's reaction to Yola, said, "Look, this woman could be the key to launching the HandyMate."

"I'm sure you're right."

"The thing is," Nick said, "if I can get the HandyMate on *¡Vamanos!* for no up-front money, it would be like getting a million bucks' worth of advertising for free."

Gretchen said, "Nicky, that woman never did anything for free in her life."

"I know that. She wants fifty percent. And she wants to call it the Otro Lado."

"You aren't, are you?"

"Not a chance. But I'll have to offer her something. She's one of the people I was hoping could supply some start-up money."

Gretchen had opened her mouth to respond when Yola appeared. "How you two doing?"

"Fine," said Nick.

"You want to know what are the specials?"

"Sure." They listened to Yola recite the specials. Gretchen ordered seafood enchiladas from the menu. Nick ordered one of the specials—something with chicken in it.

"Good choice! That's a super dish," Yola said. "I'm going to make it next week on *¡Vamanos!*. Hey, you going to come watch the taping?" Her attention was fixed on Nick.

Nick tried to catch Gretchen's eye, but she was staring intently at her fingernails. "You want to watch them make a TV show?" he asked her.

"I'm busy that day," Gretchen said, even though no day had been mentioned.

Nick looked at Yola and shrugged.

"I give you a call," said Yola. She moved off.

Gretchen leaned forward and said, "Nicky, if you let that woman put one dime into the HandyMate, you might just as well call it the Otro Lado Up-Your-Butt."

Nick, sensing that all was not well, moved into his role as the perfect, perfectly attentive date. He quit talking about the HandyMate and bombarded Gretchen with questions about her career, the subject with which she was most comfortable. It seemed to work—or maybe it was the second margarita. The tension left her shoulders, her face relaxed, and she began to enjoy herself, talking about cheerful things like bone scrapers and trepanation and cannibalism.

Yola left them alone for most of their meal, but the moment Gretchen went to visit the restroom, Yola appeared with the dessert menu.

"How was your dinner?"

"Very good."

"I knew you'd like it. You come watch me make it for TV on Wednesday, okay? Two o'clock. You know the KUAT studios?"

"I can find them."

"Yes, you are very clever."

"I amaze even myself."

"Your girlfriend . . . you are very serious?"

"I think so."

"She is very sweet." Yola placed the dessert menu on the table. "She thinks I am trying to steal you away."

"Really?" Nick liked the idea of two women competing for him.

"Women are very sensitive about these things."

"So you *are* trying to steal me away?"

Yola reached out and gave his chin a quick squeeze between her thumb and forefinger. "I see you Wednesday, Nick Fashon." She turned to find herself facing Gretchen. They were frozen for a moment, then Yola said, "He is very sweet, your boyfriend."

"Yes, he is." Gretchen's eyes narrowed, and her lips stretched across her teeth to form a grim smile.

"You better keep an eye on him!" Yola flashed a wild grin at Gretchen, turned it on Nick, then left them, the sharp clatter of her heels cutting through the dining room clamor.

Gretchen slid into her seat, eyes on Nick.

Nick picked up the dessert menu. "How about some dessert?"

"I don't think so."

"They have flan, sopaipillas, ice cream—"

"I'm not hungry."

"Oh."

"You don't actually find her attractive, do you?"

"Yola? She's not my type," said Nick. "I'm into tattooed blond archaeologists."

He looked up, expecting to find a smile on Gretchen's face, but her eyes had gone hard and serious.

It would be a long drive back to Tucson.

Seventeen

N ick, you'd better get that partner of yours under control. He is not helping your cause."

"Who is this . . . Artie?"

"I wake you up? You awake?" Artie said.

"I am now." He was sitting up, at least.

"Listen, last night Vince calls and asks me if he can collect his half of the insurance if it turns out that you set the fire."

Nick took a moment to absorb that. "He told you I torched the store?"

"He didn't exactly *say* that, but he was heading in that direction. You didn't, did you?"

"No!"

"I knew that. Anyways, you talked to Clint Pfleuger, right?"

"We met."

"Then I don't have to tell you, Pfleuger's not a guy you want to mess with. You piss him off, you'll never see a dime."

"He was pissed off before I ever met him."

"True. But the problem you got now is Vince is supposed to meet with him this afternoon. He goes in there suggesting that you set that fire, you can forget about it."

"I'll talk to him. Thanks for the heads-up."

. . .

Nick dressed and headed for Vince's condo, stopping on Speedway for a triple espresso. He finished the coffee as he pulled into Desert View Estates, a complex of three dozen identical two-story town houses near Sabino Canyon. Vince lived in 1247-B, distinguished from its neighbors by its two-tone fluorescent pink and lime-green door. The unusual color choice had created problems between Vince and the Desert View Estates Neighborhood Association. The association had declared the door inconsistent with the neighborhood aesthetic, while Vince insisted it was the only way he could distinguish his unit from those of his neighbors. As far as Nick knew, the battle was ongoing.

He walked up to the door—it was truly ugly—and rang the bell. He heard a sharp sound—a thud or a dull clap—but thirty seconds later, the door was still closed. Nick rapped on the door with his knuckles. Nothing. But he had heard something. He waited a few more seconds, then tried the door. The knob turned in his hand; the door swung open. The condo smelled of sweat and an aggressively masculine cologne.

"Vince? Anybody home?" Nick stepped inside and looked to his right, into the small living room.

The first thing he saw was Vince, sitting on the floor, his back against the front of his white leather easy chair, his mouth and chin red with blood. His right eye was swollen nearly closed, and his arms were crossed over his belly.

Nick said, "Vince? You okay?"

Vince stared back at him, breathing rapidly. His dark blue shirt was splotched with blood. Nick started toward him, then became aware of someone sitting on Vince's sofa. Nick froze.

The man was of medium size and build, somewhere between thirty and fifty years old, black hair combed straight back, skin the color of an old brass doorknob. He wore gray lizard-skin cowboy boots, black jeans, and a gray long-sleeved, western-style shirt with ivory-colored snaps. One of the sleeves was smeared with blood. His pose was languid—boots crossed at the ankles, right arm draped casually across the sofa back, a faint smile—but his eyes, the same tarnished brass as his skin, were fixed on Nick with brittle intensity.

"How you doing, buddy?" he said. His mouth hardly moved when he spoke.

Nick looked back at Vince. "You okay?" he asked again.

Vince swallowed and nodded unconvincingly.

"What's going on here?" Nick asked. He looked at the man on the sofa. "Who the hell are you?"

The man stared back at him, his face rigid.

Nick took a step toward him. "I asked you a question, *buddy.*"

The man lifted and opened his right hand to display a flat black object. At first Nick thought it was a pager or a phone, then recognized the object as a small handgun.

"You see?" the man asked.

Nick nodded.

The man stood up, a single fluid motion, and turned his brass eyes on Vince. "Do not focking disappoint me." He walked past Nick, pocketing the gun as he passed through the doorway, leaving behind an invisible fog of sweat and cologne. Nick followed him to the door. The man got into a black Dodge Ram pickup with tinted windows and fog lights mounted on top of the cab, license plate ROBO 1. He pointed his finger at Nick, winked, and drove off.

Nick closed the door and turned to Vince. "You want me to call the cops?"

Vince shook his head. He tried to sit forward, grimaced, fell back against the chair.

"I think I better see a doctor," he said.

· · ·

It's no big deal," Vince said. His breaths were audible and shallow. He was sitting on the edge of the plastic chair, holding his upper body at an awkward, slightly twisted angle.

"How can you say it's no big deal? We're sitting in a goddamn emergency room."

"I'm gonna be okay," Vince said. "I think I just bruised a couple ribs."

"You look like you've got a broken nose, too."

Vince said nothing. His good eye had a moist, vacant, injured-animal look.

"It shouldn't be too long," Nick said.

Vince swallowed.

"You going to tell me what that was about?" Nick said.

"I owe Robo some money," Vince said.

"Robo?"

Vince nodded.

"What is he? A loan shark?"

"Just a guy I borrowed some money from."

Nick shook his head. "How come you did that?"

"I needed it."

"How much do you owe him?"

"Not that much."

"It must be something. He wouldn't beat you up for twenty bucks."

"It's more than twenty." Vince took several breaths. "I owe him sixteen."

"Sixteen hundred?"

"Sixteen *thousand*."

"You borrowed sixteen thousand dollars?"

"I borrowed ten. That was four months ago. He's charging me three percent interest."

"How does three percent get you from ten thousand to sixteen?"

"Three percent a *week*."

"Oh. What was it for? You didn't put it on a horse, did you?"

"Worse. I gave it to your grandfather. For the Inch-Adder."

Nick was not sure he'd heard correctly. He replayed Vince's words in his head, analyzed them, then tried to formulate a question that did not sound absurd. He failed but asked it anyway. "You borrowed money from a loan shark named Robo so you could invest it in Caleb's belt extender?"

Vince nodded miserably. "Something like that."

Two hours and several X rays later, they learned that Vince had two cracked ribs and a broken nose.

"That must have been a nasty fall," said the youthful ER doctor.

Nick snorted. Vince said nothing. His nose looked like a malformed, overripe plum. His right eye had completely disappeared in a knot of swollen tissue, and the flesh around his left eye was beginning to turn purple. The doctor wrapped Vince's upper abdomen with a few yards of tape, applied additional tape to his nose, gave him a painkiller prescription, and told him to make an appointment for an office visit the next afternoon.

Driving back to Vince's condo, Nick remembered why he had stopped by in the first place. "You missed your appointment with Clint Pfleuger," he said.

Vince stared out the windshield.

"Artie said you accused me of setting that fire," Nick said.

"I just asked Artie some questions, that's all."

"If you weren't so miserable-looking, I'd take a shot at you myself."

Vince shrugged. "Give the pain pills another ten minutes to kick in, would you?"

"You've got to be careful, Vince. Anything you say to a guy like Pfleuger, he's going to take seriously."

Vince nodded. "Okay, okay. I didn't mean for anybody to think you did anything."

"The only way we're likely to collect is if they find out who set the fire—assuming somebody did—and prove that it had nothing to do with us."

"What if it did?"

Nick looked at Vince.

Vince said, "I mean what if, without either of us knowing about it, somebody else set the fire so that we would collect the insurance. That's what I was trying to get at when I talked to Artie. What if that's what happened?"

"Who would do that?"

Vince shrugged and winced. "Like maybe Robo. Like, what if he did it so I'd collect the insurance, so I could pay him back?"

"Robo . . . Jesus, Vince, where do you find a guy like that?"

"I, ah, I met him through Caleb. Actually."

Eighteen

William Hoff from the Tucson police had called Gretchen's number again and left another message. Nick picked up the phone, intending to call and get it over with—whatever *it* was—but his finger punched in Hardy Chin's number instead.

"Hey, I'm glad you called, man. Anybody from Pima call you?"

"No," said Nick.

"You might be hearing from them. I got on the phone this morning and made some waves." Chin laughed. "Don't let 'em bullshit you."

"I thought you said you were going to write a letter."

"First I call, then I send the letter. I'm working on it right now."

"Who did you talk to?"

"Everybody."

"Did you learn anything?"

"Not really. Anyway, you might be hearing from them. So. You called me."

"I've got a hypothetical question," Nick said.

"That's my specialty, man."

"Suppose a guy had an insurance policy on his business, and then this other party, someone with no connection to the business at all, decides to burn it down so that the guy who owns the business can collect on the policy. But the business owner, he has no idea. Would the insurance company pay?" Nick listened to silence. After several seconds he said, "Hello?"

Chin said, "I'm right here, man. Ah, how come this hypothetical firebug does this hypothetical thing?"

"Maybe so the business guy gets his hands on some ready cash."

"Does the firebug think he's doing the business guy a favor?"

"I don't know. Does it matter?"

"It matters. Look, maybe you better not say anything more."

"Okay."

"Here's my advice: if I was this business guy, I would not want any of these facts to come to light."

"Even if the business guy was totally innocent?"

"Nobody's totally innocent, man. And that's not hypothetical."

When Gretchen got home, the living room floor was littered with sheets of notebook paper, all of them covered with Nick's precise but illegible script.

"Writing a book?" she asked.

"Business plan," Nick said. "I need something in writing to present to my investors."

"You have investors?"

"I will," he said. He pointed at a row of pages laid across the top of the coffee table. "I figure negative cash flow for the next six months. I'm going to need a quarter million, at least, to get CHE off the ground."

"CHE?"

"Caleb Hardy Enterprises. Chin says that it would be easiest to just continue under Caleb's name until the estate is out of probate. He's the one who suggested selling shares of the HandyMate. Anyway, after about six months, once the HandyMate starts appearing on ¡Vamanos!, money won't be a problem. Yola thinks we can sell a couple thousand units a week. We'll be profitable in no time. I'm making a few assumptions, of course."

"I would *say* so."

Nick frowned at the tone in her voice. "I could use a little support here," he said.

"I told you before, I'm not a wealthy woman."

"I'm not talking about money."

"That's *all* you've been talking about."

"I mean, I'm not asking you for money. I just wish you'd quit acting like I'm out of my mind. You think the HandyMate is a good product, don't you?"

"It's a clever idea."

"Then how come I'm getting the feeling you don't approve? I know this isn't a sacred calling like archaeology, but it's all I've got going right now."

Gretchen had been standing in the same spot since she walked in, her boots planted at the edge of the sea of notebook pages. He could smell the desert on her.

She said, "You keep saying *we*. 'We'll need money, *we'll* be profitable.' Who is *we*?"

Nick sat back, bewildered. "I'm referring to the company. Me, my investors, and the people who will be working with me. My team. That's how you talk about these things."

"That's how *you* talk about it," she said. "You and that Fuentes woman."

Nick stared at her. "This has nothing to do with Yola," he said. "This is about raising money. It's about launching a business."

Gretchen compressed her lips and walked across the sea of papers, leaving her bootprints on his financial projections and part one of his marketing plan. A minute later he heard the shower running. What should he do? If she was going to act crazy, there wasn't much he *could* do. He was pretty sure he hadn't done anything wrong. The best course of action, he decided, would be to give her some space.

Let her work it out. And make sure not to mention Yola Fuentes again.

Nick banished Gretchen from his thoughts and returned his attention to the business plan. The sound of the shower receded. He brushed the tread mark from the marketing plan, then wrote a note to himself: *Ask Krone if ABS is dishwasher-safe.*

The next morning, Nick drove to a nearby Kinko's copy center and spent four hours typing out his business plan on one of their Macintosh computers. By adding some optimistic language and making liberal use of bullet points, charts, and white space, he was able to stretch the basic plan into an impressive-looking twenty-six-page prospectus. He printed out the original and ordered twenty bound copies. He also designed a simple business card:

C.H. ENTERPRISES
HOME OF THE HANDYMATE®
NICHOLAS FASHON—PRESIDENT

The card displayed no business address, but his cell-phone number was printed at the bottom. By early afternoon, Nick was back in his Corvette with a stack of spiral-bound plans and a box of five hundred business cards on the passenger seat. Now it was official—or at least it *felt* official. He was the HandyMate guy. He pulled out of the Kinko's parking lot and headed west on Speedway, toward Gretchen's.

The thought of seeing her again made him anxious. Dinner last night had been quiet and tense. Afterward, Nick had worked on his business plan, and Gretchen had gone to bed to read. She'd been asleep when he joined her in bed, and when he woke in the morning, she was gone. Nick did not completely understand what had gone wrong between them, but he was certain that the Handy-Mate—and Yola Fuentes—were not helping.

If he wanted his relationship with Gretchen to survive, he would have to build a firewall between her and the business and Yola. Why did Gretchen have to pull this on him now? He felt his face redden, and he realized that he was angry with her. He figured he had a right to be angry. He had lost everything, and now he was struggling to re-build his life. He could be laying down the foundation of a business empire. He needed to focus, and Gretchen was playing head games with him, letting her petty jealousy—or whatever it was—distract him. Why couldn't she just roll with it? Didn't she understand that he had priorities?

Nick realized that he had driven past the university, past I-10, and was now on Gates Pass Road, heading up into the Tucson Mountains with no destination in mind. He pulled off the road at a scenic overlook. The Avra Valley—hundreds of square miles of flat desert punctuated by a few cone-shaped mountains, trailer courts, and cotton farms—spread out before him. For reasons he could not explain, he had a sudden urgent desire to hear the Velvelettes singing "Needle in a Haystack." He looked through his tapes but could not find his Velvelettes mix. It must have been burned up. He put on a Monitors tape and cranked it up. It was Motown, it was great, but it was not what he had wanted at the moment.

He turned down the music, took out his phone, and dialed Gordo Encinas's number.

"Adobe Rags."

"Hey, Gordo, it's Nick."

"Nick. Did those jackets clear customs yet?"

"Not yet. Listen, I'm looking for some office space, just a few hundred square feet. You know of anybody who would rent to me for a few months?"

"Retail space?"

"No, just office space. I'm trying to put a deal together."

"What kind of deal?"

"Nothing to do with clothing. I'll tell you about it later. Right now I just need an address, a phone, and a couple desks."

"I know a place on Fourth Avenue."

"Really?" Nick liked the idea of having his office on Fourth Avenue, where the original Love & Fashion had opened. It was a fun neighborhood.

Gordo said, "Why don't you stop by? We'll go take a look at it."

It's a little blue," Nick said, staring at the flaking walls of the abandoned *taqueria*. The faded letters painted on the front of the building read:

TAQUERIA SONORA • TACOS, BURROS, ELOTES,
FLAUTAS, BURGERS, SHAKES • MENUDO DAILY •
SPECIALIZING IN MEXICAN AND AMERICAN CUISINE

"Nothing a coat of paint won't fix," Gordo said.

"Or a howitzer," Nick said.

"It's not so bad. Besides, you said all you need is an address and a desk."

"When you said it was on Fourth Avenue, I thought you were talking about north of downtown, not South Tucson."

"Well, it's north of downtown *South* Tucson."

South Tucson was an autonomous, predominantly Mexican-American town, located within the city limits of Tucson, approximately two square miles in area. To the people who lived there, South Tucson was a thriving, tight-knit community whose residents were proud of their heritage and were working hard to make their city a better place; but to many of the citizens of greater Tucson, South Tucson had a reputation for good, cheap Mexican food, low-ball auto repair, and reliable street drugs.

Nick looked at the neighboring buildings. On one side was a used auto-parts store specializing in hubcaps and wheels, and on the other side was a *carnicería* with two whole dressed hogs hanging in the window. Across the street was an auto-upholstery shop.

"You want to take a look inside?"

Nick nodded his assent. "How'd you come to own a place like this, Gordo?"

"I don't." Gordo twisted a key in the lock and pushed the door open. "It belongs to my cousin Johnny. He's up in Florence for the next couple years; I told him I'd try to rent it out for him."

The inside of the building was divided into three rooms, shotgun-style. Nick could still smell, faintly, the ghost odors of garlic and fried meat. The first room contained a row of cheap plastic chairs along each of the side walls, like a waiting room. The second room was full of boxes, filing cabinets, and stacks of paper.

"I thought it would be full of restaurant equipment," Nick said.

Gordo laughed. "No, this place hasn't been a *taqueria* for years. Johnny had an employment office here. Sonora Employment Services. He found jobs for people."

"Out of *here?*"

"Johnny wasn't real particular about appearances."

"What's he doing in Florence?"

"Three to five."

"He's in *jail?*"

"He had a little trouble with the Border Patrol. They stopped his van coming up I-19 from Nogales. His passengers didn't have any papers."

"They put him in jail for five years for that?"

Gordo shrugged. "He had a quarter kilo of coke under the spare tire. Anyway, his bad luck is your good fortune. What do you think?"

Nick stepped over a stack of manila files and looked into the back room. There were two metal desks, one turned upside down on top of the other. They looked serviceable. An abandoned *taqueria* in

South Tucson was the last thing he'd had in mind for launching the HandyMate, but the space wasn't bad.

"What about all this junk?"

"Move it all into the back room. You just need a couple of rooms, right?"

Nick tried to visualize himself in this space. Once the plywood covering the front window was removed, get a little light coming in . . . a coat of paint on the walls . . . maybe a couple of rugs to cover the old vinyl flooring . . . what difference did it make which end of Fourth Avenue he was on? Gordo would probably rent it to him for practically nothing.

"How much do you want?" he asked.

"Eight-fifty," Gordo replied without hesitation.

Nick laughed. The price was more than double what the place was worth.

Gordo, looking hurt, said, "Hey, I'm just trying to do my cousin a favor here."

"Eight-fifty's ridiculous, Gordo, and you know it."

"Okay, okay."

The number they arrived at was $650 per month—still more than it was worth, but Gordo agreed to defer payment for six months. They shook hands, and Gordo gave Nick the keys.

Nineteen

Gretchen laughed when Nick came through the door.

"What?" he said, confused.

"Look at you! Farmer Nick!"

Nick looked down at himself: jeans, cheap running shoes, and white T-shirt, all purchased that morning, now dirty from an afternoon of floor sweeping, wall scrubbing, and box moving.

"I don't think I've ever seen you in blue jeans."

"I just bought 'em." Nick grinned. "All my grubbies got burned up in the fire."

"What have you been doing?"

"Working on the future home of the HandyMate. I rented some office space."

Gretchen frowned. "I thought you were broke."

"I thought you'd be glad not to have me spread all over your house."

"I didn't mind."

Nick thought it best not to reply. She seemed happy and friendly at the moment. He didn't want to risk throwing her off her mood.

Gretchen said, "What did you rent?"

"An old *taqueria* down in South Tucson. It's very, ah, rustic."

Gretchen was giving him a look—knitted brow, mouth slightly

open, head tipped a few degrees to the left. He did not know what it meant, but it made him nervous.

He said, "I need a shower." He took his cell phone out of his pocket and set it on the table. "I'm expecting a call from Artie. If my phone rings, could you grab it?"

He felt her eyes on him as he headed for the bathroom.

"You're still staying here?" she asked his back.

Nick turned. "Is that okay?"

Gretchen nodded slowly.

Nick heard his phone ring while he was in the shower. He dressed and wandered out to the kitchen, where Gretchen was chopping an onion with a paring knife.

"What are you making?"

"I don't know," she said. "But it starts with chopped onion."

"Sounds good." He wanted to tell her to use a bigger knife but restrained himself.

"I'm a pretty good cook," she said.

"I know that." He sensed a crackling in the ozone. "Who called?"

"Your friend Yola."

"Oh." Nick stood very still and watched her chop. Maybe a bigger knife wasn't such a great idea.

"She wants you to call her. I wrote the number on the notepad."

Nick took the top sheet, went into the living room, and used his cell phone to return the call. The number turned out to be the Arizona Inn. The operator put him through to Yola's room.

"Hola."

"Yola? This is Nick."

"Oh, hi! Listen, I want to take you to dinner tonight."

"Tonight?"

"You and your girlfriend. Only she said she couldn't make it. What about you?"

"I . . . What did you have in mind?"

"I've got a business proposition for you. Also, I want to check out a restaurant up in the foothills. Platanos. You ever eat there?"

"I've heard it's very good."

"We'll see about that. You want to pick me up, seven-thirty?"

"Hold on a second." He muted the phone and went back into the kitchen. Gretchen was still chopping onions. If she chopped them much more, she'd have onion paste. "You don't want to go to Platanos?"

"I have plans."

"Plans? You don't even know what you're making!"

"Risotto. I'm making risotto."

Anger welled up; Nick turned away. "Yola?"

"Still here."

"I'll be there."

Twenty

Platanos owner Jose Wyler was the latest in a succession of Tucson restaurateurs with a mission to elevate Mexican peasant food beyond the ineffable. To present his haute-Mex cuisine, Wyler had chosen a decor calculated to bewilder. The interior walls were rough adobe with straw sticking out of the blocks, and chunks of genuine Sonoran Desert mud flaking off. Parts of the structure were reinforced with rough-hewn sheets of corrugated steel; the pillars were stout, irregular posts salvaged from an old bridge. The tables and chairs, by contrast, looked like something from the set of a sci-fi movie. Constructed from thin steel rods and plastic surfaces, they could not have looked more out of place—Jetsons seating in a Flintstones setting.

Nick said, "This must be what they mean by cognitive dissonance."

Yola giggled. "It's a little strange, isn't it?"

"I feel like a time traveler."

Yola was frowning at the flatware—a space-age design that matched the furniture. "Expensive," she pronounced. "My customers would steal it all the first week."

Nick, examining the menu, said, "I think it's included in the prices."

A very young man with a perfect mustache glided up to their table and introduced himself as William, the sommelier. After some discussion, Yola ordered a Chilean cabernet that William, with frowning sincerity, promised to be "very special, very unique."

After William glided off, Nick said, "He seems very earnest."

"That is important in one so young."

"Do you have a sommelier at El Otro?"

"You're looking at her. Of course, we mostly sell margaritas and beer." She waved a hand to indicate the other diners, most of whom were wearing business attire. "We don't get this expense-account business down in Sierra Vista."

Yola was wearing a burgundy silk top with a draped neckline—a once modest fashion concept updated by a cut that was low enough to display an abundance of cleavage. Her thick hair was pulled back tight and smooth. Complicated-looking garnet earrings dangled from her earlobes. Her wrists and hands were bare of ornament; everything was focused on her center, about four inches below the point of her collarbone, probably the exact point where she had applied her powerful perfume.

The sommelier returned with a bottle of the cabernet and proceeded to open it with a series of studied motions. When he poured it into Yola's glass, Nick noticed that its color matched her dress precisely. He wondered whether a different outfit would have demanded a different wine.

Moments later, the wine accepted and poured, Yola proposed a toast. "To your grandfather."

"To Caleb," Nick agreed. They both drank. Nick thought the wine a bit thin, but better than he was accustomed to drinking.

Yola put her glass down and, looking past him, exclaimed, "Jose!"

"I am speechless!" A short, slim man wearing an impeccable navy blue double-breasted suit was rushing toward them, his arms outstretched. Yola rose to meet him, and they embraced.

"Speechless! Yola, my love! You honor me!"

"I'm just checking out the competition, Jose."

"No one can compete with you! I only steal your ideas."

"No way, Jose. I hear you got a Michelin rating. How many stars?"

"Three," said Jose, smiling at the floor.

Yola laughed. "Jose, I want you to meet my friend Nick. Nick Fashon, Jose Wyler. He owns this *casucha*."

They shook hands. Jose Wyler's grip was crisp and precise. "Nick Fashon. You have been here before?"

"Never," Nick admitted.

"You will enjoy it. Please, sit down, both of you. Hector will take very good care of you. Enjoy! Enjoy!"

Jose Wyler moved on to work the next table while Hector, their waiter, took his place and recited a lengthy and ornate list of the evening's special offerings. Yola listened carefully and, without asking Nick's permission, ordered for both of them.

"I hope it's okay I order for you," she said.

"It's your show."

"Okay, I let you order dessert. So, you been thinking about the Otro Lado?"

"You mean the HandyMate?"

Yola shrugged and sipped her wine. "You are as stubborn as your grandfather."

"Look, it's not a tortilla press. The HandyMate works for all cuisines. I don't want to ethnicize it. It's got to have a name they can pronounce in New York, Alabama, and Idaho. HandyMate is good."

"HandyMate. It sounds like a cleaning tool."

Nick was rescued by the appearance of the Tres Tamal appetizer, three short chubby tamales each about the size of a hen's egg, displayed on a triangle-shaped terra-cotta platter. The golden cornhusk-wrapped tamale sat upon a drizzle of bright red chile sauce; the banana-leaf tamale was offset by a bright green cilantro salsa; the grape-leaf tamale was perched upon a scribble of pale lemon-egg sauce. The center of the platter was occupied by a bouquet of cilantro, oregano, and parsley tied with a strip of corn husk. Yola stared down at the platter, her lips parted, the HandyMate momentarily forgotten.

"So that's what a twenty-four-dollar appetizer looks like," she said. She took a few more seconds to admire the presentation, then proceeded to dissect the tamales, serving Nick a portion of each. The corn-husk tamale held a traditional pork, masa, and chili filling. The banana-leaf tamale was made with a lighter masa containing raisins, olives, and smoked duck. The third item turned out to be corn- and lamb-filled—basically a Greek dolmade with corn instead of rice. None of them tasted as good as they looked.

"But so what?" Yola said. "The thing is, you are never going to forget it." She pointed to her left eye. "People remember what they see, not what they taste. That's why food TV is so big. All these people staring at pictures of food. You know where I know Jose from? He was a food stylist for *Bon Appétit*. They did a feature on El Otro Lado eight, nine years ago; Jose was the one made the food look good for the camera. You know how he did it? Shaving cream instead of whipped cream. Strips of cardboard rolled into the enchiladas to give them that plump look. Dish soap in the Mexican hot chocolate to make it foam. He made my food look great for the camera, but you could not eat any of it. Then, a couple years ago, he quit *Bon Appétit* and moved to Tucson and opened Platanos."

Nick looked suspiciously at the bit of masa and duck on the end of his fork. Yola laughed. A hand appeared and refilled their wineglasses. Nick took a quick sip to erase the imagined taste of dish soap. Yola watched him, her mouth arranged in a short smile.

"You come watch me cook tomorrow, and I'll show you how we make food on TV. Looks good and you can eat it, too. I'm taping two shows tomorrow, one o'clock, at KUAT. You going to come, right?"

"Sure."

"Okay then." She lowered her head and looked up at him, peeking under the brim of a nonexistent hat. "So . . . no Otro Lado?"

"No Otro Lado."

"Because I have an idea. You ready?"

Nick wasn't sure, but he nodded.

"Okay," Yola said, leaning forward. "Here is my idea. We put my picture on the . . . on the HandyMate. Okay? We call it HandyMate, by Yola Fuentes. I use it on my TV show. I sell it in my restaurant. And I do infomercials for you. I will be the spokeswoman. Like Betty Crocker. You know?"

"Like Betty Crocker?"

"¡Sí! Plus, I will export for you to Mexico. I have many contacts there. All you have to do is manufacture."

"You know, Betty Crocker isn't a real person."

"Yes, but she is very popular. And you know—I just think of this—in Mexico we could call it the Otro Lado."

Teetering between amusement and horror, Nick said, "You want your picture right on the plastic?"

"No, no, we make a package." She described a shape in the air with her hands. "I am on the package. Only maybe my signature is on the plastic."

"And what do you get for this?"

"Fifty-fifty."

Hands appeared and whisked the appetizer plates and platter from the table.

Nick took a breath. "Look, I really like the idea of selling the HandyMate on your show, Yola. It would be a great way to introduce the product, and a way for both of us to realize some profit." He paused.

"I think so, too," said Yola.

"I'm sure we could work out a special deal for you, maybe even a short-term exclusive on TV sales."

Yola cocked her head.

Nick continued, "But let's be clear about one thing: the patent, the name, and the product are mine. There will be no fifty-fifty."

"No fifty-fifty?"

"No. And as far as using your image on the product, I'm not so sure that would be a good idea. I want it to appeal to a wider audience . . ."

Yola's face darkened. Nick instantly knew he'd made a mistake.

"What do you mean?" she said, spacing her words.

"I just mean . . . I think it would be wrong to attach a personality to the product . . ." He was in trouble now.

"You mean a *Mexican* personality."

"No. I mean *any* personality. French, Chinese, Eskimo, whatever."

"You are full of shit, Nick Fashon."

Nick shrugged, unable to refute her point. Yola glared at him. He half expected her to throw something—she looked like the throwing type. Then her expression shifted; she crossed her arms and sat back.

"I put in a lot of time with Caleb working on it. I am already a partner."

"In what sense? Do you have a contract? A written agreement?"

"I trusted him. When we work on the oven thing I tell you about, you remember?"

"The thermostat."

"Yes. He trust me, I trust him." Yola stared at him, her face now still as a marble bust.

"I trust you, too. But I can't just give you half of the HandyMate. It's not gonna happen. I want to be clear about that."

"You are very clear."

"I don't want you to think that I've been leading you on. Look, I have to make all the capital investment, I own Caleb Hardy Enterprises, I have to produce the actual product. All the risk is on my end. All you have to do is give it a minute or two on your show every week."

"I got some capital investment, too. I got my reputation."

"I understand that," said Nick. "But I'm going to be putting out half a million bucks"—exaggerating the amount to make his point—"just to turn out the first batch of HandyMates."

"How you going to do that?"

"Do what?"

"You got enough money?"

"Actually, I'm selling shares."

Yola's eyebrows, already painted a half inch above their correct anatomical position, rose. "You are selling shares in our company?"

The Thai Verde Curry Enchilada and Bison Machaca Platano Jose were both spectacular. If the cook had used any cardboard or dish soap in his recipe, it was not noticeable. The enchilada looked like a miniature green wedding cake surrounded by an expressionistic swirl of pureed red chile and yellow corn. The *machaca* dish was even more remarkable: a boat fashioned from the split skin of a plantain carried a cargo of shredded bison across a sea of blue-corn polenta dotted with whitecaps of thick *crema*. It was served with a stack of palm-sized corn tortillas, soft and delicate as crepes.

Yola did not have much good to say about the food. She was clearly upset. Nick wished he had simply put her off and discussed the HandyMate situation later, preferably by phone. At least she hadn't thrown any food at him. Not at these prices.

"I don't think you know what I can do," she said between bites of *machaca*. "I put the HandyMate on my show, you can't make them fast enough."

"I hope that's true," said Nick. "If so, we'll both do very well."

"Maybe I show you."

"What do you mean?"

"I show you," said Yola. "Maybe I show you how we get investors, too."

Nick spooned *machaca* onto a tortilla. "Just so long as you're clear about who owns it."

"I am very clear."

The HandyMate did not come up in conversation for the rest of the meal. They talked about the restaurant business, about food, about Caleb. They shared a bizarre chocolate-tamarind-mousse dessert. Yola picked up the check, and they left their table with bewildered stomachs and an invisible curtain between them, a situation that Nick did not regret. Getting too friendly with Yola Fuentes could be dangerous. He preferred to keep their relationship businesslike.

As if reading his thoughts, Yola suddenly turned bright and cheery.

"I like you, Nick Fashon," she said, grabbing his arm. "You're tougher than I thought. You don't let me get away with nothing."

They were standing beside the circular driveway in front of the restaurant. The valet pulled up in Nick's Corvette. Nick disengaged himself from Yola's grasp and stepped off the curb. He was reaching for his wallet to tip the valet when he noticed several dark spots on the car door. He looked closer, his jaw falling open. They were *holes.* There were *holes* in his car.

"What happened here?" Nick pointed at the damaged door.

The valet's smile evaporated. "It was not like that?"

"Hell no it wasn't like that!"

The valet took a step back, then jumped out of the way of a black pickup that suddenly roared up and skidded to a stop. Nick tore his eyes away from his injured car and looked at the man driving the truck.

"Hey. Buddy." The man pointed a finger at him, cocked it with his thumb, and winked. It was Robo, the loan shark.

Behind him, Yola erupted, letting out a wordless screech of fury followed by one of her shoes. The man ducked back, her shoe hit the side of the truck, and then she was running at him, brandishing her other shoe.

"You son of a bitch!" She launched a salvo of Spanish obscenities and threw her other shoe, which flew into the cab, just missing Robo's face.

Nick, now more concerned about Yola than his car, ran after her. Robo managed to roll up his window and lock the door before Yola reached him. Her fists hit the glass, pounding as she screeched at him in English, Spanish, and possibly Nahuatl. Nick grabbed her and pulled her back, Robo's face in the window laughing, Yola kicking at the door as Nick dragged her away.

Robo spun off, leaving behind the stench of burning rubber. Yola twisted free and ran after him, slowing and stopping only after the vehicle disappeared from sight.

"Shit!" She stamped her bare feet on the asphalt.

Nick said, "Hey, it's just some bodywork. You don't want to mess with that guy. He carries a gun."

Yola turned on Nick. "'Course he carries a gun—how you think you got those holes in your car? Thinks he's a big man with his little shooter."

"He . . ." Nick shook his head to clear it. It didn't work.

Yola picked up her shoe. "I get my other shoe back," she declared, "or he is in big trouble."

"You know him?"

"Know him? That's Roberto, my ex."

Nick swallowed. This was far stranger than any of Jose Wyler's concoctions. He took Yola by the arm and led her back to his car. The valet stood watching them.

Nick said, "My partner owes him some money. I think he's trying to drag me into it. Trying to scare me." He opened the passenger door. Yola slid in, saying nothing. Nick got behind the wheel, put the car in gear, and began to drive. He could hear Yola breathing through her nose. He said, "Your ex-husband. That's a pretty weird coincidence."

Yola barked out a laugh. "Is no coincidence. You think it is about you? Is not about you. Is about me."

Nick scowled, trying to figure out what she was saying.

Yola said, "He is just a jealous little fuck is all."

Twenty-one

Gretchen was pretending to sleep when Nick slid into bed. After a few minutes of listening to each other breathe, she said, "You smell like her."

"She was wearing a lot of perfume."

Gretchen said nothing.

"My car got shot."

"It wasn't me."

"It was Robo. The same guy who beat up Vince."

Gretchen stirred. "Somebody beat up Vince?"

"I didn't tell you about that? There's been so much going on. . . ." Nick told her what had happened. "Then the same guy—maybe the same guy who burned down our store—shoots a bunch of holes in my 'vette. And you want to know what's *really* weird? Turns out the guy, Robo, is Roberto Fuentes. Yola's ex-husband."

Gretchen sat up and turned on the light. "He really shot your car? With a gun? What have you got yourself mixed up in, Nicky?"

"I don't know. I'm worried about this Robo. Yola says he's mad because I went out to dinner with her, but I don't know. I think it has something to do with the money Vince owes him. I feel like I'm in the middle of something and everybody else knows more than me. I need information."

"You should talk to my dad."

"Bootsie? What for?"

"He still has friends in the police. Maybe he can find out about this man."

"Bootsie?"

"He's more than just an old man with bean dip, Nicky. Give him a call."

In the morning Nick went outside to look at his car. Daylight made it worse. There were six holes punched in the fiberglass body. Two of the bullets had passed through the door and lodged in his seat. He felt as if he had swallowed a fistful of cold wet clay. So ugly. So wasteful. He hoped his insurance would cover it. Fortunately, he had bought his auto insurance through someone other than Artie, so he would be spared dealing with Pima again. He punched Vince's number into his cell phone. Vince picked up on the fourth ring.

"Vince. Nick here. How are you doing?"

"I'm okay. Kind of stiff."

"You hear anything more from your friend Robo?"

"No. I don't expect to, not until next week."

"What happens next week?"

"That's when I promised to pay him."

"How are you going to do that?"

"I've got a few hundred bucks. Maybe I'll put it on a horse."

"He vandalized my car last night while I was having dinner at Platanos."

Vince took a moment to reply. "How was Platanos?"

"Not that great. Don't you want to know what he did to my car?"

"Let me guess. He ripped off the wiper blades, slashed the tires, smashed your mirrors, and broke the windshield."

"Not exactly."

"Oh. Well, that's what he did to *my* car. How come he's pissed at *you?* You owe him money?"

"No. But I was having dinner with his ex-wife. He put six bullets in my 'vette. She thinks he did it in a fit of jealousy."

"Well, there you go. That's Robo."

Back inside, Gretchen was getting ready to leave for Marana. Along with the usual jeans, long-sleeved shirt, and Red Wing boots, she was wearing an exceptionally soiled and ragged Arizona Wildcats cap.

Nick said, "You need a new hat."

"You don't like my lucky cap?"

He made a face. "It could use a cleaning."

Gretchen laughed. She seemed to have forgiven him, for the moment, for going out to dinner with Yola. "Nicky, you are a pill."

"I just think you should look good for the lizards."

"They're used to me. Oh, I called Bootsie. He says you should go see him."

"I can't just talk to him on the phone?"

"He said for you to stop by this afternoon." She grinned. "He's looking forward to it. Bootsie doesn't get that many visitors."

So who's gonna be the next asshole?"

Nick moved the phone away from his ear. "Artie?"

"First you got Vince mucking up the works, then some asshole lawyer. You actually pay him for that?"

"Artie, slow down. What happened?"

"Hardesty Chin, Jr., is what happened."

"Oh. He's the lawyer handling Caleb's estate. I told him about our situation, and he offered to look into it."

"Yeah, well, he did. Threatening to call the insurance commissioner, the governor, God, everybody. That kind of talk just ticks people off, Nick."

"Sorry. I thought he was going to be more low-key."

"What are you talking to a lawyer for, anyways?"

Nick was getting a little steamed himself. "I've got a situation, Artie. I need that money."

"And you'll *get* the money. Assuming that you didn't burn down the store."

"Artie—"

"I didn't say that. Look, you got to give it time."

"Okay, okay."

"Just keep that Hardesty Chin off my freaking back, all right?"

"I'll try."

As soon as Artie disconnected, Nick called Chin's office. Chin answered the phone himself.

"It's me. Nick."

"Nick! *¿Qué pasa?*"

"Artie Nagel just called me."

"Oh. He pissed off?"

"You made an impression."

"I know how to do that."

"Good job."

"Thanks, man. I told you you should hire me."

Driving up to Bootsie's duplex, Nick was strongly reminded of the night his store had burned down. It had happened only a few weeks ago, but it seemed like months. He could hardly remember who he was back then. Certainly not an invention marketer working out of a South Tucson *taqueria*. Certainly not a guy whose car gets vandalized by an insane loan shark. Not even a guy who would venture— alone and unarmed—to visit Bootsie Groth.

Nick parked on the street, folded his sunglasses into the breast pocket of his shirt, took a few deep breaths to calm himself, walked up to the front door, and pressed the bell. The door was opened a few seconds later by Bootsie, his lumpy body covered by only boxer shorts and an undersize tank top. It was the first time Nick had seen the old man in an upright position. He was surprised to find himself looking up. It seemed that Bootsie was big in every direction.

"Underwear guy! C'mon in!"

Nick stepped inside. It was hot and close. The sour odor of old socks and orange rind hung in the air. "AC went out," Bootsie said as Nick followed him deeper into the house. "How come I'm in my skivvies." He scratched his rump. "Notice they aren't leather?" *Hee hee.*

Bootsie led him through the kitchen and out a sliding-glass door into a small, private patio area. He lowered himself onto a redwood chaise longue. A low table beside him held a bowl of shelled peanuts, a Dr Pepper, and a telephone. He directed Nick to a folding lawn chair upholstered in macramé. Nick sat down, relieved to be breathing fresh air again.

Bootsie, looking as though he had absorbed most of the chaise into his body, said, "Can I get you something?" Clearly not an offer to be taken seriously.

"No thanks," Nick said.

"No problem. So, how you treatin' my little girl?"

"Like a goddess."

Bootsie stared at him for a few seconds, his tiny eyes glittering. For the first time Nick sensed a reserve of crafty intelligence lurking within the corpulence.

"You know what we used to call a guy like you? Slick. I don't know what they call guys like you these days."

Nick said nothing.

"Gretie tells me you're starting a new business. Not gonna re-open Love & Lingerie, huh?"

"Love & *Fashion*," Nick said, unable to stop himself.

"Oh yeah. I forgot. You named the underwear store after your-self."

"That's right."

"What's this new deal you got going? Some kind of kitchen gad-get, right?"

"It's called the HandyMate. It's a plastic kitchen utensil that my grandfather invented. I'm going to market it. Sell it on TV."

"Make a fortune off the old man's idea, huh?"

"That's what he would have wanted."

"How many of these things you expect to sell?"

"How many kitchens are there in America?"

Bootsie reached for his soda, brought it to his lips, and drank. "I don't know," he said.

"Neither do I, but it's got to be a lot."

"So . . . you gonna support my daughter in a style she's unaccus-tomed to?"

"I'd sure like to," said Nick, astonishing himself.

Bootsie set down his drink and grabbed a handful of peanuts. He dumped them into his mouth and chewed and stared at Nick. Nick held his eyes.

"I think maybe you mean that, Slick."

"I do."

"I'll be damned. Okay, Slick, Gretie said you want to find out about some guy. What's going on?"

Nick told Bootsie about his encounter with Robo at Vince's, and about his car being shot. He did not mention that he had been out to dinner with Yola at the time.

Bootsie listened carefully, his features held in neutral. Nick could see the cop in him—skeptical, hard-nosed, and focused. When Nick had finished his story, Bootsie said, "He shot your little car, huh?"

Nick did not like his car described as *little*. It made him want to quote horsepower, torque, and top end speed. He said, "Six times."

"And you want what from me?"

"I just want to know what I'm dealing with. Is this guy for real? Do the police know him? Is he really dangerous?"

"He shoots cars," Bootsie said, "you should avoid him."

"That might not be possible."

"How come you don't just report him?"

"I'd like to, but what can the police do? I can't prove that he vandalized my 'vette, and my partner won't file charges."

"Maybe, but if this prick is known to the cops, you can bet your sweet ass they'll send him a message."

"I'm afraid he'll pass the message on to Vince. Or me."

"You're kind of an easygoing fella, aren't you?"

Nick supposed that *easygoing* was a euphemism for wimp, but he let it pass.

Bootsie said, "Okay then. This jerkball have a real name?"

"Roberto Fuentes."

"And he lives here?"

"I'm not sure. Maybe Sierra Vista."

Bootsie picked up the phone, dialed a number, and asked for someone named Jacoby.

"Jocko, Bootsie here. Yeah, yeah. How's Patty doing? No shit. And the kids? You're a what? A grandparent? You're not old enough, kid . . ."

Nick quickly lost interest in Bootsie's half of the conversation. He found a high cloud to watch, a wispy, *J*-shaped stroke of water vapor suspended high above the Santa Catalina Mountains. He found himself remembering the last time he had gone hiking in the Catalinas. It was years—seven or eight, at least. There had been a time when he loved strapping on a backpack and heading up into the mountains, but these days he was just a city boy. The closest he'd been to nature lately had been his encounter with the rattlesnake at Caleb's.

He heard the name Roberto Fuentes and returned his attention to Bootsie.

". . . yeah, he uses the name Robo. Like Robocop. Only this guy doesn't sound like a cop. He might be a local, or maybe out of Sierra Vista. Yeah, just whatever you got. Uh-huh. Thanks, Jocko. You got my number, right? Later."

Bootsie disconnected and grabbed another handful of peanuts. He stared at Nick as he chewed. After swallowing, he said, "He'll call back in a few minutes. You sure you don't want something? You want a soda?" He poured more peanuts into his mouth.

"No thanks," Nick said.

"Tell me more about your whatchamacallit."

It took Nick a moment to realize what Bootsie meant. "The HandyMate?"

"Yeah."

"You want to see it? I've got a prototype out in my car."

"Bring it on, Slick."

For a guy who lived on snack food, Bootsie had remarkably little trouble grasping the concepts and applications behind the Handy-Mate. He actually extracted himself from the chaise and waddled into the kitchen to try it out. After chopping and grating several carrots, apples, and potatoes, Bootsie declared himself impressed. Nick, looking at the pile of disassembled plant matter on the kitchen counter, asked him what he was going to make with it.

"Gonna run it down the garbage disposal," Bootsie said. "Only reason I got all that rabbit food is on account of Gretie brought it. She brings me stuff she thinks I should eat. Most of it I give to the neighbors." He examined the HandyMate. It looked tiny in Bootsie's immense paw. "This is really something," he said.

"I think so, too."

"I'll buy one. How many you sold so far?"

"None. That's just a prototype. Now I have to raise money for the tooling and production."

"How you gonna do that?"

"I've drawn up a prospectus. I just need to show it around until I find some investors." It sounds so simple, Nick thought.

"Need money, huh?"

The phone rang. Bootsie hustled out to answer it. Nick rinsed off the HandyMate, then followed Bootsie outside.

Bootsie was once again embedded in his chaise, nodding and listening. "Uh-huh, uh-huh, uh-huh." A few seconds later he hung up and turned to Nick, his expression bland. "It could be worse," he said.

"What's that?"

"Roberto Fuentes. He's only been in jail once, back in the eighties, served thirty months up in Florence for involuntary manslaughter."

"What's that? He killed somebody accidentally?"

"Something like that. He got into a fight and accidentally kicked a guy to death. Fuentes claimed that he didn't mean to hurt the guy. He said he just got carried away. They couldn't prove who started the fight, so Fuentes got off easy. Anyway, he walked in eighty-seven, and since then he's been arrested and released seven times. Six of those times were for assault and battery. So far, nobody's pressed charges. Guys like your partner."

"What about the seventh time he was arrested?"

Bootsie grinned. "You're gonna like this, Slick. That other time, that was for arson."

Twenty-two

The single sheet of maize-colored paper taped to the front door of the former *taqueria* read C.H. ENTERPRISES, HOME OF THE HANDY-MATE. Nick had considered adding NICHOLAS FASHON, PROP., to the temporary sign, but he refrained. As soon as the money started rolling in, he would get a real sign. He unlocked the door and stepped inside.

"Good morning, Alice," he said to the empty chair behind the desk. He thought Alice was the perfect name for a secretary. He set the box of business plans on the desk. "File these, please, under hopes and dreams."

He imagined Alice as red-haired, a few pounds overweight, cheerful, and midway between his age and that of his mother. One day he would hire an Alice.

"I'll be in my office, shweetheart," he said. He had always wanted a secretary he could call *shweetheart*.

Nick's office contained nothing but a metal desk identical to Alice's, and two chairs. The rest of the junk was stacked in the back room. He sat behind the desk, put his feet up, took out his phone, and dialed a number.

"Rincon Plastics."

"Lew Krone, please." Nick waited contentedly.

"Krone here."

"Lew, this is Nick Fashon."

"Fashon . . . Caleb Hardy's kid, right?"

"Grandkid."

Krone chuckled. "What can I do for you, Caleb Hardy's grand-kid?"

Nick drew the check from his breast pocket. He rubbed it between his fingers, unfolded it, looked at the number.

"You can make me a mold," he said.

It was all Bootsie's doing. Nick never would have brought up the HandyMate if Bootsie hadn't asked him about it, and he certainly would not have shown him the prospectus. Gretchen had made it quite clear that he was not to consider Bootsie a potential investor. That was fine. He had gone there to find out about Robo. That was all. He'd been on his way out the door when Bootsie, all on his own, said, "So, you looking for investors, Slick? What does a guy get for his money?"

Nick had explained the setup. Every ten thousand dollars invested would buy two points, or 2 percent of the profit derived from sales of the HandyMate. It was a simple formula. Once the Handy-Mate paid off its start-up costs, all the investors would start making money.

"How long you figure that'll take?" Bootsie asked.

"Hard to say. Maybe a year."

Next thing Nick knew, Bootsie was writing a check for thirty thousand dollars. He kept saying, "I think you really got something here, Slick."

There had been a moment when Nick considered refusing the money. The moment had been brief. Bootsie would never regret his investment. The HandyMate would make a lot of money for the old man. Besides, according to Gretchen, Bootsie had money. He could afford to invest a few thousand. The problem was, Gretchen had specifically asked him not to take money from her father. How pissed off would she be? Boys-will-be-boys pissed? A dozen roses pissed? A night on the sofa pissed? How bad could it be?

Nick stared at the check. Thirty grand. Twenty-four down on the mold, six for miscellaneous expenses, and he'd be broke again in a couple weeks. He still needed money. In order of decreasing likelihood, he could borrow it, find another investor, or collect the insurance settlement.

He punched a number into his phone. Hardy Chin picked up on the first ring.

Nick said, "You're the only lawyer I've ever met who answers his own phone."

"I'm Johnny-on-the-spot," Chin said.

"Did you get that prospectus I sent you?"

"Sure I did. Looks good."

"You want in?"

"Me? I got a strict policy against investing in my clients' businesses."

"Why is that?"

"No money."

"Oh," Nick said. It was no more than he had expected. "I need ninety thousand dollars."

"I thought you needed more than that."

"I've got thirty; now I've got an immediate need for another twenty-five thousand to complete the mold, and then I'll need more. Remember we talked before about using Caleb's land for collateral?"

"That's a tough one, Nick. Like I told you. Undeveloped land, still in probate, no bank is going to write you a loan."

"No other options?"

"You might find a private lender. Somebody going to charge you, like, twenty percent."

"Somebody like Roberto Fuentes."

"He'd charge you more like twenty percent a *month*. Hey, how do you know Robo?"

"Remember that hypothetical firebug I told you about?"

The phone went silent. "Holy shit," Chin said at last. "You got to be kidding me, man."

"I wish I was."

"Listen, you better hope the cops don't get their hands on Roberto. He's just mean enough to claim you hired him. Even if it's not true."

"It's not," said Nick, putting some edge in his voice.

It rolled right off Chin. "I handled Yola's divorce. He showed up at my office one day, man, I thought he was gonna kill me."

Nick felt a shadow pass through his thoughts. He was able to resist it for an instant, then it took hold. Was it possible? He felt as if a cold, leaden presence had wrapped itself around his liver.

"You there, man?"

"Yeah . . . um, Yola says he's the jealous type."

"Jealous? Shit, he's the psycho type. Listen, don't even joke about borrowing money from him, okay?"

"I won't."

"I gotta go. *Hasta luego,* man."

Nick sat perfectly still, staring at dust motes and fending off the mental squall unleashed by Chin's comments. Was it possible? It made almost too much sense. Caleb had hooked up Vince Love and Roberto Fuentes. Vince had defaulted on his loan. And, to make things worse, Caleb, the old goat, had been hanging around with Yola. Chin had even described her as Caleb's girlfriend. Instead of having a coronary event, his grandfather might have succumbed to a Robo event.

Had they done an autopsy? Nick wasn't sure. He'd been told that the remains were in pretty rough shape, left a week or more, much of it carried off by vultures and coyotes. What would they be able to tell from an autopsy?

And what was he supposed to do about it, anyway? Go to the police, he supposed. Maybe they could dig Caleb up and take a closer look. Maybe they would find something, or maybe not. Maybe they would talk to Roberto Fuentes, but the chances of his ever being charged with the crime were remote at best.

Nick's phone rang. He lunged for it, desperate for distraction. "Hello?"

"Hey, we're about to start here. You coming?"

Yola. Damn. Nick looked at the time—one P.M. He had completely forgotten about the ¡Vamanos! taping.

"Sorry, I got tied up here."

"You coming or not? I got a surprise for you."

"I don't think I can make it, Yola. I have to meet with this guy at the plastics company and—"

"You don't want to come, you don't have to bullshit me."

"I'm not—"

"It's okay. Look, I'll talk to you later." She hung up.

This day was really jerking him around. Nick turned off his phone. He had an hour to kill before his meeting with Lew Krone at Rincon Plastics. He looked again at the check from Bootsie, aka Harmon Oscar Groth. Time enough to stop at the bank and open a checking account. That would make him feel better. At least for a while.

Nick showed up at Gretchen's place a little after six, feeling battered and drained. He'd spent two hours at Rincon Plastics working out details of the final HandyMate. It turned out they had several prototypes on file; Nick settled on the most recent version, similar to the prototype he had found at Caleb's, but with a bit more heft in the grip. He had written a check for twenty-six thousand from his new account, *Nicholas Fashon, dba C.H. Enterprises*, and Lew Krone had promised not to cash it for a few days, until Bootsie's check cleared. Nick had spent much of the afternoon making a conscious effort to avoid thinking about Robo Fuentes. It hadn't been easy.

As he walked up the three steps onto the front porch, he noticed a cardboard box full of papers and a pile of clothing. He looked closer. It looked like the new shirts and trousers he had bought from Gordo last week, and the grubbies he'd picked up at Target. What were they doing there? He looked into the box and saw his notes and the rough draft of his business plan. A Post-it note on top carried a sample of Gretchen's handwriting. He usually had trouble reading her scrawl, but this note clearly spelled out the word ASS-HOLE.

This was not good. It was very not good. He stood there, undecided what to do next, his heart banging around his rib cage like a panicked squirrel. Part of him wanted to just grab his stuff and run, to get into his car and crank up some Motown and drive. Another part was angry and wanted confrontation. Why couldn't she trust that he would return Bootsie's investment many times over? Most of him was simply bewildered. He'd expected her to be pissed, though he thought he could bring her around. But only if she would talk to him.

He tried the door. It was locked. He rang the doorbell. After about half a minute, he rang it again, then pounded. Sometimes Gretchen took a long time to answer her door. Maybe she was in the shower. Nick waited, pushing the bell every couple of minutes. After a time he gathered his possessions, crammed them into the Corvette's tiny trunk, and drove away.

·   ·   ·

Nick dreamed that he was choking on a giant hairball, and when he woke up, that turned out to be precisely what was happening. He twisted and flailed. With an annoyed croak, the cat slithered off his face and onto the floor. Nick sat up, wiping cat hairs from his lips. The room was dark, but he remembered where he was. Vince's living room, on the sofa, waiting for dawn. He could hear Vince's snores coming from the bedroom, and the sound of rain coming from outside.

He rubbed his eyes, remembering why he was there. Gretchen. He could see, burned into his mind, the one-word note she had left him. He could hear her voice saying it. Nick groaned and flopped back onto the sofa, his mind a froth of guilt and resentment.

It was too confusing and painful to think about. With a desperate effort of will, he forced his thoughts from Gretchen to the physical, unchanging solidity of the HandyMate. He imagined the machines at Rincon Plastics cranking out millions of the things. He saw himself on TV, selling a HandyMate to every cook in the nation. He conceived a line of spin-off products: the HandyMate Mini, the Super HandyMate, Le HandyMate Français, the HandyMate Outdoorsman, the MiniMate, the HandyMate Polo Edition . . . He wondered whether Caleb had worked out any such variations. He pictured Caleb's workshop, cluttered tables and overstuffed metal cabinets, piles of boxes . . . he hadn't looked at most of it. Poor murdered Caleb, killed for being friends with Yola Fuentes. Or for his connection with Vince. Or perhaps he had died of natural causes . . .

A sudden weight landed on Nick's belly. He swung his arm, knocking the cat back onto the floor.

A new idea, awesomely paranoiac, bloomed in his mind. Yola and Robo. Yola had found Caleb's body. What if she had known what she would find before she went out there? What if Caleb had been murdered by the two of them? Why? To steal the HandyMate? But how would Caleb's death get them the HandyMate? Had Caleb told Yola he would make her his heir? Why would he do that? To get her into the sack. Nick would not have put it past the old goat. But then what?

Nick turned onto his side, and the nightmare fantasy crumbled. It was not believable. If Yola and Robo had wanted to steal the HandyMate, he would not have found the prototype sitting out in plain view. No, Roberto Fuentes might have killed Caleb, but the idea of Yola being in league with him seemed absurd—especially after seeing her go off on him outside Platanos.

Thoughts tumbled. His poor shot-up Corvette. Gretchen throwing his clothes into the cardboard box, furious. Would he ever collect a dime from Pima Life? How would he pay Rincon Plastics for the mold? He needed another twenty-five grand. Could he ask Bootsie for more money? Now that Gretchen had kicked him out, he had nothing to lose. Unless he hoped to get her back . . .

Nick groaned and curled into a ball and listened to the rain and Vince's distant snoring, using the sounds to fend off his thoughts. An hour later, with the hint of dawn in the windows, he fell into a brief and fitful sleep.

Twenty-three

Tell me again what I'm doing here?"

"You owe me." Nick shifted lanes to pass a convoy of semis.

"Hey, I didn't do anything."

"You turned my life into a nightmare," Nick said.

"It's not my fault your girlfriend kicked you out."

"That's not what I'm talking about."

Vince made a sour face, reached into his pocket, and came out with a pack of cigarettes. Nick shot him a look. "It's my car," Vince said defensively.

Nick was driving Vince's Ford Explorer, watching the road through the cracked windshield. Vince had replaced the tires that Robo had shot out, but the wiper blades were a twisted mess, and both side mirrors were smashed.

"Open your window, at least," Nick said.

Vince did so.

"When did you start smoking again?"

"I don't remember."

"You're a mess, Vince."

"You don't think I know that? I could be in bed right now. Sleeping. I'm in pain, f'chrissake. I got two busted ribs, and I'm still breathing through my mouth." His nose was swollen and multihued, making the rest of his usually handsome features look undersized and pallid. He had not shaved, unusual for Vince, who was usually even more concerned about his appearance than was Nick.

"All the more reason to go for a drive instead of waiting for Robo to pay you another visit."

"He won't show up till Friday. Friday is collection day."

"How'd you do at the track?"

Vince lit his cigarette and gazed blearily out the window. Nick shook his head and guided the Explorer on to an exit ramp and turned south on Highway 80, through Benson. They rode in silence for several miles. The air was hazy with moisture from the early morning showers; the upper peaks of the Dragoons and the Whet-stones were shrouded, the fresh desert smell of creosote bush mingled with cigarette smoke. It smelled good, reminding Nick of the old days, of the life-affirming taste of that first morning cigarette.

Nick said, "You know, that Inch-Adder you invested in might not be a total loss."

Vince roused himself. "Easy for you to say."

"I'm serious. There must be some prototypes in Caleb's work-shop. After we're done shipping coffins, we can look around. I mean, if you want to pursue it."

"You're suggesting I dump more money into the thing? It was a stupid idea. Who the hell wants to buy an Inch-Adder? Somebody too cheap to invest in a new belt? I can't believe I was stupid enough to let that old man con me."

"Hey, he's *dead*, all right? Maybe he just needed more time." Nick was surprised to hear himself defending his grandfather, especially as Vince was probably correct in his assessment.

"Whatever. I just don't ever want to hear the term *Inch-Adder* again. Besides, I always thought it was a stupid name. Sounds like a small venomous snake." Vince lit another cigarette. This one didn't smell so good.

• • •

Vince was not impressed by Caleb Hardy's spread.

"Looks like a junkyard," he said as they drove down the narrow driveway.

"You see that thing that looks like a flying saucer? That was Caleb's workshop."

Vince grunted. "If he'd shown me this dump, I never would've invested."

Nick backed the Explorer up to the pole barn where the pet coffins resided. He got out, unlocked the doors, and swung them open. The air inside the shed was still cool. That wouldn't last. Another two hours and the temperature would rise into the nineties or higher.

Vince was still sitting in the truck.

Nick said, "You want to grab those orders sitting on the backseat?"

Moving slowly, Vince climbed out of the vehicle, opened the back door, and came out with a slim sheaf of purchase orders. He waddled painfully over to Nick, counting as he did so. "You dragged me all the way out here to help ship twelve lousy orders?"

"I needed your truck."

"It's not a truck. It's a sport utility vehicle."

"Whatever. I thought you might get a kick out of the place. Since Caleb made such a difference in your life, I mean."

"Thanks a hell of a lot."

"And I thought it would be nice to have some company. I guess I was wrong."

"I'm not feeling very scintillating this morning. I don't know what you expect me to do, anyway. I can't bend over, can't even pick up a phone book."

"You don't have to do anything."

"Good." Vince took a prescription bottle from his pocket, shook out a couple of tablets, and swallowed them dry.

"Codeine?" Nick asked.

"Percoset."

Nick set about packing and labeling the orders. The first purchase order was for thirty Number Ones—the gerbil size. The buyer was Cedar Manor Elementary School, someplace in Minnesota. What were those kids doing to their gerbils? Nick puzzled over it for a moment, shook it off, and packed the order.

Vince said, "You ever think about what you're doing?"

"I try not to."

"One day you're selling leather fashion accessories, the next you're in the coffin business."

"I prefer to think of it as the packaging business."

"I don't blame you."

Nick finished packing the order and went on to the next one, an assortment of sizes for Elysian Fields Pet Cemetery, one of Caleb's best customers.

"I guess I should've invested in the pet coffins instead of the Inch-Adder," Vince said.

"How did you meet that guy Robo?"

"I told you. Through your crazy grandfather."

"I know, but how did it come about?"

"Caleb convinced me that the Inch-Adder was going to be the next paper clip. He said he needed ten grand."

"For what?"

"Tooling. Christ, I don't even know what tooling *means*."

"It's the mold for injection-molded plastic parts."

"Oh. So, he tells me he's got huge orders on deck from Wal-Mart and Sears. All he needs is to show them production samples, and they'll buy hundreds of thousands of the things—you know what it looks like, right?"

"Like a plastic buckle."

"Yeah. You just cut the belt and clip it on, and you got an extra few inches. Clever damn idea. So Caleb tells me that he'll double my money in six months, and I'm like a bass on a worm. Only problem is, I don't have the money. I tell him I can raise it, only it'll take me a couple months. Caleb says he can't wait, but he has an idea. That was when he introduced me to Robo. He seemed like a nice guy."

"I haven't seen that side of him."

"The loan-application procedure was pretty straightforward. We met at a restaurant in Sierra Vista—"

"El Otro Lado?"

"I think so. Run by this good-looking Mexican broad. Anyway, Caleb and Robo and I had lunch there. Robo explained the terms of the loan. Three percent a week, no fees. I had to pay him the interest monthly, and the principle was due in six months, with no penalty for early payment. It sounded okay to me—"

"Three percent a *week*? Isn't that about three hundred percent a year?"

"Yeah, but you have to realize I only needed it for a few weeks. We were doing really well at the store, and I had some inside info on a couple of ponies . . . Shit, Nick, you know how it goes. I miscalculated. And then Caleb goes and dies on me."

"Okay, so you borrow the ten. How did he give it to you? Cash?"

"Actually, I never saw any real money. I just signed a piece of paper."

"All you did was sign a paper, and you never saw a dime?"

"Yeah. The money went straight to Caleb." Vince twisted his mouth into a pained smile and pulled the prescription bottle out of his pocket.

"You just took two," Nick pointed out.

"Oh." Vince pocketed the bottle.

"I wonder why Caleb didn't just borrow the money himself."

"He'd probably maxed out his credit line."

"Caleb owed Robo money?"

"Sure. If Caleb wasn't already in debt to Robo, why would he need me?"

"I hope he doesn't think I inherited Caleb's debt."

"He would've let you know by now."

"I suppose."

Another possibility occurred to Nick. "Do you know whether Caleb ever ordered the mold?"

Vince frowned. "I assumed so."

With the back of the Explorer crammed with boxes full of boxes, they drove toward Tucson. As soon as he could get a clear signal, Nick checked his cell phone for messages. There was only one. It was from Yola.

"Don't forget to watch my show tomorrow. Eight o'clock on channel six. You gonna like it."

Yola. He wasn't sure what to do about her. He would need her show to launch the HandyMate, but he certainly didn't want her for a partner. Yola was trouble. She was indirectly responsible for ruining his car and a contributing factor to his problems with Gretchen. And he still wondered about Caleb's death.

"You think it's possible that Robo murdered Caleb?" he asked.

Vince nodded sleepily. "Sure. Why not? I'd like to murder him myself . . . if he wasn't already dead." He'd taken a couple more pills before leaving the ranch.

Nick turned his thoughts again to Vince's arrangement with Robo and Caleb.

"Shall we find out what Caleb did with your money?"

Vince moved his shoulders in a feeble shrug, staring disinterestedly out the window.

Nick called Lew Krone. "Lew. Nick Fashon."

"Caleb's grandkid."

"Right. Caleb's grandkid. Got a question. Did you ever do any work for Caleb on a thing called the Inch-Adder?"

"Inch-Adder. Lemme think. Thing like a buckle?"

"Yeah."

"I think we worked up an estimate for him. Lemme look. Okay, yeah, I got it right here. We did an estimate."

"He never ordered the tooling?"

"No."

Nick looked over at Vince, expecting some reaction, but Vince was nodding, lost in Percoset dreams.

Twenty-four

Gordo Encinas and Artie Nagel watched Nick use the HandyMate to demolish a bagful of apples, tomatoes, and carrots. They listened as Nick led them through the business plan, nodding appreciatively at the six-, twelve-, and eighteen-month projections. At the first opportunity, Gordy said it looked like a great product, but cash was tight and he really had to go. He was out the door before Nick could phrase an objection.

Artie said, "It's darn clever, Nick. Really a neat little thing. I'd order one for my wife. What the hell. Put me down for a couple dozen. I'll give 'em away to clients."

Nick did not know what to say. Had Artie really so astronomically missed the point? He said, "Actually, Artie, we're not in production yet."

"No hurry. Just let me know. Say, how many would I have to order to have my name printed on them?"

Nick sighed. "I don't know. Actually, the reason I'm here is to talk to you about coming in on the ground floor." He tapped the prospectus, now spattered with tomato seeds. "I'm giving friends and family a first look."

Artie scowled. "How much are you looking for?"

Nick opened the prospectus to page twelve. "I figure every investor will get thirty to forty times their money back within five years."

"Or lose it all," Artie said.

"Not gonna happen. My personal guarantee."

"What good is that? You're saying if your company goes belly-up, you're going to give me my money back? How are you going to do that?"

"I'm not worried about it."

"'Course you're not." Artie flipped through the plan. "I suppose I could take a shot." He sat back in his chair and squeezed his nubbin of a chin between his thumb and forefinger. "What the hell, I'll come in for two hundred bucks."

"Two hundred?" Nick felt ill. "Jesus, Artie, don't scare me with those big numbers."

Artie laughed uncomfortably.

Nick said, "Why don't you come in for ten thousand?"

"Ten thousand?" Artie said, his eyes popping. "Are you out of your mind?"

Nick's uncle Albert in Detroit showed even less interest. The first few minutes of their phone conversation were devoted to helping Al remember that Nick Fashon was his nephew. Once they got that figured out, Al seized the opportunity to update Nick on the doings of all the relations on his father's side, including an enumeration of their children, pets, recent jobs, and television sets, of which Nick's second cousin Ben owned five, including one with a fifty-five-inch screen. Nick was forcefully reminded of why he had left Michigan. When they finally got around to discussing the HandyMate, Nick learned that it was not a product one could easily describe over the phone, and as soon as Al picked up that Nick was on the mooch, he launched into a detailing of his personal financial woes. The poor man had to buy store-brand peanut butter—or so he claimed. Nick promised to send him a copy of the prospectus anyway.

He hung up feeling more defeated than ever. He'd been in business in this town for over a decade but had somehow neglected to do any networking. He had avoided joining any merchants' groups, civic clubs, churches, or golf clubs. He didn't even have a personal banker—just a highly impersonal relationship with a Wells Fargo branch office.

He could ask Bootsie for more money, but that would kill any chance he might have of reconciling with Gretchen. He had left three messages for her, two last night and one that morning. How mad was she?

He considered camping out on her front porch, waiting for her, begging for forgiveness. It was a good plan, but should he do it tonight or wait a day or two? Waiting might be safer.

Knowing she would not be home, he called again just to hear her voice on the answering machine.

"Hi, this is Gretchen. I'm not here right now. Leave a message!"

She sounded so cheerful. He hung up.

Unable to face another night with Vince and his cat, Nick drove downtown and checked in to the Hotel Congress. Just for a night or two, he told himself. Then he would fix things up with Gretchen. He fell asleep on top of the bedspread, fully dressed, the TV on, waiting for his phone to ring, dreaming of molten plastic and cardboard coffins.

He awakened to the sound of Yola's voice. He opened his eyes and there she was, looking at him from inside the television set.

". . . today," she was saying, "we are going to talk *salsa*. No, not the music"—shaking her finger—"the *condimento*. Of course, in Mexico salsa is much, much more. Even here in the United States, we now have more varieties of salsa in the grocery store than catsup, mustard, and relish combined. We *loooove* our salsa, no?"

She was wearing a black dress with a scoop neck and a hint of sleeve. The camera added a few pounds, but they seemed to land in all the right places. The virtual Yola Fuentes was even sexier than the real one. Nick propped himself up against the headboard and watched her move around the faux-rustic kitchen set, talking about the various chilis, tomatoes, herbs, spices, and other vegetables and flavorings that went into salsas.

". . . we start today with the basic everyday salsa, what we call *salsa cruda,* composed of nothing more than tomato, fresh chili pepper, cilantro, a little lime juice, and salt . . ."

Nick noticed a familiar shape sitting beside the bowl of tomatoes. He leaned forward. Was it what he thought it was?

". . . is very simple. You simply chop the tomato . . ." She had it in her hand, and she was slicing and chopping. Nick's eyes bulged. It *was.* Where had she gotten her hands on a HandyMate? If he'd been there on the set . . . damn! What did this mean? Was she taking over the HandyMate? Had she been using it on her show all along?

". . . and I like to seed the peppers, if they are spicy. Here I am using serranos, a little hotter than the jalapeño. I cut them lengthwise and scrape out most of the seeds . . ."

Nick had never seen the HandyMate in the hands of a professional chef. Within two minutes she had put together a bowl of fresh salsa. Was she going to say anything about the HandyMate?

Nick watched the rest of show from the edge of the mattress, his fingers gripping the bedspread. Yola made an assortment of salsas, using the HandyMate for several tasks, but said nothing about it until the very end, after she used it to create a tomato rose as a garnish for a bowl of cilantro and tomatillo salsa.

"Now, I know a lot of you are wondering about this wonderful little kitchen tool. It is a new thing, invented right here in southern Arizona. It is called"—Yola smiled into the camera—"the Handy-Mate. Next week, when we talk mole, mole, and more mole, I will tell you more. Until then, *hasta luego!*"

Nick sat with his mouth open as the credits rolled.

Twenty-five

At seventy miles per hour, the bullet holes in his door began to make a sound like the howling of a tabby in heat. The sound rose in pitch as Nick increased speed until, at about eighty-two miles per hour, it abruptly ceased. That was fine with him. He took the 'vette up to eighty-five and kept it there. At that speed, in the dark, he became highly focused on the section of highway illuminated by his headlights. It helped him avoid thinking. He did not want to think, because all he could imagine was Yola Fuentes with a HandyMate.

Watch the road. He saw two green spots on the shoulder; in an instant they were gone, leaving the image of a gray fox in his memory. If the creature had darted across the road, he never would have been able to stop. Nick slowed down; his door began to howl. He sped up. To hell with the foxes.

He reached El Otro Lado just after eleven. The hostess, who looked like a smaller, dumpier version of Yola, informed him that the restaurant was about to close. Nick demanded to see Yola. A few moments later, she emerged from the kitchen in a white apron with her hair tied tightly back.

"Nick!" She embraced him happily, heedless of the murderous expression on his face. "I was just going to call you, but then I think maybe you are asleep. Hey, you see my show?"

"What the hell were you thinking?" Nick said, loading his voice with maximum venom.

Yola laughed. "You're in a pissy mood."

"You're damn right I am. You can't just start showing the Handy-Mate on TV. It isn't even in production. We don't even have a deal yet—and we aren't going to!"

"Really?" She seemed more amused than surprised.

"Yes, really. And I want that prototype. It's not your property."

Now she seemed less amused. "Your grandfather *gave* it to me."

"I don't care. Give it back to me now, or you'll be hearing from my lawyers."

Yola opened her mouth wide, hovered between anger and be-musement, then laughed in earnest. "Your lawyer? You mean Hardy Chin? Hah! Then I sic *my* lawyer on *you!* He go beat himself up and bill us both."

Nick choked on his reply.

Yola said, "Before you start yelling some more, I got some good news. Come." She grabbed his hand and pulled him toward the bar. Her hand was moist. "First we have a margarita, then I tell you good news. Freddy! Two Old Fashion Margaritas, *por favor.*" She grinned at Nick and sat down at one of the small wooden tables. "See? We name it after you: Old Fashion."

"That's your good news?" Nick sat across from her, the edge of his anger eroding. Yola seemed so glad to see him. And she looked different. Less makeup, a little tired, a little happy. A woman who had been working hard all day and was ready to celebrate.

"I got better news than that." She reached out and squeezed his wrist. "You saw the show, yes?"

"I saw it."

"Okay. Maybe you are right. I should have asked you, and I was going to, only you didn't come to the set like you said you would. You hear I called it the HandyMate? I decide you are right. El Otro

Lado is a good restaurant name, but not for HandyMate." She squeezed again. "You are *right*, Nick."

"You shouldn't have shown it," Nick said, somewhat mollified.

Yola shrugged. "I'm sorry. I was bad." Freddy delivered the two margaritas. Yola sipped hers, not taking her eyes from Nick's face. "Tell you what. You can beat me up. That's what Roberto use to do."

Nick looked away, embarrassed.

"I still have to tell you the good news."

"Fine, tell me the good news."

"We got a few phone calls after the show aired. Some people want to know about the HandyMate." She smiled and waited. When he failed to respond, she said, "Lots of calls. I talked to Xavier, my producer at KUAT. He say they got more than fifty calls, all wanting to know how to get a HandyMate."

Nick was surprised by the calls but unimpressed by the number. "That's not that many."

"It is considering that we don't give out the phone number. We don't even say to call. Some people even called here, at the restaurant. And it gets better. I got a big order. A thousand."

Now Nick was impressed. "A thousand HandyMates?"

"KUAT wants to use them as a fund-raising gift. You know, pledge a hundred dollars and you get a HandyMate with the name of the station on it. I tell Xavier we can give a discount."

Nick drew a shaky breath. A thousand HandyMates! That would be . . . he didn't *know* how much it would be. "You didn't quote them a price, I hope. I . . . I don't even know exactly what they're going to cost. I don't—" He recaptured a bit of his anger. "I don't even know how I'm going to pay for the mold!"

"You need money?"

Nick shook his head. "No. I mean . . . when do they need them?"

"Next fund-raiser is next month. But listen: the one thousand HandyMates for KUAT is just a start. You know how many PBS stations carry my show? Seventy-three. If all seventy-three stations start giving away HandyMates . . . You sure you don't need some money, Nick?"

Nick shook his head, trying to clear it. He tried to take a sip of his margarita, but the glass was empty. Yola was speaking.

"—and I talk to Xavier, you know he does infomercials for lots of people, for the Ab Buster, for the Grapefruit Diet Pill, for Voodagra—you hear about Voodagra? It is like a legal Spanish fly—all kinds of things."

"Okay, slow down a minute. Back to the order from KUAT. This is a real thing?"

"One hundred percent."

"How can they buy a thousand of something if they don't know what it costs?"

"Well . . . I have to tell them something."

"Like what?"

"I tell them ten dollar."

"Ten dollars?" Lew Krone had estimated a cost of about a dollar per unit. The profit margin would be huge.

"But I tell him I give a discount," Yola said. "You know. Like half."

"Half? Five dollars?" The numbers still looked okay.

"You think you can make them for that?" she asked.

Nick nodded. Four dollars profit per unit, one thousand units . . . perhaps times seventy-three stations . . . that would be over a quarter million dollars. Yola was holding out her margarita glass. Nick lifted his, which had somehow become full again. They clicked rims.

"To the HandyMate," she said. They drank, and Nick wondered whether he might have misjudged Yola Fuentes.

"You ever get your shoe back from your ex-husband?"

Yola laughed. "Roberto is crazy, but he is no thief. I get home yesterday, the shoe is by my front door. There is a note. He says he is very sorry."

"Let me ask you something. How did he get along with Caleb?"

Yola shrugged. "They know each other. Roberto liked him."

"They didn't have some money issues?"

Yola pursed her lips. "There was some thing. Caleb owed Roberto some money, but then I hear he pay it back."

"Yeah, by transferring the debt to my partner, Vince."

"I don't know how they work it out."

"What would Roberto have done if Caleb hadn't paid his debt?"

"Roberto is very strict, but he would not do anything bad to Caleb, if that is what you mean. I would not let him."

"He does whatever you say?"

"Some time." She smiled.

"How'd you hook up with him?"

"How people do. You know. I meet him. I fall in love. I marry him. I divorce him. End of story."

"I've heard that one before."

"Roberto can be difficult. Many times I feel sorry for him. He does not know how to relate to people. He is like the little boy in school who does not know how to tell a girl he likes her, so he hits her. But he can also be very charming."

"I haven't seen that side of him."

"Roberto has many sides. But he is not a complicated man. Have you ever been married?"

Nick shook his head.

"You should. You are a nice guy, Nick Fashon. How come you don't marry your girlfriend? You would like it. A woman to take care of you."

"I don't think I'd get a lot of TLC from Gretchen."

"You don't know. She is a good woman. I can tell."

"That might be, but at the moment she wants nothing to do with me."

"You do something bad?"

"No. Maybe. I don't know."

"You going to fix it up?"

"I don't know."

Yola regarded Nick over the rim of her glass. "You sure don't know much."

"*That,* I know." Nick picked up his margarita. "Tell me about Mexico," he said.

"Well, I was born in Hermosillo—"

"No, I mean how you would sell the HandyMate down there."

Yola tipped her head and smiled.

Here is what I like about you, Nick Fashon. You are a nice guy. Your girlfriend kick you out, but you don't come on to me. A lot of guys, they have a fight with their girlfriend, they figure it's open season. But you are faithful even after she kick you out. I like this about you. You know what else I like about you? You are good-looking."

On one level Nick sucked in her praise; on another he knew that he'd had too many margaritas. Mariachi music was playing over the sound system. He made an effort to block it out and replace it with something from his late lamented Motown collection, but instead his memory served up a tune by Jay and the Americans: *Come a leetle bit closer . . .*

"Hey, Nick Fashon, where'd you go?"

Nick shook his head to clear it, but that only made matters worse.

They had been drinking and talking for nearly two hours. All of the Otro Lado employees had gone home; Nick and Yola were alone in the restaurant. Yola's face looked soft, and her pupils were not the same size.

Nick stood up. "I think I better get going."

Yola walked out with him. As he was digging for his car keys, she said, "You know something? I think is too far to drive back to Tucson. You stay with me tonight, okay?"

Nick shook his head. "I'll be fine." He looked up at the moon, a mist-addled crescent, a fuzzy slice of peach, a bright rent in the night.

"I think you maybe have too much margarita."

"Me?" Nick tried to remember how many but failed. Maybe she was right. "You, too," he said.

"Yes, but not so many as you. And I live close." Yola guided him away from his Corvette.

"Jus' drop me at a motel," Nick said.

"No. I make you drunk, you stay with me. Don't worry, I got lots of rooms. I feed you *menudo* in the morning."

Too befuddled to unravel her argument, Nick allowed himself to be herded into Yola's SUV, a black Dodge Durango.

"Same make your ex drives," he said. "Same color, too." The license plate read ROBO 2.

"Roberto buy it for me."

Twenty blurry miles outside of Sierra Vista, at the base of the Huachuca Mountains, they turned up a steep, twisting driveway. Yola's house, a sprawling adobe structure, sat atop a truncated foothill. Nick stepped out of the SUV. The entryway was a lush jungle of bougainvillea and oleander; a breeze mounted the slope and ruffled his pant legs, the cool air smelling of juniper and orange blossoms.

"We are five thousand feet here," Yola said. "Nice and cool."

Nick followed her through the front door, which was not locked, into a spacious entryway. She led him to a long sitting room with a fireplace at one end. Several pieces of leather-upholstered furniture were gathered near the center of the room. Mexican textiles and Navajo rugs decorated the walls. The low ceiling was made of pine planks supported by heavy, rough-hewn beams. The end of the room opposite the fireplace was occupied by a grand piano with elaborately carved legs and a nativity scene painted on the underside of the propped-up top.

"I've never seen a piano like that before," Nick said.

"Is from a church in Mexico," Yola said.

"Do you play?"

She shook her head. "Roberto buy it for me."

Every time she mentioned Roberto's name, Nick felt a cold blade pressing against his neck and heard another snatch of Jay and the Americans. He sat at the piano and ran his fingers across the keys, striking random notes.

"You want something to drink?"

"I think I've had enough."

"How about a hot chocolate?" Yola asked.

A few minutes later, Nick was sitting in a soft leather chair, sipping hot chocolate from a thick mug and marveling at the marriage of poor-quality chocolate, cheap cinnamon, crudely refined sugar, and Mexican magic. Like *chorizo* and *menudo*, the drink's palatability transcended its vulgar components.

Where had Yola disappeared to? What the hell was he doing here, in her house? He should have driven himself to a motel. The effects of the margaritas were abating; the beginnings of a headache gathered behind his brow. He wished he were at home—but he had no home. A soft sound: slippers on *saltillo* tile. Yola appeared wearing a black robe made of some silky material. Her hair was tied back loosely, and she carried her own steaming mug of chocolate.

She sat down on the low table before him. Her face looked pink, as if freshly scrubbed, and she had freshened her lipstick. "I had to wash the kitchen stink off me." She smelled of soap and saffron. "How is your chocolate?"

"It's good."

"I want you to know some thing." She crossed her legs and leaned forward. The front of her robe gaped, displaying a spray of freckles on the inside of her left breast. "I did not invite you here with exterior motives."

Nick grinned.

"I say that wrong?" Yola asked, sitting up.

"It's *ulterior* motives."

"That is what I mean." Yola sipped her chocolate, licked the foam from her upper lip. She looked him in the eyes. "I did not bring you here to seduce you away from your girlfriend, or to steal Handy-Mate, or any of those things. I just think you need a place to stay, you know?"

"I appreciate that," Nick said.

"I am a nice person." Her eyes slid away, and her mouth drooped. "I have lived here alone for eight months. You are the first man to stay in this house since I make Roberto leave."

Nick did not know whether to respond with thanks or condolences. Yola stood up; the scent of chocolate and soap and saffron swirled together. She stretched, reaching for the ceiling. The hem of her robe rose, and the front parted to show her inner thigh. "I have seven bedrooms. One for me and my husband, the others for our children."

"You have kids?"

"No." Yola walked around behind his chair. "I am like you, Nick. The way life goes, my business is my child. Little children? Little children are for some other Yolanda."

"Your name is Yolanda?"

"*Sí.*" She was behind him, standing very close. Her hands touched his shoulders. Her fingers probed. "You are very tense," she said.

"I've got a lot on my mind," he said, but it wasn't true. He had only one thing on his mind.

She cupped his shoulders and kneaded. Strong hands. He imagined them kneading *masa*, stretching the dough paper-thin, baking it on the *comal*, then rolling and folding the tortilla into burros, flautas, sopaipillas.

"Is very exciting, no? To be so close to success."

Nick made a sound in his throat signifying agreement.

"I think in a few months you will be a rich man, Nick Fashon."

Her hands moved briefly to his chest, then back to his shoulders. "You must be very tired. Maybe I should show you to your room."

Nick stood up. Yola reached out and touched his lips with her forefinger. "You don't say much. You are very strong. Very attractive." She turned and began to walk away. Nick followed a few paces behind her. They entered a hallway dimly lit by ceramic sconces. Yola was a shadow, dark on dark. "These are the children's rooms," she said as they passed several doors. "Each of them contains a bed but no child." She did not stop until she reached the open doorway at the end of the hall. She turned to face him. The front of her robe fell open. "This is where the adults sleep," she said.

Twenty-six

Nick dreamed of himself sinking deep into an enchilada, drowning in a thick sauce that smelled not of chilis but of cinnamon and soap. He reached and flailed; his arms struck soft, dry fabric. He opened his eyes. The blades of a fan made languid revolutions against a plank ceiling. Sunlight slanted through a large bay window. He sat up and pushed aside a white down comforter. The bed was high, the mattress exceedingly soft. He was alone. He climbed down from the bed and walked to the window. He could see for miles across the San Pedro Valley to the Dragoon Mountains and beyond to what he thought might be the Chiricahuas.

He found his clothing where he had left it, folded and placed on a side chair near the door. He walked down the hall to the bathroom and washed his face, splashed water in his hair, combed it back with his fingers, and confronted his mirror self. How do you feel? He felt okay. He must not have had as much to drink as he had thought. Did you make any mistakes last night? He wasn't sure. Do you feel guilty?

The memory of Yola sent an erotic jolt to his groin. Nick rinsed his mouth and dressed, forcing his mind down more mundane avenues—such as wondering how he was going to get back to his car, how he was going to finance the rest of the HandyMate mold, and hoping there was a cup of coffee to be had. He hoped Yola wouldn't be too pissed at him. He did not want to dodge any spike-heeled shoes. Who was it who said "Hell hath no fury like a woman scorned"? Shakespeare or Marvin Gaye, he wasn't sure who. But he was glad he'd turned her down. It had been close.

With these thoughts, he made his way through the house to the kitchen. The smell of frying onions and chilis hung in the air. He heard voices. He pushed through a set of French doors and stepped out onto a large, sunny redwood deck that ran the length of the house and jutted out over the steep hillside. The air was cool, the sun warm. Yola, dressed in white this morning, sat at a wrought-iron table near the far edge of the deck, twenty yards away. She was not alone.

The man with her was facing away from Nick. He sat low in his chair, a gray denim jacket bunching up around his neck. A pearl-gray cowboy hat sat atop his head, slightly cocked to shade his face from the morning sun. Something about the man's attitude, the way he sat, was ringing Nick's internal alarm bells. His legs wanted him to duck back into the kitchen, but he was saved from so ignoble an act by Yola, who saw him, smiled cheerily, and waved him over. Nick approached, trying to keep his gait casual. The remains of a full breakfast—eggs, sausage, potatoes, tortillas, fruit—covered the small iron table. He could see enough of the man's face now. He stopped ten feet away, his body rigid with tension.

Roberto Fuentes turned his head slightly, a faint smile on his thin lips.

Nick looked at Yola, bewildered. She smiled up at him and shrugged. "You want some coffee?" she asked. "I get you a cup." She got up and walked quickly to the kitchen, leaving Nick alone with Robo.

"I believe you owe me for some bodywork," Nick said, amazed by his own temerity.

Robo gestured toward a chair. "How come you standing behind

me, buddy? Doan you know not to stand behind a man? Sit down."

Nick wasn't sure he could move.

"Sit down," Robo said. "I talk to you."

Nick forced his muscles to activate his limbs. He pulled the chair out from the table. Robo watched him. When Nick sat, Robo pulled a cigarette from his jacket pocket, tapped it several times on his wrist, and lit it with a small silver lighter. He inhaled and held his breath and stared at Nick.

After a few seconds he said, "So now you focking my wife."

Nick felt his heart thump several times, rapidly. He drew a breath and his pulse slowed, an engine shifting to a higher gear. Fear gave way to anger.

"Ex-wife," Nick said. Let him think what he wanted.

Robo's skin seemed to grow hard and metallic, his eyes brittle and unblinking. The stream of smoke from his cigarette bisected his face.

Nick said, "That's a pretty scary look. You must work on it."

Robo took another drag off his cigarette, expelling the smoke in two jets, one from each nostril. "You are a funny guy."

"The body-shop estimate came to eighteen hundred dollars. That's not funny."

Robo shrugged. His hard-guy look shifted to one of feigned boredom. "You doan have insurance?"

"My deductible is a thousand. I don't think it was funny what you did to my business, either."

Robo's eyebrows went up. "What I do to your business?"

Nick declined to elaborate. Maybe it would be better if Robo didn't know what Nick knew. What he *thought* he knew.

"What I do to your business?" Robo repeated.

Nick shook his head. This was not good. He was baiting a man who probably had a gun in his pocket. They were in the middle of nowhere—no other houses in sight—on the edge of a deck that dropped off into a tangle of thorny brush and cacti.

"Are you two getting to know each other?"

Both men turned and watched Yola approaching with a tray of pastries and a fresh pot of coffee.

"What I do to his business?" Robo asked her.

"His business? I don't know. Did you tell him what we talked about, Roberto?"

Robo stubbed out his cigarette and looked away.

Yola said, "He is going to pay to fix your car, Nick."

"Fock you," said Robo.

"Roberto . . ."

Robo stood up suddenly and reached into his pocket. Nick nearly went over backward in his chair. Robo pulled out a roll of cash, peeled off ten hundred-dollar bills, tossed them on the table in front of Nick.

"Fock you both," he said, and stalked off. A few seconds later they heard an engine start, tires spinning, the fading sound of shifting gears, then silence.

Yola said, "You see? Roberto can be very sweet."

Twenty-seven

Nick found a speed at which the moaning from his punctured door became tolerable, and turned his thoughts to his immediate financial difficulties. He needed twenty-four thousand dollars by next week if he wanted work on the HandyMate mold to continue. Yola, driving him back to Sierra Vista to pick up his car, had not brought up the subject of partnership again, nor had he. He wasn't sure where he stood with her, but she had promised to obtain a purchase order from KUAT. That might help him land some investors. And if he could interest other PBS affiliates in the product, he might even be able to swing a bank loan. He imagined himself walking into Wells Fargo with a hundred thousand dollars' worth of POs. That would get their attention . . . But he didn't have a fistful of POs. Not yet.

He took out his phone and checked his messages. There were four. Artie Nagel wanted him to call but didn't say why. The cop, Hoff, had left yet another laconic request for a return call. The other two messages were hang-ups.

Nick called Artie, got his voice mail, and left a message. He popped a tape into the deck, a mix he'd made of Bettye LaVette, Brenda Holloway, and a few other mostly forgotten Motown greats. He cranked up the sound, and for the next several miles, he thought nothing at all. Outside of Benson, Nick noticed that his gas gauge was nearing empty. He pulled into a Texaco and pumped the tank full of premium. When he went inside to pay, he noticed a slip of pale blue paper in his wallet. Odd. Nick liked to keep the contents of his wallet to an absolute minimum to avoid an unsightly bulge in his hip pocket. He pulled out the paper and opened it.

The attendant said, "Sorry, guy, we don't take checks."

"It's not for you," Nick said.

The check, drawn on the account of Cochise Holdings and signed by Yola Fuentes, was made out to Nick Fashon in the amount of twenty-five thousand dollars.

After arranging with the desk clerk to stay at Hotel Congress for a few more days, Nick went up to his room, bathed and changed, went downstairs to the café, and ordered a *salade niçoise* for lunch. The waitress was slim, young, and blond, and wore mirrored sunglasses and a tight cotton top that displayed several inches of midriff. The sunglasses struck Nick as odd. He did not think he had ever seen a waitress in shades. Unaccountably, she reminded him of Yola.

He ate his salad, hardly tasting it. He should be happy. He now had the means to put the HandyMate into production. True, the money was from Yola, and she would expect a lot for her investment. What exactly *did* she expect? He wasn't sure. How could she simply give him a check? Was it a gift? Something wasn't right.

He took the check from his wallet and set it beside his plate. Cochise Holdings. The signature was Yola's, but who actually owned Cochise, and what sort of business was it? Did she have partners? If so, who? Robo? Cashing this check might put Nick in debt to Roberto Fuentes. He folded the check and returned it to his wallet. Surely, there were other ways to acquire capital. He wished he knew some of them.

· · ·

The cool morning gave way to a blistering-hot Tucson afternoon. Nick drove to his office with the AC on full, chilling his front, while his back was glued to the seat by a layer of perspiration. He parked in the wisp of shade offered by a sickly mesquite tree in front of C.H. Enterprises, home of the HandyMate. Someone had ripped the paper sign off the front door. Or maybe it had been the wind and he was being paranoid. Nick unlocked the door. The air inside was even hotter. He turned on the air conditioner. The aging wall unit sputtered and groaned and hummed and began to cough out a stream of cool air. Nick stood in front of it until his body temperature returned to normal, then he sat at his desk. He sat for a few minutes staring into space, then took out his address book and began to underline the names of those he had not yet invited to invest in the Handy-Mate. He would cash the check from Yola only as a last resort.

The last name in his book was Wally Yeddis. Who the hell was Wally Yeddis? Nick thought for a moment, then remembered. Wally was the advertising salesperson from the *Tucson Weekly*, an alternative paper. What were the chances that Wally had ten grand to invest? Approaching zero. Nevertheless . . . Nick took a few fortifying breaths and dialed, but before the first ring, someone started banging on the door. Nick hung up and peered through the blinds out the front window. He could see a floral-patterned shirt and plaid Bermuda shorts covering an enormous rear end, supported by thick, white, hairy legs, black socks, and a pair of crepe-soled brown street shoes. The man's face was not visible. Although Nick could not endorse the fashion statement, his visitor did not strike him as threatening—in other words, it was not Robo. He opened the door.

Bootsie, red-faced and panting, pushed past Nick, staggered across the room, and draped his rear end over a chair. "Christ a'mighty, you know how hot it is out there?" he gasped.

Nick opened a bottle of water and handed it to him. Bootsie upended and drained the bottle. "Christ a'mighty," he said again, and belched.

"You okay?" Nick asked.

"I'm *hot!*"

Nick adjusted the air-conditioner vanes to direct cool air at Bootsie. He brought out another bottle of water, then waited until Bootsie's face went from red to pink, matching the hibiscus blossoms on his shirt.

"Feeling better?" Nick asked.

Bootsie sat up straighter and looked around the office, blinking and scowling. "This is it?"

"This is it," Nick said. "What are you doing down here? Did you drive?"

"No, Slick, I came on roller skates. 'Course I drove. What the hell, you never call me back."

Nick restrained himself. "You called?"

"Four or five times. You ever answer your phone?"

"Why didn't you leave a message?"

Bootsie's eyes grew smaller. "Why should I do that if you're not gonna call me back anyways?"

"Sorry. I didn't know you were trying to reach me."

"One hell of an organization you got here." Bootsie was looking much better. His face had reverted to its original oatmeal color, and the sweat on his forehead had dried.

"Did you just come down to look things over?"

"Not much to see. Where're all the whatchamajiggies?"

Nick wasn't able to translate.

"The Handywhatsis," Bootsie clarified.

"HandyMates? They're still working on the mold. It'll be a few weeks before we have any product."

"Looks pretty rinky-dink. Lousy neighborhood, too."

Nick shrugged. He wasn't going to argue with the old man. "What can I do for you, Bootsie?"

Bootsie pushed out his lower lip and stared at his knees. "Fact is, Slick, I came down to get my money back."

Nick managed a sickly smile as his liver—or something inside him—collapsed. "Excuse me?"

"Changed my mind," Bootsie elaborated.

"Changed . . . why?"

Bootsie met his eyes. "I gave you that money on the understanding that you and my little girl were gonna tie the knot. Now I hear you broke up with her."

There was absolutely nothing in this statement that Nick did not find outrageous. He said, "I don't . . . I didn't . . . tie the knot?"

"You left her high and dry."

"*She* kicked *me* out!" Nick sputtered.

"You broke her heart."

"Wait a second." Nick squeezed his eyes closed, shook his head, opened them. Bootsie was still there. "This is crazy," he said. "What did she tell you?"

"She loved you, Slick, but you blew it. You want to write me a check?"

"I don't have it."

"You better be kidding me."

"Why would I kid you? The money is gone; it's been paid to Rincon Plastics for the HandyMate mold. Remember the HandyMate? The reason you decided to invest?"

Bootsie was shaking his head. "It's a clever gadget, I'll give you that. But I was investing in my little girl, not some cheap plastic gizmo."

Nick stared, wordless.

Bootsie said, "You owe me thirty grand, Slick." He leaned so far forward that Nick worried he would fall on the floor. With a groan, he straightened his legs and rose to a standing position. "You better figure it out."

Nick said, "I've called her, you know. She won't call me back."

"Where've I heard that before?" Bootsie waddled to the door and grabbed the knob. "You goddamn kids don't know what's important." He turned and scowled at Nick. "You better figger out what you want, kid. You figger it out, you'll be okay. You keep mopin' around feelin' sorry for yourself and makin' excuses, then you're just another asshole. Gretie, she don't need another asshole, and neither do I." He opened the door and sunlight crashed in, followed by a wave of heat. "Christ a'mighty," Bootsie muttered. Leaving the door open, he made his way down the sidewalk to his car, a sun-bleached ten-year-old Dodge. Nick watched him wedge himself behind the wheel, start the car, and drive off.

"Christ a'mighty," Nick said, closing the door. He returned to his chair and waited for the next terrible thing to happen.

That took about five minutes. The phone rang again. It was Artie.

Twenty-eight

Vince wasn't answering his phone. Nick drove to his condo, but Vince was not answering his door. His Explorer was not in evidence. Where might he have gone? The track, maybe, or one of the casinos. Another, closer possibility occurred. Nick drove over to north Fourth Avenue and parked his car behind Vince's Explorer, just up the block from the Shanty.

Vince was sitting at the far side of the U-shaped bar, smoking a cigarette and nursing a bottle of Tsingtao. He saw Nick come in and gave him a morose salute. Nick went to join him.

"Tsingtao?" Nick asked. "I thought you didn't like those light beers."

"Communist beer," Vince said. "Capitalism sucks. Power to the people."

Nick decided that Vince must have been there for quite a while. "How drunk are you?" he asked.

Vince thought for a moment. "Semidrunk," he said. "Why?"

"I just got a call from Artie."

"Fucking Artie."

"We might have a serious problem, Vince."

"All my problems are serious."

"You ever talk to Clint Pfleuger? The investigator from the insurance company?"

"I talked to him. I also had some cop calling me every day. Why do you think I disconnected my phone?"

"What did you say?"

"Nothing."

"Nothing?"

"I don't remember. I probably told him to go fuck himself."

"Well, whatever you said, they've decided not to pay the claim."

"Big surprise there."

"And they've told the police that we did it."

Vince took a few seconds to absorb that. "We didn't, did we?"

"That all depends on what you mean by *did*. Have you heard from Robo lately?"

"Screw Robo." Vince puffed vigorously on his cigarette; Nick leaned away from the acrid cloud. "He can do whatever the hell he wants."

"What if he wants to rearrange your face again?"

Vince sniggered. "He can try." He winked, something that Nick had never seen him do before. "Check it out," he said, lifting his shirttail. Nick looked, and saw the butt of a handgun stuck in Vince's belt.

"That thing is pointed right at your nuts," Nick said.

"I got the safety on."

"You even know how to shoot?"

Vince let his shirttail fall back over the gun. "Sure I do."

Nick did not believe him.

Vince said, "Picked it up yesterday at the gun show."

"I thought there were laws to prevent clothing salesmen from owning guns."

"This is the Wild West, pardner." Vince grinned, cigarette clamped between his teeth. "Ain't nobody better mess with this cowboy. Got my Tsingtao, got my Smith & Wesson nine-millimeter."

"Nine-millimeter, huh? You even know what that means?"

Vince wrinkled his brow, pained by Nick's lack of faith in his small-arms knowledge. "It's the size," he said.

"Of what?"

Vince shrugged and stubbed out his cigarette.

"What are you going to do when the police arrest you on suspicion of arson and they find that thing stuck in your pants?"

"A guy's got a right to defend himself."

"Or to get himself killed."

"Yeah, that, too."

"When do you expect to hear from Robo again?"

Vince took a few seconds to light another cigarette. "Friday," he said.

Nick sank into the rattan chair on Gretchen's front porch, prepared to wait for days if necessary. A couple of hours, anyway. While he waited, he occupied himself by trying not to think about Yola.

It wasn't easy. He couldn't keep his mind off the twenty-five-thousand-dollar check in his wallet. And every time he thought about the HandyMate, he saw it in Yola's hands. Considering the possibility that the police might decide to arrest him for arson, he could not help but think about Robo, which took him right back to Yola.

He took out his phone and called Hardy Chin. "I got a call from Artie Nagel," Nick told him.

"They going to pay you?"

"No. Not only are they not paying, they've told the cops that they think Vince and I torched our own store."

"Oh. Well, that probably won't come to anything. Long as you didn't do it."

"Thanks a lot."

"Hey, cheer up! If the cops clear you guys, Pima will be forced to pay up. You just have to go through the process."

"Why do I think that unlikely?"

"I don't know, man. You're a pessimist."

"I'm a realist."

"Pessimist, realist, what's the difference?"

Nick did not know. He said, "Guess who gave me a big check."

"Okay, don't tell me . . . Yola?"

"How'd you know that?"

"Hey, you asked me to find you investors, I found you one."

"You're taking credit for Yola?"

"Why not? You'd never have met her except for me. How big was the check?"

"Twenty-five. It's written on the account of Cochise Holdings, whatever that is."

"Never heard of it."

"I thought you were her lawyer."

"Never heard of Cochise."

Nick saw Gretchen coming up the walk. "I gotta go."

"Wait a minute. Are you sure the check was signed by Yola?"

Nick took the check out of his pocket and looked at it. "Yeah, she signed it. But there's no address or anything on it, just the bank—Arizona National Bank, the Bisbee branch."

Gretchen's eyes found Nick on her porch; she looked startled, then gave him a tentative half-smile.

"I gotta go."

"Hold on. You should probably find out who you're getting money from."

"I . . . what are you thinking?"

"You want to make sure Roberto doesn't own any part of it. I mean, with those two, who knows? You want me to look into it?"

Gretchen stepped onto the porch. Nick pointed at the phone and held up his index finger, asking her to wait one second. Gretchen frowned and waited, shifting her weight from one foot to the other.

"Sure," Nick said. "Let me know what you find out. I mean, I'm not even sure I want to owe money to her."

"Owe money to who?" Gretchen asked. She looked down at the check in his hand.

"Just a second," Nick said to her. "I gotta go," he told Chin.

Gretchen unlocked the door.

Chin said, "You know what else you could do? You could just ask her."

"Who? Yola? I'd rather not." The door closed. "I gotta go. See what you can find out, okay?" He hung up, not waiting for Chin's reply, and tried to open the door. It was locked. He pressed the bell, then pressed it again a minute later, but she would not answer.

Twenty-nine

The next morning Nick took his 'vette to the body shop down the street from his office. The guy in charge, who looked like a bug-eyed Mexican version of Jackie Chan, looked at the bullet holes as if he had seen thousands of them—and he probably had. He scribbled some numbers on a dog-eared notepad and came up with seven hundred dollars, less than half of what Nick had been quoted up in midtown.

"How long to fix it?" Nick asked.

"Two, three days. I have it for you Friday morning."

"Sounds good. Do you have a loaner I can drive in the meantime?"

The man smiled and nodded.

The van was at least twenty years old and still, judging from the ride, on its original shocks. The driver's seat and dashboard were upholstered in matching orange shag that reeked of some cheap and powerful men's cologne. Several images of the Virgin Mary decorated the cab, including a 3D rendition encased in a clear plastic globe that served as the shift knob; and a Saint Christopher medal the size of a saucer was glued to the center of the steering wheel.

That was okay with Nick. He could load it up with pet coffins and shipping paraphernalia and move the coffin operation to his office in South Tucson so he wouldn't have to keep making the two-hour trip out to Caleb's.

He felt sick about Gretchen. She'd been right there in front of him. He'd seen her almost smile. He should have hung up the phone. No, he should have *dropped* the phone, right then and there, and gotten down on his knees and promised to return Boot-sie's money—somehow—and begged for her forgiveness. But he had not done that, and however pissed she had been before, she was even more so now.

Nick had once read that the human brain was a major consumer of calories. Thinking took a lot of energy. But trying to *not* think was more difficult yet. Staring out through the windshield of the van, watching the passing mile markers and tire shreds and phone poles and scrubby mesquite trees, trying not to think about Gretchen—*that* took a lot of energy. But when he did think of her, his stomach twisted into a knot and the oxygen went out of the air and the edges of his field of vision darkened, threatening to collapse. Nick kept driving. It was all he could do.

At the entrance to Caleb's driveway, he slowed to a crawl, easing the van over the moguls and around the rocks and across the ruts. He approached a sharp rise and eased his way over it with only the slightest bit of scraping. It would be worse on the way out because of the cargo weight, but he thought he could make it.

As Caleb's workshop came into view, Nick was suddenly beset by an image of himself lying facedown in the dirt. He was alone; any-thing could happen. What if he had a heart attack? If that was what had killed Caleb, maybe he had inherited a predisposition to heart disease. How long might it be before his body was discovered? Would he be devoured by scavengers? Which would come first, the coyotes or the vultures? Where would they start? And what about Gretchen—how would she feel? She would be sorry, damn it, and she should be. She hadn't given him a chance. She could have waited thirty goddamn seconds for him to get off the phone, but instead she locked herself in her house, not even giving him a chance to apologize or explain. It wasn't fair. He hoped she'd slept lousy last night, too.

He ground his teeth together. She was being completely unreasonable. His business was important to him, just as her archaeology was to her. It wasn't as if he'd never been inconvenienced by *her* business. If she dug up some really interesting bones, she'd forget he existed . . . although he couldn't recall a specific example. And the thing with Bootsie—he hadn't *asked* for the money. The old man had practically forced it on him. The guy was almost as nutty as his daughter. Maybe he should just stay focused on the HandyMate and fix things up with Gretchen later. He put her away and slammed a mental door, hoping it would hold for at least a few hours.

He backed the van up to the coffin barn. He unlocked the barn. The air inside still held a hint of coolness. He grabbed an armful of folded Number Fours—his biggest seller—and loaded them into the back of the van.

He found Hardy Chin at the saloon in the Copper Queen Hotel, sitting at the bar eating a bowl of chili and drinking a Corona. Nick took the next stool and ordered a Coke.

"How'd you know I was here?" Chin asked.

"Your secretary sent me."

"Secretary? That's my aunt, man. You cash that check?"

"No. You find out who owns Cochise?"

"Still working on it."

Nick sighed.

"These things take time."

"Fine. I wanted to ask you about something else. When Caleb's body was found, I assume there was a police report. They, ah, they did an autopsy on him, right?"

"I'm trying to eat my chili."

"Sorry."

Nick sipped his Coke and watched their reflection in the mirror. Tall, blond, sharp-featured Nick on the left; black-haired, broad-faced Chin on the right. It reminded Nick of Abbot and Costello.

"Why?" Chin asked.

"Why what?"

"Why you want to know about an autopsy?" He scooped up a spoonful of chili.

"Oh. I was just thinking . . . you don't think it's possible . . . how did Roberto get along with Caleb?"

Chin stared at him, the spoonful of chili forgotten. "Oh, man, don't even say that shit."

"I just want to know who I can talk to about it. If there was an autopsy, I want to know what they found. I want to know how he died."

Chin pushed his bowl aside. "He was old."

"True, but I just can't help wondering whether Robo paid him a visit. Caleb owed him money, you know."

"Sure. But I thought they straightened all that out."

"Maybe Robo didn't think so."

"If you're thinking that Roberto did something to Caleb, you're way off. They got along great. Had a lot in common."

"Like what?"

"To start with, they both had a thing for Yola."

"All the more reason for Robo to want Caleb out of the picture."

"Nah, man, it wasn't like that. Robo, he never took Caleb seriously. Hey, I hear you got a thing for her, too."

Nick said, "Where did you hear that?"

"From Yola, who else?"

"Rest assured, it's not true."

Chin shrugged. "Whatever, man. You're not the first, or even the third. Anyways, Yola would not have let Roberto hurt Caleb."

Nick thought back to the scene on Yola's patio, Robo giving him the money to fix his car. "He does what she tells him?"

"Sure. Why you think he divorced her? How would you like to be married to a woman always telling you what to do?"

"*He* divorced *her?*"

"It was mutual. They loved each other too much to be married, at least that's what Roberto told me. He's a romantic."

"You're confusing me."

"How do you think I felt? I had to handle their divorce. It's weird, man. Only divorced couple I know who still eat breakfast together."

"They do that every morning?" Oddly, this did not surprise Nick. Then something even more alarming occurred to him. "Roberto doesn't still *live* with her, does he?"

Chin took out one of his tiny cigars and lit it. "With Yola? Nah. He has a trailer a couple miles up the road."

Nick relaxed. Chin, watching him, grinned. "She likes you enough, she won't let him hurt you."

"I'm not worried about that," Nick said.

"Whatever, man."

"I still want to talk to the coroner."

Chin shrugged. "He's over in Sierra Vista. You want me to give him a call?"

That was your grandfather, eh? Sorry for your loss, son." Dr. Merle Worthington drew on his cigarette.

"I didn't know him well."

"Should make it a point to get to know your elders, son. Sometimes we don't stick around as long as you think." Worthington was in his mid-sixties but looked as if he had several decades left in him, despite the cigarettes. They were standing in the shade outside the morgue. Worthington was wearing a lab coat, a white Stetson, and black cowboy boots. "Now, what can I do for you, son?"

Nick said, "I was wondering about the autopsy. You did an autopsy on him, right?"

"Yes, I did. As I recollect, your grandpa died of heart failure."

"He had a heart attack?"

Worthington chuckled, flicked his cigarette onto the concrete, and ground it out with the toe of his boot. "You know, son, cause of death is not an exact science, especially when a body is—I don't want to upset you, son—not all there."

"I heard the coyotes had been at him."

"Lots of other critters, too. He was about one quarter et. Looking over what was left, my best guess was his heart stopped. Pretty safe bet, when you think about it."

"Is it possible he died from other causes?"

Worthington took a fresh cigarette from his shirt pocket and placed it between his lips. "Cause of death . . ." He paused to light his cigarette. "Thing you got to understand, son, is when I go, it'll probably be a heart attack or stroke does me in. And that's what they'll write on my death certificate. Only you and I both know it was these little devils actually did the killin'." He held up the cigarette, shrugged, took a deep drag. "Cause of death is like cause of life. You can't always pin it down." He frowned. "What exactly is it you're lookin' for?"

"I was wondering whether it might be possible that Caleb was killed. I mean, if it's possible that someone else was involved."

"I sure as hell hope not! We already had three homicides this month. Last thing we need in this county is another murder." He chuckled. "Not to mention an embarrassed coroner. You got some reason to think he was murdered? Yes? No? Okay, here's what I can tell you. I found no evidence of gunshot, beating, or stabbing, but I did find considerable evidence of heart disease. His arteries—what was left of 'em—looked like rusty old steel pipes. That's the price we smokers pay for our pleasure."

"Caleb didn't smoke."

"Oh? Well, what the hell do I know? In any case, I can't absolutely without a doubt for dead certain *prove* that he died as a result of a heart attack, but it's pretty damn compelling. Coronary. That's what I told the police, and that's what I wrote on the death certificate."

"What about his motorcycle?" Nick asked.

"His what?"

"Caleb had a motorcycle. It's missing. No one knows what happened to it."

Worthington sucked on his cigarette, reducing his statistical life span by another fraction of a second. "Son, motorcycles are dangerous. I want nothing to do with 'em."

Thirty

Yola's door was answered by a sturdy-looking woman in sweatpants and an oversize T-shirt with EL OTRO LADO printed across the front. Her eyes were dark with makeup. Long hair, too black to be natural, was tied back by a red paisley bandanna. Twenty years ago, Nick thought, she might have possessed the kind of hard good looks that go with Harley-Davidsons and tight blue jeans. Now, gripping a sponge mop in both hands, her narrow lips pressed tight, she just looked hard. Nick asked her if Yola was at home.

"She's resting."

"Would you tell her that Nick Fashon is here?"

"I don't want to bother her."

"Is she taking a nap? I could wait, if you don't mind."

"I don't think so."

"I really need to talk to her. How about if I just wait out here." He pointed at the metal bench beside the door. "Tell you what. I'll wait here. First chance you get, you tell her I'm waiting."

The woman closed the door. Nick did not know whether he had gotten through to her, but he sat down on the bench, checked his phone, and listened to a voice-mail message that had come in while he was out of range at Caleb's. Lew Krone wanted him to call. He dialed Rincon Plastics. Lew Krone was in a meeting. Nick left a message, then called Vince Love. The phone rang six times before Vince picked up, answering with an asthmatic cough.

"It's Nick. You okay?"

Vince cleared his throat. "I was sleeping. What time is it?"

"It's the middle of the afternoon."

"Oh. What's up?"

"Just thought I'd call, make sure you were okay."

"Why wouldn't I be?"

"Last time I saw you, you were getting drunk and had a gun stuck down your pants."

"Oh."

"You heard from Robo?"

"That's not till Friday."

"I still think you should leave town."

"I'll think about it. Look, I gotta find some aspirin or something."

"No problem." Nick hung up and watched a caravan of ants crawl across the flagstones. A few minutes later he got up and rang the bell again. The black-haired woman answered, this time holding a large pink sponge and a spray bottle. She regarded him silently.

"Did you tell her I'm here?" Nick asked.

The woman stared back.

"I'm not going away," Nick said.

The woman shrugged and closed the door. Nick sat on the metal bench and waited. A short time later, Nick's phone rang. "Hello?"

"You come all the way out here to see me?" It was Yola.

"I was already in Sierra Vista. I stopped by the restaurant, but they said you were taking the day off."

"Sometimes I do that."

"Everybody deserves a day off. Can I ask you a question?"

"Sure."

"Where are you?"

"I'm inside."

"Can I ask you another question?"

"Sure."

"How come we're talking on the phone?"

"You don't like to talk on the phone?"

"Not if I'm within shouting distance."

"I got my reasons."

"What are they?"

"Okay, you ask for it. I'm sitting in my pajamas, no makeup, I got curlers in my hair, and I haven't showered since yesterday. You know how it is?"

Nick didn't, and he didn't want to. "Okay, I understand now. But I have to talk to you about something important. Two things, actually."

"Pretend I am a hundred miles away. We can talk on the phone."

"Okay . . ." Nick was not sure which issue to broach first, so he let his mouth decide. "What do you expect to get for your twenty-five thousand?"

Yola took a moment to reply. "What do you think?" she said.

"It won't buy you a partnership."

"You do not want to be fifty-fifty partners with me, this I understand. You tell me what I get. I don't know. You are very difficult."

"According to the deal I'm offering my other investors, twenty-five thousand will get you five percent of the profits."

"That is not so much," Yola said. "Besides, you might pay yourself such a big salary there will be no profits."

"I wouldn't do that."

"I would rather have a percent of the gross."

"Not gonna happen. But don't forget, if you feature it on your show, you'll profit from the sales. You could make a couple bucks a unit. Maybe more." Nick liked talking to Yola on the phone. He was able to think more clearly.

"Yes, and I do all the work."

"You'll also get a commission for selling them to KUAT. Tell you what, I'll be honest with you."

"I expect no less."

"I can use the money, but I'm not giving away any of my company. If you don't want to profit-share, would you consider lending it to me? I'd pay you a reasonable interest rate."

He heard Yola sigh. "Okay, you win. Take my money. I lend it to you. Okay?"

This is way too easy, Nick thought. "One more question. Who owns Cochise Holdings?"

"Roberto has no part of it, if that is what frightens you."

"I'm not frightened, I just I want to know who I'm beholden to."

"Roberto has no part of it. We are divorced. Okay?"

"One more thing. My partner, Vince, has a little problem with your Roberto."

"Yes, I understand he owes Roberto money."

"Roberto is expecting to collect on Friday. The problem is, Vince doesn't have the cash."

"Then he should not have borrow it from Roberto."

"He knows that now, but it's not going to do any good for Roberto to do whatever it is he thinks he's going to do. Vince is going to need time."

"Roberto is not completely unreasonable."

"He's unreasonable enough."

"This is true."

"I'm afraid somebody's going to get hurt, and it might not be Vince. You think you could talk to Roberto? Ask him to lay off for a couple of months, stop charging interest, and give Vince a chance to get back on his feet. He listens to you, right?"

"He does not listen so good lately."

"Could you try? Don't you have breakfast with him every day?"

"I do not think we will be doing that anymore."

"Oh." Nick wondered whether that had anything to do with him.

"I got to get back to work now," she said.

"Won't you call him, at least?"

"No."

"Give me his phone number, then. I'll call him myself."

"I don't think that is a good idea."

"I'm not going to sit by and let him hurt my friend."

"Tell your friend to go away for a while."

"I tried that."

"He don't listen, huh? Just like Roberto."

"Vince thinks he can handle him."

"That is a mistake." The door opened. Nick looked up. The person standing there with the telephone pressed to her ear did not look at all like Yola—but it was. Yola wearing a mask. No. Yola with her lip swollen and cut, the flesh around her left eye mottled purple and maroon. "Many people think they can handle Roberto," she said into the phone. "Roberto does not like to be handle."

Fingers locked on the steering wheel, breathing shallowly through his nose, his eyes locked on the highway, seeing Yola's bruised face . . . I should go there, he thought. Find Robo's trailer and . . . and what? Robo carried a gun. Even without the gun, he could probably kick the shit out of a guy like Nick. The last time Nick had been in a fistfight, he'd been fourteen years old and had broken his hand. That was about all he knew about fighting: you don't punch a guy on the skull with your fist.

Anyway, it wasn't his fight. Or was it? Nick had spent the night under Yola's roof. He hadn't slept with her, but a guy like Robo wouldn't believe that. Nick was responsible for Yola's beating, just as he was responsible for Vince's bruises. It was all about him. If not for Nick, Vince never would have met Caleb, never would have taken on Caleb's debt to Robo, never would have bought himself that gun. Nick had to get that gun away from Vince before something really terrible happened.

He had to do a lot of things. Find out who burned down Love & Fashion. Find out if Caleb had been murdered.

Every thought led back to Roberto Fuentes.

Nick took a few deep breaths and forced himself to notice the the millions of poppies growing along the roadside, the dusky green of mesquite trees dotting the floor of the San Pedro Valley, the cloudless blue Arizona sky. There were things more important than Roberto Fuentes. The HandyMate. He had to pay Rincon Plastics. Use Yola's money? That line of thought took him back to Robo. Think about something else. Bootsie. He had to return Bootsie's money so he could fix things up with Gretchen.

Gretchen. There it was. That was what was *really* bothering him. A few weeks ago he had thought to spend the rest of his life with her; now he wasn't sure he would ever see her again.

His phone rang.

"Hello."

"Nick? This is Lew Krone. How are you doing?"

"Not so good."

"Well, you'll be doing better in a minute. Are you sitting down?"

"Yes."

"I think I've found a pretty good customer for your HandyMate."

"Oh?"

"One of our customers is a premium buyer for Pillsbury." Krone waited for Nick's response.

"Premium?" Nick said.

"You know those offers on the back of cereal boxes? Send in four box tops and ninety-nine cents and you get some sort of doohickey? Those are called premiums. Anything from a plastic action figure to a calorie counter's notebook. They give them away—or sell them— by the *millions*."

"Millions?" Nick realized he had drifted across the line; he took his foot off the accelerator and steered back into his lane.

"Millions. So this buyer was here to talk about producing a set of measuring spoons, a giveaway they're planning for the Pillsbury

Bake-Off, and he happened to notice your prototype sitting on my desk. I hope that's okay . . ."

"Keep talking," Nick said. He guided the van onto the shoulder and brought it to a complete stop.

"Bottom line is, he loves it. He wants to put a mail-in offer on every bag of flour and box of biscuit mix they sell. Do you know how much flour Pillsbury sells?"

"A lot?"

"Let me put it this way. If one out of every thousand bags of flour generates an order for your HandyMate, you will do very, very well. Let me put it another way. The buyer told me that their initial order would be for no fewer than eighty thousand units."

Nick cleared his throat. "Initial order?"

"Those were his words."

Thirty-one

Millions of HandyMates. A HandyMate in every kitchen. Wheelbarrows full of money. An office with a view of the Catalinas. A secretary named Alice. There were few problems that could withstand a barrage of money. He would be able to repay Bootsie, which would help fix matters with Gretchen. He could cover Vince's debt to Robo. He could replace his lost Motown records. Life would be perfect.

As he drove into Tucson, Nick's thoughts returned to short-term financing. He still had to come up with the cash to complete the mold-making, and his visit with Yola had done nothing to reassure him about the consequences of using her money. On the plus side, having an order in hand for eighty thousand units should make raising cash considerably easier. In fact, there was one obvious source that he hadn't previously considered.

After dropping off the coffins at UPS, Nick headed straight to Rincon Plastics. Lew Krone greeted him with a large smile.

"Caleb's grandkid, congratulations!" They shook hands for what seemed like a long time. "I knew you had a winner, Nick. I'm just glad I could be the one to bring in your first order. The first of many, I'm sure."

Nick agreed, then told Krone about the impending order from

KUAT TV. "I just wish Caleb could be here to see it," he said.

Krone nodded. "That would really be something. But the fact is, if your grandfather hadn't died, and if you hadn't come in to see me, I wouldn't have had that part sitting on my desk, and the buyer might never have seen it."

"True," said Nick, giving himself a mental pat on the back. "So—how is the tooling coming along?"

"On schedule, as far as I know. We'll need the rest of the money in a few days, of course."

"Of course. Actually, I wanted to talk to you about that. Ah, fact is, I don't have it."

Krone's smile faded.

"I have several investors on hold right now," Nick said quickly. "My problem is that they all want a piece of the action."

"You can hardly blame them," Krone observed.

"No, but I don't want to be parceling out chunks of my inheritance just because of a little cash-flow problem."

"I can understand that."

Encouraged, Nick plunged ahead. "So I was thinking that, considering that we've landed this big order, Rincon Plastics might provide me with some short-term credit. If we price it right, the order from Pillsbury should be enough to pay for the rest of the mold, with money left over."

Lew Krone was sitting back in his chair wearing a bemused smile. "We're not in the moneylending business, Nick."

"I'm not talking about borrowing money. Just time."

Krone regarded him blandly. "When you get to be my age, the distinction is somewhat abstract."

"You want the business, don't you?"

"Naturally."

"There must be a way we can work together to make it happen."

Krone nodded in agreement. "There is. Of course, we'd have to protect ourselves."

Nick experienced an all too familiar tightening of his scrotum. "What did you have in mind?" he asked.

Krone smiled and clasped his hands. "You know, I had this conversation with your grandfather once concerning a different item. You remember that part you asked me about last week? The belt extender?"

"The Inch-Adder?"

"Yes. I had some discussions with a major mail-order retailer. They were interested in featuring the item in their catalog. Caleb was having difficulty financing the tooling for the part, so we developed a program for him. We offered to absorb all expenses, handle the sales, the marketing, distribution—everything. All Caleb would have had to do was sit back and collect a rather generous royalty."

"In exchange for what?"

"Since we would be doing essentially everything, we would, of course, own all rights to the product."

"What happened?"

"Nothing."

"Caleb told you to take a hike."

"Essentially. And as a consequence, nothing came of the product. Caleb wouldn't let go, so he ended up with nothing." He held Nick's eyes and waited.

Nick said, "I am not giving up rights to the HandyMate."

Krone shrugged. "I wish you luck, Caleb's grandkid."

Thirty-two

The next two days passed uneventfully. Nick met with three bankers, described his situation, and let each explain to him why it would be impossible to lend him any money at this time. He left several messages for Gretchen, ignored as many from Bootsie, and finally had a conversation with Lieutenant William Hoff of the Tucson police.

Talking with Hoff on the phone was a lot like listening to his messages. The man sounded like he was drugged. He asked Nick a few pro forma questions—whether he had any reason to suspect arson, whether there had been any cleaning supplies or electrical devices in the basement, and so forth. With each question Hoff sounded increasingly uninterested in the answers. Nick imagined him as a man moments away from retirement, slumped over a desk, struggling to stay awake, reading the questions from a manual on arson investigation.

After Hoff ran out of questions, Nick asked, "How do you think the fire started?"

Hoff said, "This one was apparently started by an electrical short."

"Then you don't think it was set deliberately?"

"Possibly not," said Hoff.

"Pima is refusing to pay our claim. They're saying we burned down our own store."

"It's been known to happen."

"Yeah, well, I guarantee you I didn't burn up my own shoes and record collection," Nick said.

Hoff did not reply for several seconds. Nick wondered whether he had fallen asleep. "Hello?"

"Uh, yes. What did you say about shoes and records?"

"I lost all my stuff in the fire. My shoes, my books, my record albums. I lived above the store."

"What kind of records?"

"I had a collection of Motown vinyl."

"Oh." Hoff sounded disappointed. "I like jazz. I like Billie Holiday. I like Charlie Parker. I liked Miles Davis before he got all weird. He's dead now, too."

"So I've heard." Nick did not want to talk jazz. A jazz fan talking about his passion could be as unstoppable as a diarrhetic bowel movement. "Is there anything else?"

"Uh, no . . . actually, there is. Would it be possible for you to stop by the station? I'd like you to take a look at something, see if you recognize it."

"What is it?"

"I don't know, but it may have caused your fire. A tool of some sort. It looks like a miniature hedge trimmer. Did you keep anything like that in your basement?"

Nick tried to visualize the basement. They'd had several boxes of display props, which included everything from canoe paddles to an antique miner's pick to a 1949 typewriter. He didn't remember a hedge trimmer, but it was possible.

"You just want me to look at it?"

"Yes."

Maybe if this Lieutenant Hoff proved that the fire wasn't arson, they could force Pima to pay up. Nick promised to stop by the first chance he got.

Feeling somewhat buoyed, Nick called Lew Krone to ask about the purchase order from Pillsbury. Two of the bankers had indicated that with a purchase order in hand, they might be able to work out some short-term financing. Krone told him that the actual purchase order might not arrive for some time. "Large corporations move slowly," he said. "And when they do place their order, they'll want it yesterday. In any case, the PO will be written directly to Rincon Plastics. We would be acting as your sales organization. Pillsbury buys it from us, we buy it from you, you buy it from us. We have to protect ourselves."

"I need the PO to get the financing."

"You're in a difficult situation, Nick. I wish I could help you."

First thing Friday morning, Nick picked up his Corvette at the body shop. They had done a beautiful job. He paid them with the cash he'd received from Robo, congratulating himself on the three-hundred-dollar profit. For a while he simply drove around town, enjoying being back in his car. He was tooling through Saguaro National Park when it occurred to him that something else was supposed to happen on Friday. Vince and Robo. Robo was expecting to be paid, but instead of having money, Vince had a gun.

Nick pulled over and phoned Vince. Lots of ringing but no answer, not even a machine.

Vince's Explorer was parked in the carport, but he did not answer the door. The blinds were closed; Nick could not see inside. The door was locked. He unlatched the side gate and let himself into the tiny backyard. The patio door was also locked. Nick banged on the glass. No response. Maybe Vince really wasn't home. Maybe he was hurt, or worse. Nick grabbed the handle and jerked it up and down several times, hoping to dislodge the lock, but to no avail. He would either have to break the glass or find a key. If Vince had hidden a spare key, where would it be? He looked under the mat. Too obvious. He checked the shallow ledge above the door. He looked under the potted jojoba, and in several other likely hiding places. Returning to the front door, he continued his search but turned up nothing. Maybe he should call the cops before some inquisitive neighbor got the same idea. No, not yet. He went back to reexamine the patio door, then got the tire iron from his car. He wedged the tip of the iron under the patio door and stepped on it. The bottom of the glass door popped up over the rail and dropped out of its housing. Nick set the door aside and stepped into the sour smell of cat and stale coffee. He moved from room to room, fully expecting to find Vince's remains on the floor somewhere, but the condo contained neither the living nor the dead. Nick sagged with relief. He ran himself a glass of water from the tap and drank it. Vince could not have gone far without his truck. Nick decided to wait around for a while. He silently practiced explaining to Vince why he had ruined his back door.

Twenty minutes later, he began to wonder whether Vince would return at all. Where was the cat? In looking around the condo, Nick had noticed that there was no toothbrush or razor in the bathroom. He remembered that Vince owned a battered set of Mark Cross luggage. A quick search of the closets turned up no suitcases. He did, however, find the nine-millimeter Smith & Wesson that Vince had been showing off at the Shanty.

This was good news. Vince had left town. The fact that he had left his Explorer behind probably meant he had gone far enough away to fly rather than drive. And he had left his gun behind. Apparently, Nick had gotten through to him.

The doorbell rang. Nick went to the front window and peered

through a crack in the blinds. It was Robo: black sunglasses, black jeans, black boots, and a black guayabera. Death come calling. Nick ran back to Vince's bedroom, grabbed the Smith & Wesson, and returned to the entryway. He wasn't planning to open the door, but that might not stop Robo. He flicked off the safety and waited. A few seconds later, he heard Robo working on the lock. The doorknob turned, the door swung in, and Robo stepped inside. It took him a few seconds to see Nick, who was standing very still with the gun at his side.

Robo lifted his sunglasses. "I am not looking for you, buddy," he said.

"Nobody else home."

Robo cocked his head. "No?"

Nick shook his head.

Robo's black eyes went to the gun in Nick's hand. A wide grin spread across his face. It was the first time Nick had ever seen him express happiness.

"You gonna shoot me?" Robo inquired, as if delighted by the prospect.

"Is that what you want?"

"I doan know. What are my choices?"

Nick was not sure. He did not like the way Robo was standing, leaning forward slightly, weight on the balls of his feet. They were eight feet apart, close enough that if Nick let his guard down, Robo would be on him in an instant.

Nick raised his arm, pointing the gun at Robo's midsection. "I think you'd better leave." His voice sounded hollow and distant.

"Or what, you shoot me?" Robo asked, still with the grin.

"That's right."

Robo lowered his eyebrows and scrunched up his mouth; his narrow mustache became a crowded squiggle. He held his hands a few inches out from his sides. "What about if I take away your gun?"

"That's when I shoot you," Nick said.

"What if I shoot you first?" Slowly, Robo lifted the hem of his guayabera, showing Nick the small automatic clipped to his belt. Nick concentrated on keeping his hand steady. Robo made a sudden movement, crouching slightly and jerking his right hand toward the gun. Nick took a step back, his finger tightening on the trigger but not enough to fire the gun.

Robo straightened up and laughed. "See, now you can't shoot no more. You are froze up. I freeze you."

Was he right? Nick's hand and arm felt like lead. Was it physically possible for him to pull the trigger?

Robo said, "Now I draw my gun, just like cowboy. If you are still pointing yours at me, I shoot you. Otherwise, you put the gun down, I doan kill you."

Nick saw Robo's hand move toward his waist, reaching for his gun. He felt Vince's broken ribs. He saw Yola's blackened eye. If he dropped the gun, he would be next. Or he could get shot. Neither option appealed to him.

Nick's finger pulled the trigger; the Smith jumped in his hand; a sharp sound slapped his eardrums.

Robo said, "Fock," looking down at his left leg. Both men took a moment to assess the damage. The bullet had grazed the inside of Robo's thigh a few inches below his zipper, slicing open his jeans and removing a three-inch strip of flesh, blood blooming bright red and fading to maroon as it was absorbed by the black denim. "You, you are a focking maniac."

"That's right." Nick was shaking. "I'm a focking maniac."

Robo looked up. "Now you mock me. You are in big trouble now."

Nick applied all his willpower to holding the gun steady. If Robo made another move for his gun, Nick would have to shoot again, and he was not at all sure his second shot would be any more accurate than the first.

Robo glared at him, his hand pressed to his thigh, then turned and limped out the front door. Nick followed and watched him get into his pickup. Robo started the truck, put it in gear, and lurched backward. The oversize steel bumper obliterated the front end of Nick's Corvette. The sound of crumpling fiberglass went straight to Nick's belly, nearly doubling him over. Robo shifted and screeched off, spinning his tires, leaving two blue wisps of burnt rubber to dissipate in the still afternoon air. The front end of the Corvette was in ruins. Nick wanted to cry.

Thirty-three

After arranging to have his car towed back to the body shop, Nick wedged the patio door into place. It wasn't very secure, but it would have to do. He found a set of keys on the kitchen counter and drove off in Vince's Explorer. Under the circumstances, it was the least Vince could do for him. The Smith & Wesson rode along on the passenger seat, wrapped in a newspaper.

Nick drove through downtown past the boarded-up hulk that had once been his home, then turned south on Fourth Avenue and parked in front of his new headquarters. Once inside, he closed the blinds, turned up the air conditioner, unwrapped the gun, and set it on his desk. He sat staring at it for an indefinite period. A few weeks ago he had been selling fashion accessories, now he was shooting people. What next? Maybe he would be arrested for arson and sued by Bootsie Groth. Gretchen would never talk to him again, and the HandyMate would never reach the market. He would wind up in jail or—even worse—end his life living in a caboose selling pet coffins for beer money. Suddenly everything terrible and wrong seemed possible, even probable. Maybe he should follow his own advice to Vince and skip town. He picked up the gun. Now that he wasn't buzzing with adrenaline, its weight surprised him. Its hard surfaces felt alien and alive. Had he actually pointed this device at another human being and pulled the trigger? Apparently so. He aimed the gun at the rattling air conditioner, at a stain on the wall, at the front door. He had always assumed that people who owned guns did so to feel safe and powerful. At the moment, he felt neither. He put the gun in his desk drawer, closed it, picked up the phone, and dialed Gretchen's number. As usual, he got her answering machine.

"Hi, it's me. Still trying. You could call me back some—"

"Hello?" Her voice, achingly familiar. Nick's throat went rigid. "Hello?" she repeated.

"It's me," Nick said.

Silence.

He cleared his throat. "Can we talk?"

"Isn't that what we're doing?"

Words tumbled out. "Look, I know you're mad at me, and it's my fault. I made a mistake."

"Are you sure?"

"I— What do you mean?"

"Are you sure you made a mistake? Maybe it wasn't a mistake."

"I should have talked to you before I accepted the money from your dad."

"I would have asked you not to take it. In fact, I did."

"I was wrong."

"You made a choice, Nicky."

"It was a bad choice. I was out of my mind."

"I think you knew exactly what you were doing. You chose to pursue your HandyMate, and you were willing to step on me to do it."

"I didn't see it that way."

"Are you sure?"

"I want to see you."

He heard her sigh. She said, "Nicky, it's not just my dad's money."

Nick's viscera sagged.

She said, "It's everything."

"Could you narrow that down . . . just a little?"

He heard something that may have been a suppressed laugh. He could still make her laugh. That was good.

She said, "Look, how can we *live* together if we don't have time to *be* together?"

"That doesn't"—he almost said *make sense* but caught his tongue at the last possible instant—"mean we can't see each other at *all*."

"I just feel you need to work through your problems. Figure out what you want to do with your life." Putting it all on him.

"I have to see you."

"No."

Just like that. Kicked in the gut.

"Why not?"

"Because all you care about is Nicky, Nick. Because you think about nothing but your business. Because you're obsessed. Because you took my father's money and put it into some crackpot invention."

"It's not—"

Gretchen wasn't done. "And because you go to the nicest restaurant in town—the one you were supposed to take *me* to—with that Yola creature. And because when I'm *looking* at you, I can't *think* straight. I'm still in love with you, and everything is *wrong*. That's why I can't see you."

Nick's heart was pounding. All he could remember of what she'd said were the words *I'm still in love with you.*

"I love you, too."

"You're not listening. I can't even talk to you."

"What do I have to do?"

"Get my dad's money back to him, then we can talk." Her voice softened. "I'm sorry. It just can't be any other way."

"I understand," he said, but it wasn't true. He didn't understand her, and he didn't think he ever would.

But she still loved him.

.   .   .

For as long as he had possessed a driver's license, Nick had sought solace behind the wheel. It didn't matter where he was headed; while he was driving, he was doing something. He was moving. Anything might happen. Each hilltop, each bend in the road, held promise.

The road also helped focus his thoughts. But not always. Sometimes the miles flowed by leaving nothing in their wake, not even the memory of their passing. He drove through Tombstone, trying to remember where he had told himself he was going. He had to be going someplace.

The packrats were making inroads; there were three separate nests under construction in the workshop. After a century of neglect, the steel parasol would be completely filled with scraps of wood and grass and cactus—a packrat megalopolis. Nick wandered through the maze of tables and cabinets, imagining Caleb working, muttering to himself, his mind wandering in strange new directions. Did Nick have anything in common with his grandfather? A strong entrepreneurial streak, a bit of stubbornness, little else. He could not see himself living in such isolation. He was no inventor. He picked up a small metal box with two knobs, one on each side, and a lever on the top. He'd never noticed it before. Turning one knob caused the lever to move up and down, which made the opposite knob rotate. Nick found a screwdriver and removed a plate from the bottom of the box. Inside was a complicated arrangement of plastic gears. He worked the knobs and the levers, trying to figure out how it worked, but could make no sense of the gear system. The box had no apparent function. Perhaps it had never been intended to be useful. He set it aside, found a shovel, and set about cleaning out the rat nests. The rats would take over eventually, but not on his watch.

The physical labor helped Nick settle his thoughts. He could learn something from these rats, he reflected. Destroying their nests would set them back but wouldn't slow them down. They would immediately start rebuilding. It was what they did. No pack-rat ever brooded for days or weeks on end over the loss of its domicile. It simply began again.

An hour later, sweaty and parched, Nick let himself into the caboose. Nothing would taste quite so good after an hour of cleaning out rat nests as an ice-cold beer, and there was one waiting for him in Caleb's solar-powered refrigerator. He opened the refrigerator door, expecting to wrap his hand around the ice-cold neck of a Corona, but found nothing. He felt a prickling on the back of his neck. Last time he had visited, there had been one last bottle of Corona. He had saved it for a moment such as this, and now it was gone. He looked around the caboose. Everything seemed to be the same except for the missing beer. Was it possible he was mistaken? No. But who would drive all the way out to this desolate compound to steal one bottle of beer? Who would drive out for *any* reason? The only living people he knew who had *ever* been there were Chin, Yola, and Robo. And the old prospector, Herb Jenks. Nick went outside and examined the earth in front of the caboose. Sure enough, he could pick out a narrow tire track, probably made by Caleb's missing Harley-Davidson. He could see where the bike had been parked, and heel prints from a large shoe or boot.

He now thought he knew who had taken the beer, and what had happened to Caleb's Harley. Not Yola—her feet were too small. Not Robo, who would have done more than grab a beer. As for Chin— Nick just couldn't see him on a motorcycle. That left Herb Jenks. How, then, had Jenks come into possession of the bike? Caleb might have sold it to him. Or Jenks might have stopped by for a visit, found Caleb dead on the ground, and helped himself to the bike. Or he might have had an argument with Caleb and killed him. According to Chin, Jenks loved to fight when he got drunk. The fact that no one had seen him since Caleb's death was suggestive. But why had Jenks returned to the scene of the crime? For beer?

I should go to the cops with this, Nick thought. Then he imagined their reaction. The last thing the Cochise County sheriff wanted was to turn a simple heart attack into a murder mystery. Nick's theory would not receive an enthusiastic welcome, especially from Worthington, the coroner, for whom reopening the case would mean inconvenience at best or embarrassment at worst. No, the cops would do nothing.

Nick stood in the sun staring at the caboose. Did he really care about what had happened to Caleb, or was he upset about the missing beer? He'd been jerked around in so many directions lately he didn't know what was important anymore.

Chin's law office was closed. This was turning out to be a remarkably unproductive day. Nick walked down to the Copper Queen, where he had interrupted Chin's lunch a few days earlier. Chin was nowhere in evidence. Nick ordered a bowl of chili and a beer. He ate slowly, stirring matters in his mind with the deliberate violence of a farmer turning compost. He had to make a decision soon about who he was going to allow to steal the HandyMate from him—Lew Krone or Yola Fuentes. He was leaning toward Rincon Plastics. At least they were clear and direct about what they wanted. And they would come up with enough immediate cash for him to pay off Bootsie; in fact, buying out Bootsie was one of their requirements. And that might open Gretchen's door. He felt a twinge. How had he ever let things go wrong with her? Was it just the thing with Bootsie, or were there other issues? He called up the memory of her face. The image was losing focus. What would it be like to see her again? To touch her?

Nick finished his meal and returned to Chin's office. The door was open. He walked in to find Chin working intently on his laptop computer.

"Hey, Nick, you play golf?"

"Never took it up."

Chin turned his laptop so that Nick could see the screen. A man in plus fours was preparing to tee off.

"I've been invited to join the country club," Chin said. "I'll be their first member of Asian descent. A great honor. Only problem is, I don't golf."

"You're trying to learn it on your computer?"

"Just the basics, man." He depressed a key; the man on the screen swung; the ball bounced into the rough. "See? I'm learning what not to do."

"And saving on greens fees."

"You got it." Chin turned the laptop back to its original position and sat back in his chair. "You sure come here a lot. ¿*Qué pasa?*"

"I've just been out to Caleb's. You haven't by any chance seen that prospector friend of his, have you?"

"You mean Herb Jenks? Nah. He doesn't show up in Bisbee that often." Chin set up his next shot. "Why?"

"Somebody was there. There were some things missing, and I saw motorcycle tracks."

Chin looked up from his game. "What was missing?"

"A bottle of beer."

"That's it?"

"I'm not sure. He might have taken something else, but I don't know what."

"You're thinking it was Jenks?"

"We still don't know what happened to Caleb's Harley. Is it possible he sold it to Jenks?"

Chin shrugged. "Most likely it was just some outlaw biker tooling around the back roads. We get a lot of them around here. He stumbles on Caleb's place, pokes around a bit, and can't find anything worth stealing except the beer."

Nick nodded. It sounded reasonable.

Chin said, "By the way, I got some good news for you."

"I could use some of that."

"I found out who owns Cochise."

Nick frowned, wondering how this could be good news. "Let me guess. Roberto Fuentes."

"No, man. One of Yola's other boyfriends." Chin's grin was wide and tight with suppressed information.

Nick said, "How long are you going to leave me hanging?"

Chin's grin remained undiminished. "Nicholas Fashon," he said.

His own name, first and last, did not register immediately. Then he got it. "Explain," he said.

Chin sat forward. "Cochise Holdings is a bank account, forty-nine thousand nine hundred ninety-six dollars and eighty-four cents total, with Yola and your grandfather as signatories." He sat back and waited for Nick to ask the next question.

"Yola and Caleb?"

Chin nodded.

"How come you didn't know about this? You're Caleb's executor."

"Like I told you before, Caleb didn't write everything down. Only reason I found out about it at all is I got a friend over at the bank."

"So you're telling me that Yola gave me a check written on a bank account that I own half of?"

"You got it, man."

So, Caleb had some money after all. Nick remembered Yola talking about some sort of thermostat he'd invented, claiming that she and Caleb had been partners. Apparently, it was true. Fifty grand. And his half would be enough pay for the rest of the mold. "How do I get my hands on it?"

"You've already got it. She gave you a check, right?"

"Yeah, but she didn't tell me it was my own money."

"She probably forgot to mention it."

"So I'm square with her, right? I don't owe her anything?"

"I think you owe her about a buck and a half."

Thirty-four

Nick was nearly back to Tucson when it occurred to him that instead of using the twenty-five grand to pay for the mold, he might use it to repay Bootsie. This concept did not sit easily. If he repaid Bootsie, he would have to give up control of the HandyMate to Rincon Plastics. On the other hand, if he used the money to pay for the mold, there was a good chance that he'd be able to repay Bootsie within a few weeks out of the profits from the sales to KUAT and Pillsbury. He might even be able to pay Bootsie a premium. Would that earn him points from Gretchen? Probably not. What was important to her—insofar as he understood her agenda—was that he repay Bootsie at the earliest possible opportunity. She wanted him to undo what he had done, and the more painful the process, the better. Nick felt himself growing angry. How could she be so stupid? The HandyMate would be a huge success. Bootsie would make a ton of money. Nick would be a hero. Why was she making it so hard for him?

What he should do, he decided, was talk to Bootsie again. Maybe the old man wasn't so brain-dead that he couldn't see the mistake he'd make by pulling out. If Nick could get Bootsie on his side, the old man might be able to convince his daughter that Nick wasn't such an opportunistic, lying sack of shit after all. It was worth a try.

· · ·

You bring my money?" Bootsie was red-faced, naked from the waist up, and breathing heavily. His upper body was shiny with perspiration; his legs were clad in a pair of heather-gray sweatpants that had been manufactured with a much smaller individual in mind.

"Working out?" Nick asked.

"As a matter of fact, yes. You oughta try it sometime. Put some muscle on." Bootsie glared, daring Nick to dispute his point.

Nick somehow managed not to laugh. He lowered his eyes to Bootsie's jutting, perfectly round button of a navel. He wanted to ask whether it had always been an outie, or if its protuberant quality was a consequence of obesity.

Bootsie said, "I'm guessing you don't have my money. What do you want, Slick?"

"I have some good news," Nick said. "Mind if I come in?"

Bootsie grunted, not buying it, but he backed away from the door and let Nick inside. "Gotta finish my routine," he said. Nick followed him through the house into the backyard, where Bootsie had set up a weight bench.

"Long as you're here, you might as well spot me," Bootsie said. He sat on the end of the bench and laid back. The sides of his abdomen draped over the edge of the bench. He reached up and wrapped his big hands around the barbell, which held two small twenty-five-pound disks. "Well?" he demanded, glaring at Nick, who, suddenly comprehending what was expected of him, took his place behind the head of the bench and rested his hands lightly on the barbell.

Bootsie took several deep breaths, lifted the barbell from its rack, lowered it slowly to his chest, and pushed it back up again. Nick kept his hands under the bar, prepared to help if the weight became too much for the old man. Bootsie performed four more lifts, each one moving his face from pink toward the infrared. On the sixth rep, his arms began to shake and he froze halfway up. Nick grabbed the bar and lifted it onto the rack. Gasping, Bootsie sat up.

"God . . . damn . . . it," he gasped. "I . . . had . . . it!"

"Sorry," Nick said.

"I . . . used . . . to lift—" He shook his head and took several breaths. "Your age . . . I could bench three-fifteen."

"That's a lot," Nick said.

"How much you bench-press, Slick?"

"I don't know." Nick had never lifted a weight in his life. "Do you work out every day?"

Bootsie shook his head. "First time in ten years." He emitted a wheezy giggle. "I damn near . . . killed myself . . . draggin' this thing outta the garage." He rested his elbows on his knees and focused on breathing.

Nick asked, "What made you do that?"

Bootsie stared at the ground. "I just figgered it was time to get in shape."

"Aren't you kind of, ah, mature for that?"

"You think maybe I should wait a couple years? Jesus, where'd you leave your brain?"

Nick laughed uncomfortably.

Bootsie said, "You want to know how come I'm exercising? I'll tell you, Slick. I might have to go back to work. Bag groceries or something. You want to know how come? On account of I invested my nest egg with some gigolo con artist and I don't expect I'll ever see a dime of it. That's how come. Unless you got a check for me. You got a check for me?"

"If you want a check, I'll write you one right now," said Nick. "But you'd be a fool to take it."

Bootsie looked up, surprised.

"This thing's about to take off," Nick said. "I've got orders for nearly a hundred thousand units. Pillsbury is going to feature the HandyMate on every bag of flour it sells. And I'm going to sell them to every public TV station in the country as a fund-raising premium. It's going to be huge."

"You give up on Gretie?" Bootsie asked.

Nick swallowed, trying to fill the sudden vacuum in his belly. "No," he said. "This is how I'm going to get her back."

"You think you're gonna get her back by making a bunch of money?"

"I'm going to get her back by being who I want to be. Look, you were married a long time, right?"

"Forty-four years to the same woman, God bless 'er," Bootsie said.

"She like you being a cop?"

Bootsie shook his head.

"This is just a guess, but did she ever want you to quit and get another job?"

"We talked about it."

"But you didn't, right?"

"What else was I gonna do? I was a cop."

"And what if you had quit the force and took another job? What would your wife have thought of you? Would she have loved 'Bootsie Groth, security guard,' or 'Bootsie Groth, insurance salesman'?"

Bootsie stared at Nick for several seconds, his eyebrows lowered. Nick feared he had crossed the line, but Bootsie suddenly looked away.

"Maybe you're not so goddamn stupid after all," he said.

"I just have to see this thing through," Nick said. "If I have to take a chance that Gretchen won't ride it out with me, then that's what I've got to do. Now, my question to you is, do you want your money back now, or do you want to double it in six months?"

"You know what I want?" Bootsie said. "I want you to help me haul all this junk back in the garage. Think you can handle that, Slick?"

"I can handle it," Nick said.

Lew Krone looked down at the check. "Congratulations, Caleb's grandkid. You put it together."

"You inspired me."

"I did? Didn't mean to." Krone picked up the check. "We should have that mold ready in a few days. You'll have samples by Thursday."

"How is that order from Pillsbury coming along?"

"Just talked to the buyer. They want to know if we can emboss their name into the part."

"You mean make a custom mold for them? What did you tell them?"

"Told them they'd have to order a minimum of three hundred thousand units."

"And?"

Lew Krone sat back in his chair and showed Nick a huge yellow grin.

Knowing he wouldn't be able to sleep until he confronted Yola, Nick got back in the Explorer and headed to Sierra Vista. The drive passed like a dream; he walked into El Otro Lado feeling as if he had stepped onto a stage set, dead tired but strangely energized. The waitresses and customers seemed small and barely animate. The ceiling felt low, and the walls appeared closer than he knew them to be.

Walking past the hostess, he crossed the dining area and pushed through the double doors into the kitchen. He stopped, taking in the confusion of aluminum pans, white countertops, and fast-moving, aproned people. After a few seconds he spotted Yola working over one of two oversize cooktops. She was wearing a white apron, like everyone else in the kitchen, and her long hair was tied back in a loose roll. As if sensing his presence, she turned her head. Her eyes widened, and she smiled at him as if he were the answer to a lifetime of dreams and prayers.

"Nick!" She handed her spoon to the nearest warm body, rattled off a set of instructions, and gave Nick an enthusiastic hug.

"You're looking a little better," he said. Heavy makeup concealed the bruising around her eye, and the swelling in her lip had gone down.

"Yes." She touched her lip.

"Have you heard from him?"

"I talk to him on the phone. Roberto is very upset with you. You should not have shot him."

"I didn't have a lot of choice."

"Roberto can be difficult. He does not know how to act sometime."

"How is he doing?"

"He is very angry. I worry about you, Nick."

"You should worry about Roberto." Nick heard bravado in his voice and wondered where it was coming from. What if he ran into Robo in the parking lot? He wished he had brought Vince's gun.

"I worry about all men." She smiled, Mona Lisa with a split lip.

Nick said, "I cashed your check."

"Good. That is why I give it to you."

"Sure it is." He took out his checkbook and scribbled out a check for $1.58. Yola watched, her face growing puzzled. Nick tore out the check out and set it on the table.

"You are giving me money?"

"I'm giving you change."

"I do not understand."

"I'm taking Caleb's half of Cochise Holdings. There was forty-nine thousand nine hundred ninety-six dollars and eighty-four cents in the account." He pointed at the check. "That's your change."

Yola shook her head sorrowfully. "I do not understand," she said again.

"I think you do." Nick stood up.

"I'm sorry if I give you too much money," Yola said.

Nick turned and started to walk away.

"If I deceive you," Yola said to his back, "it is only to make you like me better."

Nick passed through the kitchen and the dining room and out the front door into the parking lot, keeping his eyes open for a black Ram pickup. He climbed into Vince Love's Explorer with the shattered mirrors and twisted windshield wipers, pulled out onto the road, and headed back toward Tucson, feeling thoroughly scrambled and unsatisfied. He tried to analyze Yola and her motivations but made little progress. He was tired. After a time he slipped into a trancelike state, random thoughts coming and going quickly, each mental image sustained for an instant by the hum of the tires, obliterated by each beat of his heart.

Thirty-five

Three days later Nick's phone began to ring. One of the first calls was from Gordo Encinas.

"Nick! Gordo here. Listen, I've been thinking about that thinga-majig you showed me. The HandyMate? I might be able to come up with a few bucks after all—if you're still looking for investors."

"What changed your mind?"

"I've just been thinking about it is all. You're a sharp guy. I just think investing in one of your projects might be the smart thing to do."

"Did you hear something?"

"No! Well, I did happen to catch that woman on TV. The Mexi-can cook?"

"Yola Fuentes."

"Yes! You know, it's very different watching her use it. Making real food. I mean, what did you show me? How to chop up an apple? What do I want with chopped apple? Anyway, I have some money."

Nick thought about it for a few seconds. He could use the cash, but it was far less urgent now that he had paid for the mold. Also, he was irritated that Gordo had passed on the opportunity earlier, when his need for cash had been immediate.

"Thanks for the offer, Gordo, but I'm not selling any more

shares." He couldn't help adding, "We picked up a million-dollar order from Pillsbury last week. You missed the boat, Gord. Sorry."

Nick also took calls from several premium and ad-specialty reps—sales organizations that specialized in selling promotional items. Word had gotten out about the order from Pillsbury. Nick put them all off, saying that they were still developing the HandyMate marketing team and would be in touch soon. Two plastics companies called, both promising to produce the HandyMate cheaper than Rincon. One even offered to replicate the mold at no cost in exchange for a percentage of the HandyMate business. Nick promised to keep them in mind. At the very least, he could use them as leverage on Lew Krone.

By the end of the week Nick felt confident enough to install a real phone line, lease a computer, and call Pertsy and Caroline. Caroline answered the phone and promised to start work the next morning. Nick explained that her first paycheck might be a few weeks in coming. Caroline had no problem with that, which made Nick feel very good about himself. The only soft spot in the week was Gretchen—or rather her absence.

He had left her a few phone messages but never heard back. She wouldn't talk to him again until he cut Bootsie a big fat check. How long would that be? Realistically, two months, maybe more. Even if the Pillsbury PO arrived tomorrow, they would still have to produce and ship the order. If Pillsbury wanted a custom mold, that alone could take six weeks. Then another four to six weeks to get paid . . . he was looking at *three* months. Maybe he had blown off Gordo Encinas too soon. His cash-flow problems were only beginning. He didn't doubt that the business could survive—worst-case scenario, he would have to cut a new deal with Rincon—but he wasn't sure he could go that long without Gretchen. For a few seconds, Nick's thoughts tumbled like fruits in a slot machine, then a strategy clicked into place. He called Hardy Chin and got the answering machine.

"You have reached the law offices of Hardesty Chin, Jr. We are sorry, but we are not available at this time. Please leave a message after the tone."

Nick said, "Hardy, this is Nick. I have to talk to you. I—"

Chin picked up. "Nick? How you doing?"

"I'm fine. Listen, I need money fast."

"Nick, I—"

"Here's what I want you to do. I'm selling Caleb's land. I don't care how much we have to discount it, I don't care that it's in probate, I don't care how much more I could get for it if I wait. There has to be some way to turn it into cash. Now."

"Look, Nick—"

"You're a lawyer, right? You figure it out. I don't care if I don't get half what it's worth. I've got a tiger by the tail here with this Handy-Mate, and I'm not letting go. You hear what I'm saying?"

"I hear you," Chin said.

"Good."

"But we have to talk. Can you come up here?"

"When? Not today, I hope. Can't you get things rolling without me?"

Nick heard muffled voices, as if through a hand held over the phone, then Chin's voice loud in his ear.

"Things have changed here, Nick. Look, can you get down here this afternoon? Say, four o'clock?"

"You know how many times I've schlepped back and forth the past few weeks? I know that road way too well. Can't it wait?"

"Nick, I wouldn't ask you to make the drive if it wasn't . . . let's just say you won't be disappointed, okay?" Chin laughed, sounding a note of hysteria in the final high-pitched gasp.

"What's going on, Chin?"

"Just be here at four, man. Okay?"

"Okay, okay. But let's get back to Caleb's land for a moment. I want you to sell it, as quickly as possible."

"We'll talk about that this afternoon, Nick. And don't worry about the money. Just be here." Chin hung up. Nick stared at the phone, all momentum lost. What could Chin want to show him? He smelled Yola's deceitful hand in there somewhere. He checked the time. Still morning. He had things to do—but what? The telephone rang; Nick answered.

"Mr. Fashon?" Voice like a sluggish recording. "This is Lieutenant Hoff with the Tucson police . . ."

"Oh. I was supposed to come see you, wasn't I?"

"I'd like to wrap this up," Hoff said.

"Sorry. There's been a lot going on here."

"I'll be here all afternoon. Why don't you drop by?"

Nick thought, What the hell. Get it over with. What else was he going to do, other than brood about his irritatingly mysterious appointment in Bisbee?

"You're downtown, right?"

"That's right," said Hoff. "On Stone. Ask at the front desk, they'll send you up."

"I'll be there in half an hour."

Lieutenant Hoff smelled faintly of smoke, as if he had just come from the scene of a fire. He was younger than Nick had expected—around fifty-five. He had thinning gray-blond hair, a hollow, bloodless face, and pale eyes that managed to convey equal amounts of despair and nihilism. Probably a drinker. Probably divorced. Probably suicidal. Nick liked him immediately.

Hoff's metal desk was one of four crowded into a ten-by-fifteen office space—the Tucson Arson Investigations Unit. The other three desks were unoccupied; Hoff and Nick were alone.

"How are our friends at Pima Life treating you?" Hoff asked.

"Not well," said Nick. "Like I told you, they think we set fire to our own store."

"Assuming that you didn't, that's unfortunate."

"Well, I didn't. And I don't know who did."

"What makes you think someone did?"

"I . . . well, Clint Pfleuger told me it was arson, and you're investigating it . . . I don't know. It seems kind of unlikely."

"I've investigated a lot of fires," Hoff said. "Look at my desk." The desktop held several dozen large straw-colored envelopes, the heavy-duty type, flaps tied down with red strings, the backs heavily notated with dates and scrawled observations. "These are my current cases. Guys torching their own restaurants, warehouses, you name it. Here's a guy set fire to his pickup truck. Spread to the neighbor's garage. Him we're gonna nail. But a lot of them walk."

Hoff selected one of the envelopes, opened it, and extracted a pink three-by-five index card. He tapped the edge of the card on his desk, set it down, folded his hands over it. His fingernails were long and rimmed with black. The backs of his hands had several patches of unnaturally smooth, hairless skin, as if he had been badly burned once. Nick imagined him at the scene of a fire, sorting through the smoking debris barehanded.

"Your fire," Hoff said, "is not typical."

"You said you wanted to show me something."

"Yes." Hoff stood up. Nick started to follow, but the detective waved him back into the chair. "Wait here." He plodded out of the office and down the hallway as if carrying a great weight. Nick felt sorry for the guy. He wondered what Hoff's story was, and hoped he would never know.

A few minutes later Hoff returned carrying a large plastic Ziploc bag containing a twisted, blackened object about twelve inches in length. He set it on his desk before Nick, then took his seat and waited, saying nothing.

"What is it?" Nick asked after a moment.

"I was hoping you could tell me."

Nick looked closer, poking at the object through the plastic bag.

"I don't know," he said. "It just looks like a burned-up . . . *thing*."

Hoff leaned forward and, using a pen, pointed out several features of the object. "This end had an electrical cord attached. We found traces of it, melted of course. And this section here contained some electronics inside a hard plastic casing." Engaged in the details, he became more animated. "It's about the right size and shape for a human hand, indicating that it may have been some sort of handheld tool. And the other end—it's hard to see—it looks a little like a toothed blade. That's why I was thinking a mini hedge trimmer. But it's so small. One of our guys suggested it might be a hedge trimmer for bonsais." Hoff coughed out a wheezy laugh. "Whatever it was, it started your fire."

The object suddenly became eerily familiar.

Hoff said, "It almost looks like a metal comb . . ."

Nick whispered, "Holy shit, Batman."

"Excuse me?" Hoff became alert, leaning forward, his eyes hard on Nick, who was examining the object intently.

Nick said, "That's a Comb-n-Clean."

"A what?"

"Comb-n-Clean. My grandfather Caleb was an inventor. You don't have to wash your hair, just use his electric Comb-n-Clean. But there was a problem. It could set your hair on fire." Nick stared at the blackened husk of the electric comb. "Vince had a few boxes of junk down there, some of Caleb's prototypes . . . he must've left it plugged in."

Hoff nodded and made a notation. "Did you keep any flammable liquids in the basement?"

"No. I already told you that."

"Are you sure? You were in the clothing business, right? Did you keep any benzine around? Dry-cleaning fluid? Spot remover?"

"Spot remover." Nick nodded. "We did have a can of spot remover. We were trying to get mildew stains off some leather purses. It didn't work. That was a few months ago."

Hoff smiled and sat back. He had what he wanted. "Did you store it in the basement?"

"Maybe. I don't know."

"There you go. You've got your accelerant—the spot remover. And you've got your ignition source." Hoff pointed at the scorched electric comb. "Ka-boom."

"So you're saying one of us is the arsonist?"

"Did you burn your building down?"

"No!"

Hoff shrugged. "That's what I thought. Your partner told me the same thing. Not arsonists. Just careless. That's different. Leaving a faulty appliance plugged in doesn't get you put in jail. It could happen to anybody." He seemed to be melting into his chair.

"What do you do now?"

Hoff sank deeper. "Write a report, go home, put on a CD."

"And you're saying that the fire was accidental?"

"That's what I'm putting in my report. You really like that Motown crap, huh?"

"Yeah, I do."

"You should give Charlie Parker a listen."

"I like Charlie Parker, too. You think I can get my insurance company to pay the claim?"

Hoff opened and closed his mouth twice, trying to speak but too weary to put it together. He pushed himself upright in his chair, took a deep breath, and said, "I'll send them a copy of my report." He smiled weakly, sinking again. "Thanks for stopping by."

"That's it?"

Hoff's head moved up and down. "Case closed."

That was too easy, Nick thought. He hoped that Hoff was not typical of the local police. If so, there would be very little crime solving. Someone had plugged in that comb. Someone had gone into the basement, plugged in the comb, and placed the can of spot remover beside it. When the comb warmed up and started to spark . . . What was it Hoff had said? *Ka-boom.*

Vince Love.

Nick turned south on Fourth Avenue. He didn't remember getting into the Explorer. Driving on automatic pilot. Cars and houses and trees and things marched anonymously past.

Vince had burned down the store. No one else could have known that the Comb-n-Clean was a fire hazard. No one else even knew it was there. Vince had gone into the basement and deliberately started the fire. He had destroyed Love & Fashion, the building, and all of Nick's possessions. And lied about it. Nick felt as if his stomach had turned brittle and collapsed. You think you know a guy and then . . . Clint Pfleuger had been right all along. It was insurance fraud.

Nick pulled over to the curb and parked across the street from the *taqueria.* Insurance fraud. Could he collect the money now that he knew it was Vince who had torched the store? He needed the cash. He imagined himself accepting the check, cashing it, using it. How ethical and moral a person was he? It was easy to be honest over, say, a few hundred dollars. He could never find a wallet and fail to return it to its owner. But this was a lot of money, money he needed. And despite the fact that Vince had started the fire, Nick himself was an innocent. He was as much a victim as if it had been a bona fide, unorchestrated electrical fire. Or a lightning strike. Why shouldn't he collect his half of the insurance?

Nick unlocked the door, entered his office, closed and locked the door, turned on the air conditioner, and plunked himself down behind his desk.

Of course, he wouldn't be the only one getting paid. Vince would get half. The thought of him accepting a check made Nick shudder. And the thought of Vince paying off Roberto Fuentes made him feel even worse. He didn't think he could stand it.

Perhaps, he thought, this would be the toll exacted by the gods, or fate, or whatever, for taking the money. Even though the ethics of his situation fell squarely into the charcoal gray—there would be a price. There was always a price.

The front doorknob rattled, then someone knocked, three door-rattling bangs.

"Just a second." Nick's hand went to his top left desk drawer, where he had left Vince's gun. Just in case he got a visit from Robo. He lifted the revolver from the drawer and slipped it into his pocket. It felt huge; it would stretch the lining. He went to the window and peeked past the blinds. Bootsie, dressed to the nines in a sagging, robin's-egg-blue polyester suit, a straw driving cap, and a bright yellow shirt that looked as if it might have been ironed once, stood waiting outside.

Part of Nick—the part worried about Robo—relaxed, while another part of him tensed. He could imagine no good reason for Bootsie to visit. Another change of heart? He practiced his smile, getting his cheeks good and loose, then took a fortifying breath and opened the door.

"Bootsie!" he said. "What are—" He went rigid. Bootsie was not alone. Nick cleared his throat. "Hey," he said. Standing to Bootsie's right, looking small by comparison, stood Gretchen, a puzzled frown on her beautiful face.

Thirty-six

Hey yourself, Slick." Bootsie clapped Nick on the shoulder and pushed past him into the office. Nick's eyes stayed with Gretchen.

She said, "This wasn't my idea."

"What wasn't?"

"Coming here." She crossed her arms.

"Oh. You want to come in?"

"He told me we were going to the dentist." Gretchen uncrossed her arms and walked past Nick, not touching him, into the building. "He wanted company."

Bootsie said, "You got anything to drink, Slick? A Coke or something?"

"Water okay?" Still looking at Gretchen.

"If that's all you got," said Bootsie.

"Water for you?" Nick asked Gretchen.

She shook her head. Nick went to the back room and grabbed a bottle of Arrowhead from the cooler.

Bootsie said, "Thought we'd stop by, see how you're doing." He opened the bottle and sucked down half of it. "Gretie's never been here."

Neither Nick nor Gretchen said anything.

"HandyMate World Headquarters," Bootsie said. "Home of the million-dollar order. Could be the next Microsauce."

"Micro*soft*," Gretchen said.

"Whatever." Bootsie winked at Nick. "No respect. She treats her old man like an eight-year-old."

"More like a *six*-year-old," Gretchen said.

Another wink. "See what I mean?"

Nick swallowed. What did Bootsie hope to accomplish here? It seemed as incomprehensible as international politics or the speech of ravens. Just hang on and get through it, he told himself.

Bootsie said, "Anyways, all these big orders you got comin' down the pipe, I think you got a winner here, Slick."

Gretchen turned to Nick. "When did he start calling you *Slick*?"

"I don't remember."

"If you're doing so well, why haven't you given him back his money?"

Nick gestured at their surroundings. "I'm working out of a South Tucson *taqueria*. What makes you think I'm doing well?"

Gretchen shot a finger at her father. "*He* says you're the next Microsauce."

"I've got some orders, sure. But I still have cash-flow troubles. I did have some money for a moment. I tried to give it back to him. He wouldn't take it."

Bootsie had planted himself behind Nick's desk. He was grinning.

"Is that true?" she asked him.

"Absolutely."

Gretchen rolled her eyes. "Daddy . . ."

"I'm gonna die a millionaire," Bootsie said. "You should be happy."

She looked at Nick. "He told me he wanted me to go with him to the dentist. That's how come he's wearing his school clothes."

"You get dressed up to see the dentist?" Nick asked.

"He gets dressed up for anyone with more than four years of college. Except me."

"It's about respect for the profession," Bootsie growled. "Doctors, dentists, and judges I wear a jacket. Lawyers, I don't give a crap."

Nick and Gretchen locked eyes for a moment. Nick thought he caught the ghost of a smile.

Gretchen asked, "Daddy, do you have a dentist appointment or not?"

"Yeah, I got a dentist appointment."

"When?"

"I think it's tomorrow. I must've got the day wrong."

"I skipped a faculty meeting for this, Daddy."

"You hate those meetings anyway. You should thank me." He pushed himself up out of the chair. "Gotta use the little-boys' room. 'Scuse me." He lumbered toward the restroom.

Gretchen had her arms crossed again.

Nick said, "I'm going to make this work, Gretchen."

"Make what work?"

For a moment, Nick wasn't sure. Then a spurt of stubbornness caused him to say, "The HandyMate. The business."

Her face changed as if suddenly subjected to tremendous atmospheric pressure.

Nick said, "I have to make it work, Gret. I have to have *something*. And as far as your dad's money is concerned, if I give it back to him now, it would be almost like stealing. He's about to make a lot of money. I've got an order coming for three hundred thousand units. And that's just the beginning."

Gretchen nodded sadly. He got the impression she was giving up on him.

"I'm happy for you, Nicky," she said.

"It's the second most exciting thing that's ever happened to me."

"What was the first?"

"Meeting you. Pawing through my Peruvian purses."

"That were made in China."

"I sold a lot of those."

"You should be ashamed of yourself." She was smiling.

"I miss you," Nick said. "Constantly."

"I miss you, too. Too bad you're such an asshole."

Nick heard the toilet flush, then Bootsie's ponderous footsteps. Bootsie said something. Trapped in Gretchen's eyes, Nick didn't hear him.

Bootsie raised his voice. "I said, what's that you got in your pocket, Slick?"

"What?"

"Your pocket." Bootsie pointed.

"Oh!" Nick reached back and felt the gun sagging his hip pocket. He took it out and laughed self-consciously.

"Watch where you point it," said Bootsie.

Gretchen took a step back.

Nick handed it to Bootsie. "It's a nine," he said.

"A *nine?* You been watching too much TV, Slick. Christ a'mighty, it's actually loaded. What're you doing with this thing?"

"It's Vince's."

"That don't answer my question."

"I've had a problem with that guy I was telling you about. Roberto Fuentes."

"He still giving you troubles?"

"Well, last time I saw him, he threatened to shoot me."

Gretchen said, "Nicky!"

Bootsie looked from Nick to the gun, then back again. "You even know how to use it?"

Nick compressed his lips. "Well . . . I *did*," he said.

"What the hell's that mean?"

"I didn't have any choice. Like I said, he was threatening to shoot me. Anyway, he's not dead or anything. Last I heard, he was still walking around. That's why I've been keeping the gun."

"Jesus Christ, Slick. You *shot* somebody?"

"I sort of winged him."

"You got a death wish?"

"If I hadn't had the gun, I might be dead right now."

"Jesus, Slick." Bootsie removed the clip from the gun and ejected the cartridge in the chamber. "Guys like you get killed all the time." He put the clip in his pocket and set the gun on the desk.

"Nick . . ." Gretchen was standing with her hand covering her chin and mouth, her eyes wide. "What are you involved in? You actually *shot* a man?"

"It was sort of an accident." At least he had her attention.

"Nick, I can't— I don't understand what you're doing." She dropped her hand from her mouth and turned on Bootsie, suddenly angry. "Why did you bring me here?"

Bootsie shrugged. "It was on the way to the dentist."

"Your appointment isn't till tomorrow."

"Oh yeah."

"I have to go." She was out the door, not quite slamming it, but closing it with more force than was necessary.

Bootsie and Nick looked at each other.

"What were you thinking?" asked Nick.

Bootsie shrugged. "I just thought you two kids ought to see each other."

"Great. That's great. So you trick her into coming here, then symbolically emasculate me—as much as tell her I'm an incompetent, dangerous fool."

Bootsie stared at Nick with his mouth open. "What—the gun thing?"

"How do you think she likes me now?"

"I don't— Ah, crap. I just don't get you kids. What the hell, she don't listen to me anyways. So what are you gonna do, Slick?"

"Do?"

"Aren't you going after her?"

"She obviously wants nothing to do with me."

"Not true. I bet she's standing out there waiting for you."

"So you're the expert on women now?"

"What do you got to lose?"

He's right, Nick thought. But goddamn it, why should he have to go chasing her? Ah hell. What choice did he have? He opened the door. Gretchen was standing on the other side, facing him, wearing a peculiar expression.

Nick said, "I—" Gretchen slammed into him, knocking him back into the office. Nick lost his balance and went down with Gretchen on top of him. For the briefest instant he thought she was attacking him, but she rolled away to reveal another figure standing in the doorway.

Robo.

Nick scrambled to his feet.

"Hey. Buddy," Robo said. "I hear you are a big businessman now." He closed the door and looked around the office. "Kind of a dump." He was dressed in the same gray denim jacket and felt hat he had worn at Yola's. His eyes were concealed by a pair of dark wraparound sunglasses.

Gretchen was still on the floor, sitting up, a confused and frightened expression on her face. Bootsie sat unmoving behind Nick's desk, Vince's unloaded handgun a few inches from his hand. Robo spotted the gun; his right hand disappeared into his jacket and reappeared with a small automatic pointed at Bootsie's forehead. Bootsie moved his hand away from the unloaded gun, his eyes locked onto Robo's, his face devoid of expression.

Nick eased himself between Robo and Gretchen. "What can I do for you, Roberto?" His voice sounded remarkably level, even to him.

"What do you think?" Robo asked.

"I think you're angry with me."

Robo pursed his lips and wagged his head back and forth. "I doan get angry. I get even."

"You wrecked my car twice. How even do you want to get?"

"Maybe I shoot you in the leg a couple times."

Robo limped across the room and picked up the gun from the desk. Nick shifted position, staying between Robo and Gretchen. He caught a whiff of Robo's nose-wrenching cologne.

Robo noticed that the clip was missing. "You doan keep your gun loaded?"

"Loaded guns are dangerous," Nick said.

"I take it anyways." Robo dropped the gun into his jacket pocket. "That okay with you?"

Nick shrugged.

"You hear from your friend Vince Love?"

"Not lately," said Nick.

Robo shook his head, disappointed. "I doan understand people who doan meet their obligations. I ask myself, What is the world coming to? What do you think? You doan think about this? You know what? If I could not pay my debts"—he pointed the gun at his temple—"I think I shoot myself. How you like that?"

"That's one way to go," Nick said.

"You focking-A right." Robo tipped his head and raised his sunglasses, looking past Nick's shoulder. "How come you hiding my pretty friend?" He lowered the gun. "Hey pretty girl. What is your name?"

"Gretchen," said Gretchen.

"You his girlfriend?" Robo asked.

Gretchen stared back at him.

Robo laughed and looked at Nick. "She know you focking my wife?"

The room became silent. Robo lowered his sunglasses.

Nick looked at Gretchen, whose face had turned to stone. She would not meet his eyes. He said to Robo, "Why don't you just shoot me now?"

"That what you want?"

Nick reconsidered. "No. But if you're not going to use it, would you put it away?"

"You doan like the gun? Okay, I put it away." Robo slipped the gun into his pocket.

"What do you want?" Nick asked.

"It is very simple. Your grandfather, he owed me some money. You know about this?"

Nick nodded.

"And then he give the debt to Vince Love."

"You mean he conned Vince into accepting it."

"This is between your grandfather and Vince Love, but yes, I agree. This debt was not a good thing for Vince Love."

Considering that it had led Vince to torch the store, it had been a very bad thing for Nick Fashon, too.

"Here is what I am going to do," Robo said. "I unwind the loan. Go back to before. Your friend Vince Love does not owe me the money. The debt is Caleb Hardy's. What do you think? You like that?"

Nick could see where this was going.

Robo said, "I take your friend off the hook. I transfer debt back to you. You owe me nineteen thousand six hundred. That's today. Tomorrow is more. Okay?"

"Not okay," said Nick.

Robo shrugged. "Is okay with me. Tell you what, I give you special. One-time-only offer. You pay me today, I knock off two percent."

Nick shook his head. "Not gonna happen."

"Then we got a problem, you and me."

Bootsie said, "He said it's not gonna happen."

Robo turned on Bootsie. "You talk to me, old man?"

"Yeah I talk, you piece of garbage."

"Take it easy, Daddy," Gretchen said.

"He your daddy? You better listen to your little girl, Daddy."

Bootsie stood up and leaned across the desk toward Robo, his face coloring. "I dealt with two-bit assholes like you every day for twenty-six years. I used to haul in a dozen just like you every Friday night."

"You a cop?" Robo laughed. "You too old and fat to be a cop."

"I'm not too old and fat to put down a frijole-gobbling *pistolero* like you, Jose."

Robo's face darkened. "My name is not Jose. It is Roberto."

"You look like a Jose to me, *Jose*." Bootsie was getting redder. "Hard to tell, though, hiding behind those cheap shades."

"You want my eyes, *puerco*?" Robo whipped off his sunglasses. His cologne had become more aggressive, amplified by stress and perspiration. Dilated pupils blacked out most of his irises, and red veins webbed the whites of his eyes.

Chest heaving, Bootsie came around the far side of the desk. Nick grabbed at Bootsie's arm, trying to pull him back. Bootsie batted his hand away. "Back off, Slick."

"See my eyes? I show you something else." Robo's hand came up holding his little gun.

Bootsie stopped. "You need that to handle an old man like me?"

They were standing four feet apart, just out of arm's reach but close enough to make it impossible for Robo to miss his broad target.

"I doan waste time with you, *puerco*."

"I read your sheet, Jose. You never shot nobody."

"Nobody *you* know about, *puerco*."

"Little gun like that, what, twenty-five-caliber? Wouldn't hardly slow me down."

"You want to try one? How about I shoot you in the face? You like that?"

"Go ahead, Jose." Bootsie pressed his index finger into the center of his bulbous forehead. "Right there." He removed his finger, leaving a white spot on the florid expanse.

Robo raised the gun. "Maybe I do it."

"You think so?" The spot slowly faded. Bootsie swayed forward, his eyes fixed on Robo.

Robo said, "Ah, fock you, old man." He lowered the gun. Bootsie's hand shot out; both the gun and Robo's own hand disappeared into Bootsie's oversize fist. Robo's mouth fell open and emitted a strangled quack. Bootsie jerked his arm back, sending Robo across the room into a file cabinet. Robo hit the steel cabinet with his face and slid to the floor. He was still for an instant, then shook it off, pushed himself up, and scrambled to his feet. Nick looked for the gun, but Robo's hands were empty. Bootsie, gasping for air, had it clutched in his meaty paw, pointed at Robo's astonished face.

"Just sit . . . tight . . . Jose," Bootsie said between inhalations. "I've . . . shot . . . a few . . . like you . . . It's easy."

"Daddy?" Gretchen's voice came out a squeak.

"I'm okay, sweetie," Bootsie gasped. He braced himself on the desk. "Just gotta . . . catch my breath." He seemed to be breathing better, and his face was losing some of its carmine brilliance.

Nick picked up the phone.

"What are you . . . doing . . . Slick?"

"Calling the cops."

Bootsie shook his head. "Hold on a sec. Maybe we oughta think about that."

Nick put the phone down.

"Maybe—" Bootsie coughed. Robo tensed, ready to launch himself if the old man let down his guard, but Bootsie recovered without letting his attention waver. He wiped his mouth on his sleeve. "Maybe we should ask Jose here what we should do. What do you think, Jose? Should we call the cops? Should I shoot you? How we gonna get you to leave poor Slick here alone? What do you think we should do?"

"I think you should go fock yourself."

"That's what I figured," Bootsie said, shaking his head.

"Or he can pay me what I am owed."

"He doesn't owe you anything, Jose."

"Somebody owes me."

"That might be. But it's nobody here in this room. Look, if we can't come to an understanding here, I'm gonna let Nick call the cops. But you should know that I was on the force twenty-six years. I still got friends there. How do you think they're gonna take it when they hear you pulled a gun on me? You prepared to deal with that?"

Robo, saying nothing, glared at him.

"You've been lucky so far, *Roberto*. Only one little bid upstate, two and a half years, and nothing for the past seventeen. You've been real lucky. That can change."

Robo was listening.

"I want you to leave him alone, *Roberto*. You understand what I'm saying?"

Robo's eyes glistened with emotion.

"And that money you think you're owed? That's a write-off. You understand me?"

"This money I am owed."

"Not by my friend Nick. Understand? I'm gonna need some indication I'm getting through to you, son."

Robo nodded with great effort. Nick imagined he could hear vertebrae grinding.

The nod was enough for Bootsie.

"Okay, Jose. Get the hell out of here."

Robo stood up and held out his hand. "You want to give me my gun back?"

Bootsie smiled and shook his head.

Robo dropped the hand to his side, went to the door without looking at Nick, opened it, and walked out into the afternoon sun. Bootsie watched the door swing shut. He continued to watch it for several seconds, as if expecting Robo to come charging back, then made his way back around the desk and sank into the chair.

Gretchen rushed to her father. "Are you okay?"

"I'm fine," said Bootsie. He set Robo's gun on the desk. "Never been better." He grinned. "Didn't know the old man still had it in him, did ya?"

"You could've been hurt, Daddy."

"By him? I use to handle lots worse. A guy like that, he's all noise."

Nick stood watching them. Robo was out of the picture—perhaps—but he still felt like something was missing. Probably his testicles.

"Besides," Bootsie said, "if I'd had a problem, Nick here woulda stepped in—right, Slick?"

Nick searched for a note of sarcasm in Bootsie's voice but could not find it.

Bootsie said, "You handled yourself good, kid."

Nick thought, I did?

"Didn't freeze up, stayed loose and ready for anything. I liked the way you got yourself between him and Gretie." He gave Gretchen's arm a squeeze. "That was real good."

Had he really done that? Nick couldn't remember. Gretchen was staring at him, her eyes flat.

"I owe you an apology," Bootsie went on. "I shouldn'ta unloaded your gun. I shoulda known you wouldn't be packin' it without good reason. My mistake, Slick." He winked. Bootsie was trying to make Nick look good. Judging from the mask on Gretchen's face, it wasn't working.

Nick said, "It wasn't a mistake. If you hadn't unloaded that gun, somebody might have been shot. Just one thing . . ."

"What's that?"

"You let him leave with it in his pocket."

Bootsie frowned, then shrugged it off. "No big deal. It's not loaded, I got the clip. Besides, he's probably got a half-dozen more at home."

"That's not very reassuring."

"He won't bother you. I think we scared him good."

"I think we just made him madder."

Gretchen said, "Is it true?" Her eyes were hard and glistening.

"Is what true?"

"What he said. That man. Are you having an affair with his wife?"

"No!" Desperate, he gave her his best look of stricken innocence. "Who is she?"

"Who?"

"His wife."

"I don't . . . Yola. He used to be married to Yola."

Gretchen put her right hand over her mouth; her other hand was balled into a fist.

Nick said, "I didn't—"

She turned away from him, walked three strides to the door, fought with the knob for a long two seconds, jerked it open.

"Gretchen . . ."

The door slammed, a punch to Nick's heart. He closed his eyes and pulled his fists against his chest and listened to Bootsie's asthmatic breathing.

After a few seconds, Bootsie said, "Well, Slick, looks like you got yourself a problem."

Nick opened his eyes and watched Bootsie heave himself up out of his chair and follow his daughter out the door.

Thirty-seven

This time he had lost Gretchen for good. Despite Bootsie's contrived praise, Nick knew that he had performed abysmally. He had let Bootsie treat him like a wayward child on the gun issue, and he had failed to take command of the situation when Robo appeared. He had demonstrated to Gretchen that he wasn't half the man her father was. And then there was the Yola problem. There was no recovering from that. How could he prove to Gretchen that he hadn't slept with Yola? She wouldn't believe him. She had left him with nothing, not even a sad smile, and he had let her go.

Rethinking the whole scene left him furious with Bootsie. As for Robo—Robo was like the weather: avoid it when you can, dress for it when you can't, and sometimes get killed by it. Maybe he should think of Bootsie that way, too. If Robo was a tornado, Bootsie would be an earthquake. And Gretchen? Nick decided not to pursue the metaphor.

As he neared Bisbee, Nick began to wonder again what might be waiting for him. The phone call from Chin had been very peculiar. Why had he refused to tell him what it was about? He'd said he had something to show Nick, had said, *Don't worry about the money.*

Nick imagined the possibilities. Maybe Chin had found a secret bank account in Caleb's name. Millions of dollars. That would be nice. Or he had located Caleb's motorcycle . . . no, he wouldn't make Nick drive all that way to look at a motorcycle. It could be something bad. Really bad. Like a conflicting patent on the HandyMate. What if Caleb had stolen the idea and Nick was being sued by some crazy inventor from Alaska? It was no more unlikely than any other scenario. *Don't worry about the money.* Did that mean that money was no longer a problem, or that no amount of money could save him? Nick wished he had asked a few more questions.

Hardy Chin's aunt was not at her desk. Nick heard voices and laughter. He knocked on Chin's door and opened it. Chin was behind his desk wearing the same cream-colored western-cut sport coat, snap-button chambray shirt, and bolo tie he had worn the first time Nick met him.

"Nick!" Chin stood up, his face morphing from laughter to sobriety. He cleared his throat and his gaze shifted. Nick followed his eyes to the man sitting across from him. The man turned toward Nick. He was deeply tanned, clean-shaven, and weathered. Maybe sixty years old. His white hair was hacked short. A turquoise stud in his left ear matched his irises in both size and hue. He grinned, displaying a collection of gold, silver, and enamel. His bright eyes disappeared in starbursts of wrinkles. Maybe he was older than sixty.

Chin said, "I want you to know I didn't know, Nick."

"Didn't know what?"

Chin's eyes went back to the older man. Was Nick supposed to know him? The man was dressed in well-worn denim and a sleeveless black leather tunic. Wiry, sunbaked arms, chest covered with a mat of curly white hairs, powerful, long-fingered hands. He was holding something. A HandyMate. Nick's thoughts spun, then caught. This had to be the missing prospector, the guy who had stolen Caleb's motorcycle. Somehow he had gotten hold of a HandyMate prototype.

Nick said, "Herb Jenks?"

The old man's eyes widened, then he roared with laughter. Chin was grinning, too, although he still looked worried. The old man slapped his knee, and his laugh degenerated into a weird cackle that sent a horrified chill up Nick's spine.

"Herb Jenks!" the old man gasped, his eyes tearing from laughter. "Why, Herb Jenks is dead and buried, boy." He stood up and threw his arms around Nick and gave him a mighty squeeze. "You don't recognize your own flesh and blood?"

Thirty-eight

Dead? Kee-rist, do I look like a zombie? Still can't believe you-all mistook old Herb for me." Caleb Hardy chuckled. "'Course, I knew you would once the critters got to him. Most folks just can't see past a beard."

Nick said, "You killed Herb Jenks?"

"Kill Herb?" Caleb shook his head, smiling sadly, explaining the obvious to his idiot grandchild. "Why would I do that? Herb and me, we went way back. I wouldn't harm a hair on that old man's head. I just come home one day—I'd been over in Deming for the duck races—you ever seen ducks race?"

"Not recently."

"Oughta go next year. Hell of a good time. Anyways, I come home and there's Herb, dead as roadkill. Heart attack, my guess. Herb never did know how to take care of himself. Poor guy, forty years diggin' holes in those damn mountains and nothing to show for it. He used to say, 'When I'm dead, then I'll know where all the gold is hid.' That's what gave me the idea to just be dead for a while. Figured I might get more done dead than alive, and damned if it don't seem to have worked! Why don't you sit down, boy? You look half dead yourself."

Nick groped his way to the other chair and sank into it. Caleb's grinning visage filled his eyes. He closed them and squeezed his lids until he saw confetti. When he opened them, Caleb was still there.

"I ain't gonna disappear on you, boy. Hey, you think you're surprised, you should've seen that old man at Rincon Plastics."

"You saw Lew Krone?"

"Swung by there this morning." Caleb brandished the Handy-Mate. "First one out of the block. Y'know, you didn't get it quite right. Must've used one of the old prototypes. Oh well, it's still one hell of a thing. You did a good job. Hear you even managed to fend off Yola, more or less."

Nick looked at Chin.

"I told him you'd been having some issues with Yola," Chin said.

"Gotta say, though, I ain't any too pleased with how you took care of my place. I come home, mice living in my pantry and my plants dead and only one lousy beer in the icebox. You could've at least kept my fridge stocked, boy."

Nick turned to Chin and asked, "Why isn't he dead?"

Chin shrugged.

"And *you*"—Caleb turned on Chin—"you let little Yola get her hooks into him. Almost gave away the farm. Woman like that'll suck the blood out of you faster'n a lawyer. Speakin' a which, grandson, did you know that Mr. Hardy Chin here is not really a lawyer?"

Chin's eyes widened, and he sat up straight. "Goddamn it, Caleb! I am so a lawyer."

"You ever pass the bar?"

Chin scowled at his thumbnail.

"What have you been charging Nick here for your so-called legal advice?"

"Nothing," said Chin.

"Well, you sure ain't been working for free."

Chin cleared his throat. "Actually, I've been billing your estate."

Caleb's mouth fell open. "My *estate?*"

"I haven't seen any bills," Nick said slowly.

"I've been deferring the bills until after probate."

Caleb's grin returned. "It looks like you've really put one over on yourself, counselor."

Chin looked as if he had swallowed something unspeakable.

"Let me ask this again," said Nick to Caleb. "Why aren't you dead?"

"On account of I didn't *die.*" He used one of the short prongs on the HandyMate to scrape under a fingernail. "Only that's not what you're asking, is it?"

Nick waited.

Caleb rotated the HandyMate, running his fingers over its precision-molded surface. "I always knew I had a million-dollar idea in me, boy. Only surprise was that it turned out to be this little old thing. I figured to hit it rich with the NoseGard or maybe one of the bass lures. You know how I came up with this puppy? Lost my damn bottle opener. Yep. Meantime, I had this nylon spatula that I'd left too close to a burner once, and it got part melted, and I looked at it and saw if I did a little carving, it might just snap the top off a beer. Uh-huh. One thing led to another, and pretty soon I wasn't hardly using anything but my HandyMate to do all my cooking. You know this thing will pop the pit right out of an avocado?"

Nick shook his head.

"Does a few other tricks you geniuses missed, too. You like seeds in your grapes?"

"I buy seedless grapes."

"Maybe you'll change your mind once you see this puppy at work. So, you want to know how come you haven't seen me around in a while. Fact is, I've been down in Mexico having myself a little sabbatical. A man's got to take a little time for himself."

"You just took off? Didn't mention it to anybody?"

"More or less. I'm sorry if you were worried, boy. I just didn't think you cared." Again the weird cackle. "Fact is, things worked out just like I planned. Well, almost. I didn't mean for your whole building to burn down."

Nick said, "That wasn't your . . . wait a second . . ." He replayed Caleb's words. "You what?"

"It was an accident," said Caleb. "I just wanted to help poor Vinnie out. He was having this problem with Roberto—"

"Wait, stop, no." Nick held up his hands. "Are you saying *you* started that fire? You burned down my store? You burned all my stuff?"

"Like I was saying, it was an accident. Vinnie was having this problem with Roberto—"

"Because *you* conned him into taking on *your* debt. By the way, why did you do that? You had twenty-five grand in your Cochise checking account."

"I did?"

"You didn't know about it?"

"Well . . ." Caleb scratched his leathery neck. "I knew there was something in there. But that ain't the point, boy. You want to make it in business, you got to use other people's money. Against my religion to finance my own businesses."

"So you put Vince in debt to Robo for 'religious' reasons?"

Caleb shrugged. "He knew what he was getting into."

"I doubt it. He probably thought he might actually get some return on his investment."

"And he will, boy. He will." Caleb fixed his eyes on Nick's and stared until Nick rolled his eyes up and away. "He will," Caleb said again. "Anyway, we were talking one day, and Vinnie mentioned that you fellas had a lot of dead stock in the basement and a pretty good insurance policy on the store. I sort of read between the lines. Figured I'd just create a little smoke damage, y'know, to generate some cash and get poor Vinnie off the hook. I didn't know it was gonna get out of hand that way."

"You're saying Vince asked you to start the fire?"

"No, no. I just anticipated his desire."

"You anticipated his desire."

"Yup."

"Did you decide to burn down my store before or after you killed Herb Jenks?"

"You don't listen so good. Old Herb died on his own. I didn't start the fire till later."

"On the way to your sabbatical."

"Exactly. I was kinda surprised when the whole building went, but then I got to thinkin' it might not be such a bad thing. Might get you focused on my doohickeys. As long as you were all caught up selling leather underwear—"

"We were *not* selling leather underwear!"

"Hey, I'm not stupid, boy. I read that article, and I know leather underwear when I see it."

Nick threw up his hands; he flipped his head back and stared hard at the ceiling. Beam me up, Scotty.

Caleb prattled on. "Far as your stuff, hell, I didn't know you *lived* up there. Didn't know anybody lived up there. I got to apologize for that."

Nick brought his chin back down. "Big of you," he said.

Caleb emitted a cackle straight out of Bedlam. "It's just *stuff*, boy. You can always get more *stuff*."

Nick rested his elbows on his knees and covered his face with his hands. "I can't believe what I'm hearing," he mumbled into his palms.

"So," Caleb continued, "I just figured it was a two-birds-with-one-stone situation: Vince can pay off Roberto out of the insurance money, and you're freed up to manage my estate. It was the perfect solution."

Nick peeked through his fingers at Chin. "How come he's not dead?"

Chin pushed out his lower lip and produced the faintest of shrugs.

Caleb said, "Hey, no need to take that attitude, grandson. No harm done. We all got what we wanted."

"How do you figure that?"

"Well, I got my HandyMate up and rolling. Chin here, even if he's not really a lawyer, got himself a new client; plus he got one back he thought was dead. Vince got Roberto paid off—or he will, as soon as that insurance money comes in—and Roberto gets his money. Everybody gets what they want. Even Yola. She gets to put my HandyMate on TV."

"You're forgetting somebody," Nick said.

"Who? You? Hell, boy, you get it all! I'm not changing my will none. I go, you're golden."

"How soon might that be?"

Caleb's mouth widened into a precious-metal grin. "Could be a while," he said.

"In the meantime," Nick said, "I've lost my business, my partner, all my possessions, and my girlfriend."

"Look at it this way, boy—you got your granddaddy back!"

Nick stood up.

"Where you going?"

"I don't know." Nick passed through the door into the reception room and out onto the sidewalk. His legs felt long and rubbery, and all the buildings seemed to be leaning toward him. He walked up the street past the panama-hat shop, past the restaurants and gift shops and art galleries. He walked by Caleb's motorcycle—how had he missed seeing it before? He walked two blocks, searching for his red Corvette before he remembered that his car was back in the body shop. He had arrived in Vince's Explorer. And he had not parked uphill of Chin's office, he had parked on the downhill side.

He turned back toward Chin's to find Caleb standing a few feet behind him.

Nick said, "I don't need you."

"Never thought you did."

"What do you want from me?"

Caleb said, "Tell you what. How about I buy you a cool one."

Thirty-nine

The tavern was shadowy and quiet, and it smelled of stale beer and cigarettes. Caleb and Nick took two stools at the back end of the bar.

"Couple a Coronas, Vern," said Caleb. "And don't you dare stick a lime in 'em."

"Wouldn't do that," said the bartender. He opened a pair of long-necks and placed them on the bar.

"Herb used to drink here," Caleb said, "till he got hisself eighty-sixed. Ain't that right, Vern?"

"That's right."

"He's dead, y'know."

"Herb is? Oh well. Heard you were dead, too."

"It was only temporary," said Caleb. He lifted his bottle and held it toward Nick. "Cheers."

"What are we celebrating?"

"My resurrection?"

"More like my ruination."

Caleb sighed, shaking his head. "You got to work on that outlook, boy."

Nick sipped his beer. "My problem isn't my outlook. It's you."

Caleb nodded slowly, not in agreement but in understanding.

"Well, I'm sorry if you feel that way. I really am. If I'd known you were going to take things so hard, I'd a done things different."

"No you wouldn't. You're insane." Nick turned away. Why had he followed the old man into this bar?

Caleb laughed; the sound was like sandpaper on Nick's brain. He spun on Caleb and shouted, "You are! You ruined me! You wrecked my life!"

Caleb, startled, leaned back, nearly falling off his stool. "Whoa there! Take it easy, boy."

"And quit calling me *boy!*"

"Okay, okay, calm down. Look, I had my troubles, too."

"Like I should give a damn."

"You got to understand, Nick, I was in a pickle. Roberto demanding money—"

"You managed to shrug that off onto Vince."

"Yeah, but Roberto made it clear that if Vince couldn't pay, the debt would revert to me. And I had Yola demanding a share of the HandyMate—never should've gotten involved with that woman. Hot little number, though, ain't she?"

"She thinks so."

"Her and lots of other people. You think that Fuentes woman's hot, don't you, Vern?" Caleb asked him.

The bartender looked up. "You don't mind leaving your balls behind, maybe."

Caleb laughed. "Vern, he don't trust nobody. Anyway, like I was saying, I had lots of reasons to skedaddle. Then I find old Herb Jenks dead on my doorstep. Now, how do you suppose that made me feel?"

Nick waited.

"I'll tell you, Nick. It made me feel *old*. I stood there staring down at poor Herb, and damned if it didn't feel like I was looking down on my own self. Dead and gone. And I thought, What the hell am I doing sitting out here in the damn desert frittering away my last few years on earth when I could be on the open road having a good old time? So then I started thinking, What if I just hop on my bike and go? What would happen? Who would take care of my place? Who would take care of the coffin business? What would happen to all my great ideas? And then I saw it." He paused and sipped his Corona. "You ever have a really great idea hit you"—he slammed a fist into his palm—"like that? Well, that's how it hit me. Boom! One second I'm a dried-up old man with a bunch of half-assed inventions wasting away in the outback, the next moment I'm a genius. I ask myself, What if I take off for a few months? Give the coyotes and vultures a couple more days, and everybody will think Herb is me. Get Yola and Roberto off my back, and my estate goes to my sharp, energetic grandson. I knew you had it in you, Nick. I just knew it. Figured if I ever come back, you'd have everything under control, and if I didn't come back, well, it was all gonna be yours anyway."

"You had it all figured out."

"Damn right I did. Only thing that bothered me was your friend Vince. I'd kind of left him high and dry with Roberto. That was when I decided to get him some insurance money before I left."

"You delayed your trip just long enough to burn down my store? How thoughtful."

"Like I said before, I'm sorry about that. Didn't mean for the whole thing to go up."

Nick closed his eyes. "What do you want from me?"

"I want you to stay on," said Caleb. "Help me run the business."

"I don't think I can do that."

"Sure you can. You've got to. Look, I've got all these doohickeys I thunk up, but I don't know beans about selling them. I need a guy like you. I mean, look what happened when I went away. I'm gone a couple months, and you've got the HandyMate in production with a million-dollar order in hand!"

"Not quite a million," said Nick.

"See? See what I mean? You've got a head for numbers. You're a practical, down-to-earth, hard-nosed businessman."

Nick laughed, and it came out sounding nearly as demented as Caleb's cackle.

Caleb said, "It's true. You are. Especially compared to me."

"I suppose it's all relative. But I'm not interested."

"Why? You don't want to get rich? Or is it that you don't want to work with your poor decrepit old grandpa?"

"It's more a matter of not wanting to work with an irresponsible, scheming, lying arsonist."

Caleb drew back, frowning, his chin tucked down. "That's cold, son."

"Which part of it isn't true?"

"I never lied to you."

"You did your damnedest to mislead me."

"I thought I explained that to you."

Nick stood up. "I was a happy man."

"So go back to being happy."

"It's not that easy." Nick walked out, leaving his grandfather looking after him.

Walking out on Caleb for the second time made him feel better. Or maybe it was the beer. Nick drove out of Bisbee feeling a kind of numb satisfaction. He was just outside the city limits when he was hit again, a sneaky follow-up punch with enough behind it to double him over: he had *nothing*—no prospects, no family, and very few friends. In fact, now that he thought about it, he had no friends at all. Vince was gone. Bootsie, already disgusted with him for blowing it with Gretchen, would be even angrier upon finding his investment in the hands of an insane hermit. As for Gretchen—as long as she thought he had slept with Yola, he didn't have a chance. In her mind, he was not only a cheat, he was an impoverished cheat. His best course of action might be to steal a pick and shovel, head into the mountains, and prospect for silver and gold. He could become the new Herb Jenks.

Nick imagined himself wandering through the canyons, scraping at the rocks with his pick, making simple meals of salt pork and beans, sleeping under the desert sky. Was this how Herb Jenks had been driven into the hills? The fantasy lasted about thirty seconds. It wasn't him. But what other choices were available? It occurred to him to follow Caleb's example—he could fake his own death and move to Mexico. He would be no less a pauper in Mexico, but he would, at least, have plenty of company. He could become a Nogales street beggar. Or he could turn to crime. Rob a bank. He still had options.

Approaching Tombstone, imagining himself as a Bonnieless Clyde, he happened to glance in the mirror and see, a quarter mile back, the distinctive grille of a black Dodge pickup, fog lights mounted over the cab.

Curiously, Nick felt neither startled nor afraid. Since everything else had gone wrong, it made perfect sense that Robo would appear. He felt detached, as events were happening on a television screen. A homeless pauper pursued by a crazed, jealous loan shark. Could be a movie of the week.

I wonder what will happen next, Nick thought. If Robo killed him, all his problems would go away. The thing to do, though, would be to take out a big life-insurance policy first. He could name himself as the beneficiary and become a dead rich man. Or rather a rich dead man, as his demise would necessarily precede his wealth.

He slowed as he entered Tombstone. Maybe Robo wasn't really tailing him. It could be a coincidence. He turned left on a cross street, then right on Allan Street. Robo followed, close enough now that Nick could see his face through the tinted windshield. No coincidence.

Covered boardwalks ran along both sides of Allan Street, giving the town an Old West look. To complete the illusion, Wyatt Earp and Doc Holliday crossed the street in front of him, long-barreled revolvers strapped to their hips. Probably actors from a reenactment of the gunfight at the OK Corral. The boardwalks were crowded. Nick slowed, then came to a complete stop to let a gaggle of tourists cross.

Robo pulled up close behind him. Did he really expect to frighten Nick into paying him the money? Maybe the money had nothing to do with it. Maybe it was about Yola. Or about Robo wallowing in the pure rage of a man whose desires have been thwarted. If that was it, Nick could understand. Maybe they had something in common there. He wished he was more like Robo—instead of feeling sorry for himself, he could just go out and hurt somebody. He thought about Robo beating up Vince, and Yola, and then he recalled Robo backing his truck into Nick's Corvette. He could still hear the fiberglass tearing. The remembered sound sent a jolt of adrenaline to his heart; his fingers whitened on the steering wheel.

The tourists passed, leaving the street clear, but Nick did not move.

Robo leaned on his horn.

The blare of the horn tripped a synapse in Nick's stressed-out brain. He jammed the gear selector into reverse and crushed the accelerator. Tires spun, then caught. The Explorer lurched back, crumpling the pickup's grille and bumper. Robo's face disappeared, eclipsed by an exploding air bag. Nick kept his foot on the gas, tires smoking, skidding the pickup back up the street. The Dodge slewed to the side and ran up against the boardwalk, breaking one of the posts supporting the overhang.

Nick jumped out, ran back to the pickup, opened the door, yanked Robo out of the cab. Robo had turned gray, his hair and face covered with white powder from the airbag. He was too stunned to resist as Nick swung him against the side of the truck, brought his right fist back, and drove it forward into Robo's belly. Robo doubled over and slid down the fender to a sitting position on the tarmac.

Nick stepped back, breathing hard, his body humming.

Holding up his hand in a placating gesture, Robo said, "Take it easy, buddy . . ." He rolled onto his hands and knees. "What I do to you?" He got his feet under him, then launched himself. Nick was ready. He brought up his fist in a short arc and caught Robo a glancing blow on the chin, but it wasn't enough to prevent Robo's head from driving into his gut, driving him back into a hitching post. Nick wrapped his arms around Robo's abdomen, and the two men staggered out into the street looking like an inverted, self-flagellating, half-human version of Pushme-Pullyou. Nick, afraid to let go, tried to squeeze the breath out of Robo, but Robo's fists hammering into Nick's thighs were taking their toll. With desperate strength, Nick heaved himself upright, lifting Robo up off the ground, then spiked him headfirst into the ground.

He stepped back, ready for more, but Robo, facedown on the street, wasn't moving. Nick became aware of eyes on him, several dozen people lining the boardwalk. If they'd come to Tombstone to watch a gunfight between the Earps and the Clantons, they were getting a bonus.

Robo still wasn't moving. Nick approached cautiously. He put his foot against Robo's shoulder and rolled him over onto his back.

Robo's eyes opened and focused. "Hey, buddy," he said. He smiled and looked down toward his waist. Nick followed his glance and saw the gun in Robo's hand. A weight punched Nick high on his belly, sending him stumbling back. His heels hit the edge of the boardwalk, and he sat down. He hadn't heard the gun go off, but his ears were ringing and his shirt was soaked with blood. Sitting took too much effort. He fell back onto the rough planking and stared up at the underside of the sagging overhang. He could see, with remarkable acuity, a black widow in the rafters. He heard screaming and voices, and then Doc Holliday was bending over him, pressing something against his belly, and telling him that everything would be okay.

<u>Forty</u>

Two old men, one fat, one thin, playing cards and talking. Nick could not understand what they were saying. He closed his eyes and made them go away.

A slide show, a collection of faces. Gretchen, Bootsie, Caleb. A man wearing a white coat and large metal-rimmed eyeglasses. Intermission. Gretchen again, and Hardy Chin. A nurse with short red hair. Gretchen, crying.

The first time Nick woke up and stayed awake long enough to remember it, he was alone in the hospital room. He knew he was in a hospital because of the television mounted high on the wall, the rails on his bed, the tube attached to his wrist, and the vast discomfort in his abdomen. He wondered how long he had been there. He moved his legs. Still working. He counted his arms. Two. He closed each eye in turn, opened and closed his mouth, reached up and felt his head. A large, soft bandage covered most of his skull. He hoped they hadn't shaved his head.

He looked to his left, out a window containing nothing but blue sky. To his right was a curtain. He could hear a faint beeping from outside the room, and voices. He wondered whether he was capable of getting out of bed. He lacked sufficient motivation to make the attempt. He was not uncomfortable. He could detect no pain. Why move?

He remembered Tombstone. He remembered one still image of the gun in Robo's hand.

Time passed slowly, first one minute, then five. Nick discovered a remote control on the table beside his bed and turned on the television. A man in a flannel shirt demonstrating how to install a ceiling fan.

"Trying to get some *sleep* over here," came a gravelly voice from beyond the curtain.

"Sorry!" Nick turned off the sound but left the television on. He watched the ceiling-fan installation. He thought that he could install a ceiling fan if he had to. He fell asleep and dreamed of ground wires and blade rotation.

His next conscious episode began with Bootsie's booming voice.

"Hey Slick, you awake?"

Nick opened his eyes. He swallowed, worked his tongue around his mouth, and said, "I wasn't."

"Sorry. Thought I saw your eyelids flutter."

Nick cleared his throat. "I was dreaming."

"Oh. How you feelin'?"

"I'm not sure. How long have I been here?"

"Six months."

Nick said, "Huh?"

Bootsie laughed. "Just messing with you, Slick. They Medevaced you in two nights ago. Y'know, we already had this conversation."

"I don't remember it."

"You remember what happened to you?"

"I got shot."

"You got shot twice."

"I did?"

"Once in your belly and once in the bean."

"I don't remember getting shot in the head."

"Just a graze. It was the slug in your liver that just about killed you."

"Oh. I'm going to be okay?"

"You're tougher than you look."

Nick did not feel tough. "What about Robo?"

"He's just down the hall. Broken neck. But they say he's gonna get his legs back. Amazing what they can do with therapy these days. My guess is he won't be bothering you anymore."

"You said that once before."

"Life's full of surprises, Slick. Speaking of, I met your dead grandpa."

Nick's eyes went to the television. The man in the flannel shirt was installing a light kit on the ceiling fan. He must have been asleep for just a few minutes. Either that or he was stuck in one of the cheap rooms where the television showed nothing but ceiling-fan installations twenty-four hours a day. Maybe he was dead and this was hell.

Bootsie said, "Seems like a heck of a nice guy. Tells me you two are going to get rich."

"Yeah, right." Nick returned his attention to Bootsie. "You said Robo's right down the hall?"

"Yep."

"How come he's not in jail?"

"What, for shooting you in self-defense? What you should be asking is how come *you're* not in jail. About forty witnesses said they saw you deliberately smash into his truck, drag him out of the cab, then beat the crap out of him."

"Oh. I guess it looked that way."

"You know how many strings I had to pull to get the Cochise County sheriff to lose interest in you? Fact is, if your friend Roberto wants to press charges, you might still have a problem. Kinda think he'll let it go, though."

Nick was having trouble focusing. He opened his mouth to ask another question about Robo, but what came out was "Is it true that you named yourself after a dog?"

Bootsie blinked rapidly, shifting programs. "What's your point, Slick?"

"I don't know," said Nick. He really didn't.

"He plays pinochle," said Bootsie.

Nick became confused. Had he fallen asleep again? "Who?"

"Caleb. He plays pinochle."

Maybe he was *still* asleep. He wondered how far back in his memory he would have to travel to reach reality. His eyes returned to the television, where the man in the flannel shirt was looking into the camera and moving his mouth. Nick thought he could perform the ceiling-fan installation, but the talking, that looked way too hard.

"You play?" Bootsie asked.

If I choose not to reply, Nick wondered, will my mouth say something?

Bootsie said, "You okay, Slick?"

Nick nodded, and his eyelids fell.

Nick's next waking impression was of carmine lips. Yola. He stared at her face for several seconds. When it did not disappear, he looked away, at the ceiling, and there discovered a blue afterimage of her smile.

"How are you feeling?" she asked.

"What do you want?"

"To see how you are doing."

"I'm going to live, they say."

That seemed to delight her. "Everybody is okay then," she said.

"How do you figure that?"

"You are getting better, Caleb is alive, and Roberto will be coming home very soon. He will not be walking so good, but he will be home."

"Home with you?"

"Yes. He loves me, you know."

"Of course he does."

"This will be a good thing for him. It will calm him down. We will get married again. You will not have to worry about Roberto no more."

"I've heard that before."

"Yes, but you have never before heard it from me. You must understand, Roberto is very sorry he shoot you. He had to show he was not afraid. You know, you are a lot like him."

"I don't think so."

"You are wrong. You are like two little boys, shooting each other. You are wrong about me, too. I am a very nice person."

"I never said otherwise."

"Yes, but you have thought it."

Nick woke up in the middle of a conversation. Bootsie was saying, ". . . says you should be able to go home tomorrow. Gretie brought over some of your clothes—"

"Gretchen was here?" Nick asked.

"She's been here every day. I told you that before. You blanking out on me again?"

"No," Nick lied.

Bootsie clearly did not believe him. "Well, don't worry about it. The doc says it's a common reaction to trauma. Says you'll probably get all your noodles back, but it'll take time."

"Did I talk to her?"

"Gretie? Nah, every time she comes by, you're out of it. Fact is, I think she prefers it that way. Once she heard you woke up, she got real busy with her job. Liked you better unconscious." *Hee hee hee.* "Anyways, she went and got your stuff out of that hotel you been staying at—"

"They let her take my stuff?"

"You were behind on the rent. They were happy to get rid of it. Anyways, they say you can go home tomorrow—"

"I don't have a home."

"You can stay with me. I got an extra room."

Nick thought for a moment. "Do you still have that gun you took away from Robo?"

"I got it."

"How about you just shoot me?"

"Now, don't be talking like that, Slick. I know you're not that far gone. Besides, you might hurt my feelings."

Nick closed his eyes and tried to imagine living with Bootsie Groth. Better he should camp out in the *taqueria*.

"You going away again, Slick?"

"I'm trying. It's not working."

"You still got a chance with her, y'know."

"I doubt it."

"You're wrong there. She's a little perturbed with you, true. Can't blame her, I mean, you messing around with that Mexican gal. Met her, too. Gotta say, I can't blame ya." Bootsie leered and laughed— *hee hee hee*—then sobered and said, "You want to marry my little girl, you better straighten up and fly right."

"Who said anything about marriage?"

"You did."

"You're dreaming."

"No way, Slick. You told me you were going to support my little girl in a style she wasn't accustomed to. Right there on my patio."

It sounded vaguely familiar. "It doesn't matter," Nick said. "I couldn't support a goldfish right now. Besides, as long as she thinks I was messing around with Yola—which I wasn't, by the way—she won't have anything to do with me."

Bootsie shrugged. "I won't argue with you, but I know my little girl. You take your time and play your cards smart, she'll come around sure as the full moon."

Bootsie might as well be promising the second coming, Nick thought, but a part of him wanted desperately to believe. Gretchen had visited him in the hospital—was that out of love or pity? Maybe he still had a chance with her. Maybe not.

"The thing is with Gretie, ever since she was yay-high to a grasshopper, she had this stubborn streak. Tell her she can't have something, you never hear the end of it. Tell her she has to eat her green beans . . . you ever see her eat a green bean?"

"She hates them."

"Thirty years, ever since her mother made her eat one. You just can't make her do anything she doesn't want to. You keep that in mind, she'll come around. You just got to decide what you want, son. You know how it goes with a woman. You got to work on her as hard as you worked on that HandyMate."

"She's not a kitchen tool."

"There you go! You got a good start on it. Now all you got to do is decide what you want and go after it."

"I know what I want," Nick said.

"You do? Let's hear it."

"I want everything like it was before. You remember that night Gretchen and I came over for dinner and we ate chips and bean dip? That's what I want. I want Gretchen, and I want my store back."

Bootsie raised his eyebrows. "That's it?"

"What's it?" Caleb's voice. Nick turned his head to see his grandfather, dressed in riding leathers and wearing sunglasses.

"What this boy wants," Bootsie explained. "He wants to marry my daughter, and he wants his store back. And he wants some bean dip."

Caleb pocketed his glasses and looked at Nick. "You want bean dip, you must be feeling better." Looking at Bootsie, he said, "I thought she was mad at him."

"She'll get over it," Bootsie said.

"Well hey!" Caleb beamed. "Congratulations, boy!"

"I'm glad you and Caleb found each other," Nick said after a few seconds of vertigo. "You're both certifiable."

The two old men laughed, Caleb's cackle in utter disharmony with Bootsie's *hee hee hee.*

Caleb, first to recover, composed his features and asked, "You sure you've thought this out, Nick? You really want your store back?"

"I want my life back."

Caleb said, "My offer to you stands. I'm about to make a pile of money on the HandyMate. I could use you, Nick."

"You already have."

Caleb sighed. "I guess I deserve that. Tell you what. You put in a lot of time and effort on the HandyMate and never paid yourself a dime of salary. Might be I could come up with some back pay for you. Maybe enough to set you up in a new shop. What d'you say?"

Nick said nothing. His brain had gone numb.

Caleb reached out and gave Nick's shoulder a squeeze. "You think about it, kid. Hey! What time is it?" He pulled a watch from his pocket, then grabbed the remote and turned on the television.

Yola Fuentes looked out at them, smiling and chattering and using a HandyMate to cut the kernels from a fresh ear of corn.

"This was taped yesterday," Caleb said. "She's making green-corn tamales."

Yola displayed the HandyMate, demonstrated how to scrape the last sweet juices from the ear of corn, then turned the cob-scraping task over to her assistant, an older man in a chef's hat and apron who bore a remarkable resemblance to Caleb Hardy.

Forty-one

Four weeks before Christmas in a small storefront on Fourth Avenue near the university, Nick celebrated the grand opening of his new shop, called simply Fashion.

For the occasion, Nick wore a new pair of black linen trousers, a natural-color silk T-shirt, and an unconstructed alpaca/ramie-blend sport coat from Peru. He put a selection of Motown CDs in the stereo and tweaked each display to show off his goods in the best possible light.

Most of his stock had arrived in time, including a collection of calfskin intimate apparel. He had decided that Bootsie's idea was not half bad. The front window held a display of leather underwear artfully arranged with a collection of longhorn skulls and potted cacti. At the very least, it would get him noticed.

Beside the cash register was a cardboard coffin filled with twelve dozen HandyMates, a gift from Caleb Hardy. Each HandyMate was printed with the name and address of the store. Caleb's idea was to give every customer a free HandyMate with any purchase. Nick did not think that kitchen tools were the best vehicle for promoting leather underwear, but he had promised to hand them out. Maybe the HandyMate had some underwear-related uses he had yet to puzzle out.

The store was about half the size of the one that had burned down. Nick had wanted to keep it small, since this time he was on his own. Vince, who had fled to Las Vegas, returned to Tucson just long enough to pack up his possessions and collect his half of the insurance settlement. Vince had shown little interest in renewing their partnership, and Nick had made no effort to change his mind. He'd had his fill of partnerships. Last he heard, Vince was back in Las Vegas running an espresso stand on Fremont Street.

Nick opened the doors at noon. There were no waiting crowds of fashion-conscious leather freaks. That was fine with him. He had done nothing beyond some minimal word-of-mouth and a banner above the door to announce the opening. It would take time to rebuild his customer base. Everything took time. Recovering from the bullet wound in his abdomen had taken months; there remained a distant but profound ache that bothered him when he lifted anything heavier than a phone book, or sometimes in the middle of the night for no reason at all.

He was still working on Gretchen. He called her every few days. Not too often. Keeping the calls light and friendly, staying in touch, not putting any pressure on her. A week ago she had agreed to meet him for coffee. They talked about her work—she was involved in another survey south of Green Valley, extracting as much archaeological information as possible before the earthmovers razed another six hundred acres of desert to make room for yet another housing development. Nick gave her an update on his new store and invited her to the grand opening. He watched her drink a double latte, watched her lick the foam from her upper lip and tried not to show how desperately he wanted to do it for her. What was she thinking? What was she feeling? Could she really be as relaxed and uncaring as she appeared? He thought not. Her eyes were moist, and her laugh was a little too loud, and her hands did not know where to be.

At one point she said, "I talked to Yola."

"Oh?" His intestines knotted. "When?"

"You were still in the hospital."

"What did she have to say?"

"It was an interesting conversation. Basically, she said, 'I want you to know I did not fuck your boyfriend.'"

"That is true."

"I'll give her this: she has a way with words."

They had parted that afternoon with a gentle hug. It was the first time he had touched her in over four months.

At twenty minutes after twelve, Nick greeted his first customer, a young woman seeking a Hanukkah gift for her boyfriend who was, she announced, a vegan. The very fact that she had walked into a shop specializing in leather accessories did not bode well for their relationship, Nick thought. He sold her a silk and alpaca sweater, one of the few items in the store that did not require an animal to be put to death. Moments after she left, it occurred to him that several silkworms had, in fact, sacrificed their lives for the sweater. Good thing for her he had a generous return policy.

As the afternoon wore on, a few more customers drifted in. Nick sold a couple of belts, a driving cap, and a four-hundred-dollar deerskin vest. Gordo Encinas showed up to pay his respects, and Hardy Chin came by with the latest news about Caleb's burgeoning HandyMate empire.

"He's got an order pending from the U.S. Army. They want a simplified version of the HandyMate in every mess kit. The only problem is that they want a camouflage pattern molded into the plastic, and they're very specific about the colors and shapes."

"I'm sure Caleb will figure out a way to do it."

"Maybe. Only I get the feeling he's not all that keen on doing business with the government. Too much paperwork."

"He should have stayed dead."

"I'm not sure he'd disagree with that. By the way, he says to say he's sorry he can't stop by today. He's taping four more shows with Yola."

Chin bought a leather key fob, the least expensive item in the store, wished Nick luck, and left.

Shortly before closing time, his last customer entered the store.

"Can I help you?" Nick asked.

"I certainly hope so," said the young woman. "I am in desperate need of a leather thong."

"You've come to the right place." Nick smiled and led her to the display. "I happen to have that item in black, red, brown, and bone."

"Oh, I think the bone would be very nice." Gretchen lifted the scrap of leather from a cattle skull and held it to Nick's hips. "Very nice indeed."

ACKNOWLEDGMENTS

Thank you to Chris Acevado for El Otro Lado; to Margaret Falk for the boardwalk; to Jonathon Lazear for the tunes; to Brad Miller for the estate planning; to Don Roth for the plastic; to Kathy Saatzer for the dish soap and cardboard; and to Steve Brewer, Mary Logue, and Deborah Woodworth for reading it rough.